The Merry Month of Murder

The Fyttleton Mysteries #2

Nicola Slade

www.darkstroke.com

Copyright © 2020 by Nicola Slade
Image: Adobe Stock © Parato
Design: Services for Authors
All rights reserved.

No part of this book may be used or reproduced in any manner
whatsoever without written permission of the author or Crooked
Cat/darkstroke except for brief quotations used for promotion or in
reviews. This is a work of fiction. Names, characters,
and incidents are used fictitiously.

First Dark Edition, darkstroke, Crooked Cat Books 2020

Discover us online:
www.darkstroke.com

Join us on instagram:
www.instagram.com/darkstrokebooks/

Include **#darkstroke** in a photo of yourself
holding this book on Instagram and
something nice will happen.

*For my sister-in-law, Ruth Pimm,
remembering when we whitewashed the
cellar at The Red House!*

*And for all my nearest and dearest –
always.*

Acknowledgements

When *The Convalescent Corpse* was published I was delighted that so many lovely readers wanted to know What Happened Next. I thought I'd better find that out too and had a few surprises when I did, so here it is.

Unlikely as it might seem the inspiration and background for The Brother Grimm and Uncle George's Undesirable Legacy have their origins in real, actual fact! I'm indebted to two friends who shared family legends with me, but I suspect they would rather remain anonymous.

About the Author

Nicola Slade is an award-winning, bestselling author of historical and contemporary mysteries and romantic fiction, all set in and around Winchester and Romsey in Hampshire – which is where she lives. *The House at Ladywell* – a contemporary romantic novel with historical echoes – won the International Chatelaine Grand Prize for Romantic Fiction at the CIBA awards in April 2019.

She is the author of the mid-Victorian Charlotte Richmond mysteries and the contemporary Harriet Quigley mysteries. *The Convalescent Corpse*, published November 2018, an Amazon best-seller, is the first in a new series, The Fyttleton Mysteries, set in 1918.

The Convalescent Corpse is the first book in The Fyttleton Mysteries.

The Merry Month of Murder is the second book in The Fyttleton Mysteries.

The Merry Month of Murder

The Fyttleton Mysteries #2

DRAMATIS PERSONAE

The Family at Sandringham Lodge
Alix Fyttleton:Looking for Mr Darcy
Christabel Fyttleton:Unexpectedly has time on her hands
Adelaide Fyttleton:Covets a strange legacy
Margaret Fyttleton:(Mother) Novelist & wet blanket
Lady Elspeth Gillespie:(Granny) Handy with a whitewash brush

The Guests at Balmoral Lodge
Mrs Lydia Trellis:Child bride. Eating for two
Miss Myrtle Preston:Sister of a wounded hero. Eating for three
Mrs Nesta Camperdown:Subdued wife and mother. Not eating much
Miss Judith Evershed:Mathematics mistress with an outsize headache

The Staff at Groom Hall Convalescent Hospital
Sister Janet Wisden:A vast improvement on her predecessor
Dr Fergus Munro:Teller of tall tales

The Patients at Groom Hall Convalescent Hospital
Major Monty Preston:Brother, wounded hero, stout fellow
Lt Peter Camperdown: Very young wounded hero.
Captain Digby Trellis:Accountant who failed to notice a tank heading his way

In the town
Miss Portia Diplock:A bugbear
Mr Edgar Makepeace:Kind-hearted and upright solicitor
Miss Bertha Makepeace: Kind-hearted and upright do-gooder
Henry Makepeace: Also kind-hearted. And upright
Wilfred Seymour:A cheerful youth, not planning to become an undertaker
Aldwyn Camperdown: A loose Canon
Miss Elise Acton:A woman brought low
Two girls called Vera:Both intent on joining the household

Medical staff and maypole dancers; patients and parsons; housemaids and handymen; newly arrived point-of-lay chickens; elderly hens affronted at the arrival of the newcomers; a large, hairy dog; cats; more cats; the Brother Grimm (don't ask); and Uncle George's undesirable legacy

Prologue

I stared, horrified, at the body sprawled on the grass at my feet.

When the doctor pronounced that life was extinct, I felt as though the surrounding crowd had, as though by some mystic force, retreated to a safe distance. It was as though the three of us were left alone in the circle: the doctor, the dead body, and me.

It had all been going so well. We had weathered the winter, at first paralysed by grief at my brother's death in France but gradually we had managed to cope with sorrow, with our perennial lack of funds, and with wartime restrictions until we had forged a new kind of life. With the arrival of spring we had begun to feel hopeful, even to be happy now and then…

'Well? Did you hear me, young woman?' The elderly doctor was barking at me and I blinked. 'I asked if you could give me the name and address of this poor soul.'

And that's the trouble with being the sensible one – everyone always steps back and expects you to deal with any difficulties.

Even a dead body…

Chapter One

Tuesday, 30th April 1918

It was teatime on Tuesday, and nobody had died yet. Nor had anyone risen from a watery grave or descended into the muddy ditch that was grandly known as the ha-ha. This was an improvement on the events of last month.

I shan't go into detail about the above occurrences, all of which really did happen, but I'll sum it up; partly, I admit, to try to get it straight in my own head. It's just as well I had no idea at the time that things were going to go from bad to worse and that we'd end up having to deal with a dead body.

Again.

Of course, that's not strictly accurate. By the Tuesday teatime all kinds of things had already happened and instead, it all really began the previous Friday afternoon, when my sister Alix bounced into the house full of news.

Although we eventually had to cope with a maypole, country dancers, and a tangle of bodies, we were refreshingly free of death and disaster until the following Friday.

To begin with, I am Christabel Fyttleton, middle daughter of the late Percival and the present (in person though rarely in spirit) Margaret Fyttleton. I'll be nineteen years old in September and I'm also the middle granddaughter of Lady Elspeth Gillespie, only child of the last Earl of Inverboyne. Although we tend to keep quiet about it, Granny is the most accomplished poacher anyone could ever wish to meet, having honed her skills at her family's crumbling ancestral pile in Aberdeenshire. Now widowed, her brief career as a debutante in aristocratic society was cut short by extreme shyness, lack of fortune and marriage to an eccentric academic. What happened when she was presented to Queen Victoria is better forgotten.

We live in Ramalley, a small market town in Hampshire, between Winchester and Southampton and our current concern is how to make ends meet. I say current concern, but I should really say perennial, not helped by increasing war shortages and rationing. Next door to us is Groom Hall, a small convalescent hospital for officers who are on the brink of returning to everyday life; an aim that could be considered the triumph of hope over experience when you remember that although some will always bear the visible wounds of the war, they all suffer in other ways from undergoing untold horrors. Circumstances led us recently to open a guest house in the semi-detached other half of our own Victorian villa, when we invited female relatives of the wounded officers to stay with us as lodgers.

Don't worry, there's not much more scene-setting. My elder sister Alix will be twenty in November. She spends her mornings as companion and dogsbody to an irascible old lady in town, duties that she performs with unfailing cheerfulness, undaunted by the knowledge that the old lady has quarrelled with all her previous employees. I've never found anyone capable of arguing with Alix (apart from Addy and me, but that's different) because she blithely ignores hints and merely opens her blue eyes wide in surprise if anyone is horrid to her. This quality has led to the old lady's grateful relatives paying Alix a very handsome salary which includes an equally handsome lunch, the old lady being a great one for her food. This is a helpful saving to our housekeeping budget, particularly as the old lady's cook often insists on giving my sister lavish leftovers, half a joint of beef being a recent example. Alix's afternoons are spent as a volunteer up at Groom Hall, the convalescent hospital.

My younger sister, Adelaide, is fifteen. Until a few weeks ago she was a pupil at St Mildred's, a small, very inefficient private school for girls, where the mistresses were as reluctant to teach Addy, as she was scornful of their ability to do any such thing. All that ended when a serious drainage problem, combined with a timely legacy, allowed the Headmistress to close the school and escape thankfully to Weston-super-Mare.

The remaining members of our household at Sandringham Lodge (which, believe me, is nowhere near as grand as its ambitious name suggests) are Granny, the aforementioned poacher, widow of Professor Cornelius Gillespie, (eminent scholar and completely useless land agent). Granny is our strength and stay in the everlasting struggle to keep the home fires burning despite the constant hindrance of Mother, our eccentric remaining parent. We have very good reason to try to forget our errant Papa, so we rarely speak of him.

Mother is known professionally by her maiden name, Margaret Gillespie, and is a respected author of learned but dull biographies of notable women. The biographies are on hold at the moment because she is also the author of the wildly popular short romances by Mabel de Rochforde. Mother is not comfortable in society and does not deal at all well with real people or real life, so she prefers to dwell in a world of rosy fiction. This peculiarity of hers suits us perfectly as we would much prefer her to have no idea that we are now earning a small income from the lady lodgers in the adjoining Balmoral Lodge. (Like our own house it's not nearly as grand as it sounds.)

If Mother knew we had any money coming in she would spend it all on books, quite ruthlessly ignoring the prior claims of food, coal, electricity, gas and clothing, all of which she considers irrelevant. Because of this attitude we have taken great care that she should have no idea about the lodgers or indeed that Addy has left school.

Those are the main points of interest about our family; we try to keep the more eccentric aspects to ourselves.

We are now near the end of April, almost into May and the novelty of being lodging housekeepers has worn off and become our normal way of life. Humdrum, you might say. Major changes in the staff at the convalescent hospital took place just before Easter, which was early this year, and since then patients have come and gone. A serious leak from a downpipe at Groom Hall and an unfortunate infestation of mice meant that the new Sister-in-Charge decided the place needed some urgent renovation along with a good spring-cleaning and some redecoration. The leak was repaired at once but when the most recent batch of patients left a week ago, Sister closed the hospital for a few days in order to effect these changes. Alix brought home a note of apology to us for loss of income, because no officers meant no patients and no patients meant no lodgers for us. Such a thoughtful course of action (the note) was a welcome change from the previous regime.

Granny replied graciously, and Addy and I presented Sister Wisden with two of our latest kittens to keep down the mice as a thank-you. All our cats have royal names, so Sister was a little startled to be introduced to John Balliol and Robert the Bruce, though she luckily turned out to be a cat lover and they soon became Johnny and Robbie and settled in happily. Johnny is an accomplished mouser while Robbie, perhaps not surprisingly, is a great one for catching spiders.

We welcomed the few days' respite from dealing with the lodgers next door (knowing it was only temporary and therefore not a threat to our income) and luckily we now have some savings in hand following a recent windfall. We've enjoyed a brief holiday after all the hard work of being landladies. Refreshed, we now await with interest, and some trepidation, the new clutch of wives and mothers. Their sons, husbands or brothers will arrive by a new transport due any day now from the big military hospital at Netley near Southampton. It will be interesting to discover how their relatives, our new paying guests, turn out.

Our first and most difficult lodger had been transformed from a dragon to a lamb after Alix was particularly kind to her and we discovered that she had been harbouring two of our kittens. They're supposed to stay on our side of the door between the two houses, but it is a well-known fact that cats can move with ease through solid walls, and we were glad to hear she had found them comforting during an anxious time.

Luckily, that first party of lodgers adored the kittens, but I've taken the precaution since of amending the particulars set out on the invitation card displayed up at the Hall. This now includes the words Household contains cats and a dog. Any potential lodger who prefers not to find her room invaded by cats, or who objects to the presence – often unseen but never unheard – of a large hairy dog of uncertain parentage, is welcome to try her luck in the overcrowded town. I didn't feel it necessary to mention the four ageing hens, or that we have four point-of-lay hens arriving imminently to increase our egg yield. We don't have a cockerel to make the dawn hideous but even so, hens are not everyone's cup of tea, though very few people object to a new-laid egg for breakfast.

The mother and daughter who were members of that first party had brought their visit to a triumphal conclusion with the daughter's wedding, by special licence, to one of the convalescent officers. Three weeks to the day from when they first laid eyes on each other the radiant bride walked down the aisle of Ramalley Priory, watched by her even more radiant and tearful mother! Cynical observers (well, all right, the Fyttleton sisters) might say that the bride having been recently jilted at the altar, and the bridegroom being a widower with an eye to the bride's wealthy parents, had been a factor, but we were happy to have played a part.

The final guest of that initial attempt at being landladies was Miss Evershed, a schoolmistress who, after an unfortunate incident, was still recuperating and likely to be here for the whole of the summer. Judith Evershed's misfortune was Adelaide's salvation and a cause for celebration to Alix, Granny and me. Judith had undertaken to tutor Addy in preparation for her examinations in a couple of months' time, an arrangement that suited us all. Addy was thriving under a tutor who appreciated her intelligence and, moreover, knew how to keep her eccentricities in check. Alix,

Granny and I could relax for a while and the new arrangement relieved the frustration Judith felt at having to take a rest from teaching for the summer. She had recovered from a bad fall but was still troubled by headaches and several doctors had insisted that she must rest.

Friday, 26th April

As the back door crashed open, I glanced at the clock and poured out the cocoa I'd just made. Alix had been in attendance on her old lady but today was different.

'Hurrah,' she cried, reaching for the cup I held out to her. 'You're a life-saver, Christy, and I'm free now for at least ten days, and with full pay too. I've just pushed and pulled Mrs Redfern into the Bournemouth train together with her long-suffering maid and a mountain of luggage, to stay with the old lady's sister. She'll have a lovely time squabbling with everyone there.'

This was typical of Alix; she really was pleased that the quarrelsome old lady would enjoy her favourite pastime during her holiday. She drank deeply, savouring her cocoa, then she gave another excited bounce. 'I bumped into Sister Wisden at the station just now. She was going shopping in Winchester just as I'd waved off the Bournemouth train. You'll never guess what's happened.' She whisked through to the hall to hang up the coat and hat she'd thrown on to a chair while she drank.

Granny looks severe until you detect the glimmer of amusement that lurks in her blue eyes and she nodded in Alix's direction while she stirred the custard for tonight's jam roly-poly. Addy and Judith were in the dining room poring over some knotty problems in an old examination paper and neither deigned to come out to see what was up, so I put Alix out of her misery.

'Are you going to tell us?'

'A new doctor has been appointed to the hospital,' she said triumphantly. 'He'll arrive tomorrow morning.'

'On a Saturday morning? What's he like?' This really was

interesting news. The previous doctor at Groom Hall had been persuaded (forcibly) to take overdue retirement and another retired, elderly surgeon from Southampton had filled in while they awaited the appointment of a permanent medical officer. Much hung on the new doctor's ability to raise morale in staff and patients and to restore the hospital to full efficiency (if that's actually possible). The news was momentous enough to persuade Addy and Miss Evershed to abandon the delights of trigonometry and wander hopefully into the kitchen on the lookout for biscuits and excitement.

'His name is Dr Mungo, or Moncur, or Munro or Moncrieff, maybe. It sounds Scottish at any rate,' Alix declared with relish. 'He's been wounded and has a lost an arm or a leg or something, but he's recovered enough to take charge up at the Hall.'

At this announcement the other occupant of the kitchen raised his head. This was Henry Makepeace who, festooned with domestic animals, the dog asleep on his feet, a cat on his lap, and a kitten draped round his shoulders, was sitting at the table proof-reading my latest chapter. (I write adventure yarns for boys and young men and Henry is a good source for ideas and research.)

'Do you know him, Henry?' Addy had noticed his reaction too. 'What's he like? Small and dark and bad-tempered, perhaps, like Mr Mackintosh at the Post Office? He must be Scottish with any one of those names, so I expect he'll be red-haired and sing songs in Gaelic and wear a kilt.' She paused for breath. 'Can you wear a kilt if you have a wooden leg? Do you think he'll have it carved like a pirate?'

'Why on earth…?' Even after knowing us for a while Henry finds it difficult to follow Adelaide's random flights of fancy. He too has a badly injured leg and until recently he was Captain Makepeace, a convalescent patient up at the Hall. On being invalided out of the army he has taken up an offer from an older cousin living in our town and is now continuing the legal studies that were interrupted by the war. Henry has rapidly become a fixture in our family, for his own sake as well as having been a good friend at school to our darling brother Bertie who was killed last November.

'Well?' Addy frowned at him and the rest of us waited. I was intrigued to see a glimmer of amusement in his eyes and wondered what he knew about the newly appointed doctor.

'If he's been wounded it probably means he's young,' Alix suggested.

'Doesn't always follow,' Henry disagreed but at Addy's gathering frown he shrugged. 'I've come across a Dr Mungo, a Dr Moncrieff, and a Dr Munro. Dr Mungo was quite elderly, and Moncrieff was in his forties, but he died of cholera in Mesopotamia around eighteen months ago. The other one, though, if it's the chap I met last year, was quite young; a nice fellow.' He gently unhitched another kitten that was climbing up his trouser leg and then had to remove a cat from the manuscript he'd been reading. 'I'd better be off. I only stopped for ten minutes on my way back from the station on an errand for Cousin Edgar. And no, I never heard Munro sing, Addy, so I can't tell you what language he warbles in.'

She glared at him but relented enough to wave goodbye. As I saw him to the back door, Addy called out to him. 'Don't forget you're coming to tea on Sunday, Henry.'

'I'm not likely to.' He smiled at her. 'I've never had a birthday party, though the year Jonty and I had a kind-hearted nurse she tried to arrange one for me, but Father soon put a stop to it. That sort of thing, he said, would encourage us to be milksops.'

As always, when he thought of his older brother Jonathan who was killed at Passchendaele, a shadow fell on Henry's face, but he brightened and nodded to me to show he was all right, then went off to town with a jaunty spring in his step. (Well, jaunty for Henry, whose wounded leg will trouble him all his days.)

When I went back into the kitchen, Alix looked up with an exclamation.

'There, I almost forgot. Sister Wisden asked me to find out whether you'd like to help sort out some boxes of books, Christy. They arrived this morning, she said, from the auctioneer in town; he thought the patients might enjoy them. Apparently, they're running out of space in their store and these books haven't sold, so it was the jumble sale, or the hospital.'

'Doesn't sound very inviting.' I grumbled, but she knew I was caught. Boxes of books? How could I resist. 'When does Sister want us to do this?'

'The patients are arriving after luncheon tomorrow, so I said we'd go up to help with the books in the morning,' Alix explained. 'We might catch a glimpse of the new doctor; I'm sure he'll be there in time to greet them.'

'You should go and help with the books too, Adelaide,' suggested Judith Evershed, to Addy's disgust. 'Please don't make that face, I've told you several times that it reveals an extremely immature nature. Besides, if the wind changes, you'll be stuck like that.' She turned away for a moment though not before I caught the glimmer of a smile. Judith Evershed finds my sister very entertaining even though she is impressed by Addy's intelligence. 'I have plenty of work and can occupy myself very well tomorrow morning. It will do you good to help Christabel and you never know, you might find some interesting books.'

Instead of settling down in bed that night, I reached for my dressing-gown and sneaked up to Alix's attic bedroom. She showed no surprise and pulled back the covers to let me tuck in beside her.

'What's up?' she asked.

'We've had relatives turn up sometimes even before the patients have arrived at Groom Hall, so with any luck we could have a house full of lodgers tomorrow or the next day, even though it's the weekend,' I said, snuggling down and pulling the eiderdown up to my chin. It's still quite chilly at night. 'We'll be run off our feet looking after them and we still haven't decided what to do with our windfall. We need to talk about it but there never seems to be time.'

The windfall in question had arrived a few weeks earlier and we were very cagey about it. Alix, Granny and I are the only people who know that there's a large (well, large for us) amount of money in the bank. Suffice to say that most families have a black sheep and that although we are painfully respectable, not all our relatives can be described thus, hence our discretion about the source of our new-found security. Such as it is.

'It's safe enough at the moment,' I temporised. 'It's in Granny's account and she and I are the only signatories so nobody else can touch it. I don't want to squander it...'

Alix snorted with laughter at the very idea, as we are frugal in the extreme, which is just as well when you think about our combined income. Besides, having a larger-than-life father who was officially recorded as having drowned when the Lusitania sank three years ago, had taught us always to have an emergency fund in reserve – though never previously such a comfortable cushion against unexpected catastrophes. And never previously with the gratifying knowledge that Papa could not get his hands on it. I crossed my fingers at the thought; you never know...

'I think a hundred pounds of it should be absolutely untouchable, except in a case of really dire emergency.' Alix nodded and I went on, 'I'd like to send Addy to the High School for a year, starting in September. Judith is happy to coach her for the exams this summer, which is good news for us, but Addy's far too young to think of going to Oxford yet, even if – when – she gets through. As for university, we should put aside another portion of the windfall to cover that.'

'The High School is a really good idea,' Alix agreed. 'A year at a decent school would do her a power of good; she needs to learn how to get along with ordinary girls.'

'Exactly,' I'd known she would understand. 'Even without the windfall we can afford the fees because we've been paying for St Mildred's and the cost will be about the same and much better value for money. After a year we can review the situation; she might have set her heart on something new by then. I'll discuss it with Judith when I have time.'

Saturday, 27th April, early morning

I looked in at the drawing room after breakfast and felt a deep sense of gratitude that we could afford a maid as helpful as Bella. The room was ready for Sunday's tea party; spotless and as elegant as possible in view of the slightly battered furniture and the faded chintzes in curtains and covers. I knew that the house next door was equally spick and span.

My mission was to wrap up Henry's birthday present so it could be stowed away out of sight and I could tick off one more task from my never-ending list. His actual birthday is the first of May but that's on Wednesday, a working day, so we've invited him, and his cousins too, for a tea party here tomorrow instead.

'We should take more photographs of the people we love,' I said soberly and glanced at the picture of Bertie, forever young and brave and smiling in his subaltern's uniform, taken just before he went off to war. Our dearest, darling brother. I blinked away a tear and blew a loving kiss to him then admired the framed photograph I was wrapping for Henry. We three girls smiled at the camera, looking happy and well-dressed at the wedding of that earliest lodger. Her father, a major, had been a patient at Groom Hall as had her new husband, and in a fit of triumphant generosity the bride had, on the morning before her wedding, presented us with a good part of her maidenly wardrobe.

'I'll need different clothes once I'm married,' she had told me in a surprising burst of confidence; surprising because we had previously barely heard a word from her. 'You won't be offended if I offer you these things, will you?'

Offended? No Fyttleton living would be offended at being given such lovely things so I'd thanked her enthusiastically and at once took possession of the blue silk for myself, having admired it from afar. Most women nowadays would think twice about casually handing out one good, wearable dress, let alone three such beauties, but she had wealthy parents and was marrying a man of comfortable means. I've observed that people like that always seem to afford new clothes, even in these straitened times.

That's why we look so charming in the photograph, though of course you can't see the actual colours: Addy in a green linen frock with cherry coloured knots of ribbon, Alix in a soft pink silk, and me – complacent and thrilled all in one – in the dull Liberty blue that suited me so well. The bride had handed over straw hats too, along with silk flowers for trimmings. I do hope she'll be happy with her wounded hero husband.

I hadn't realised I'd spoken out loud as I wrapped the happy photograph until behind me, Judith Evershed drew a long, sighing breath.

'It's not always that easy.' She looked wistful and I raised an eyebrow.

'Judith?'

'There was someone.' Her voice was sad. 'He did give me a photograph, but I keep it under lock and key. It's not a good idea to have it on show.' She hesitated and her dark eyes misted. 'He had the photograph taken when he was commissioned into the army.'

'I – don't understand,' I was puzzled.

'It was the wrong army,' she said quietly and in a flash I remembered that she had spent some time teaching in Germany before the war, shortly after she left Oxford. She had once made some remark about a dance at the local castle and – yes, there had been mention of the young officers attending.

'Oh, poor Judith. Have you ever heard anything?'

She shook her head, desolate for a moment, and I squeezed her shoulder as I left the room.

In the kitchen I made scones and put them in the oven, then whipped up a batter and set it aside in the larder, ready to become Yorkshire pudding, pancakes or toad-in-the-hole, or possibly all three for luncheon and dinner, because I had wheeled some sausages out of the butcher.

The dog capered about when he saw me slip my coat on, but I shook my head at him. 'I'm sorry, Bobs, I'm only wearing my coat because it's chilly outside. I'm just going to see to the hens.'

Undaunted, Bobs followed me down the garden, though Boadicea, the dowager cat, who had raised an inquisitive head, sniffed disdainfully and went back to sleep. Hens are no novelty to her even if Bobs is always eager to greet them.

As usual, our four middle-aged hens stared balefully at the dog and demanded their breakfast from me. Well, I say four of them, but one of them had astonished us a couple of weeks earlier by becoming broody.

'Broody?' Alix had opened her eyes wide in disbelief. 'Kaiser Bill? Isn't she too old?'

Together we had looked at Bill (so named when a neighbour gave her to us, because we had thought such a big chick must be a male). There could be no doubt. Even as we'd stared at her Kaiser Bill, completely ignoring us as usual (unless we come bearing food), was fussily plucking some feathers from her breast to line her untidy creation of straw and moss. We had felt obliged to do our best for her; we knew we wouldn't be able to bear her mournful clucking otherwise. A chance meeting with the friendly farmer who lives just up the road had solved the problem when Addy came home bearing a clutch of eggs.

'He's not too sure they'll hatch,' she had explained. 'Their broody hen met a sticky end last night when the fox got in the hen run, which is why there are only half-a-dozen eggs because some were smashed. He says we're welcome to try.'

Looking at Kaiser Bill now happily sitting on her adopted eggs, I hoped everything would work out in the end. I bent to have a sniff and was relieved to find that at least the eggs didn't smell bad, so perhaps there was hope.

'You might be lucky, Bill,' I told her and stroked her head which is never a good idea because, like her namesake, she's belligerent and rude.

When my scones were done, I left them cooling on the rack and slipped unnoticed upstairs where I was able to spend a while typing out my latest serial. The week's holiday from running a guest house had given me an excellent chance to finish my previous one and send it off to the magazine editor, and I was now just over halfway into Mulberry Boys March to War, its provisional title. Luckily my editor only requires short books.

There was no sign of Granny when I arrived in the kitchen, so I assumed she was reading or knitting in her room, but Alix and Judith Evershed were lingering over a cup of Camp coffee and Alix waved her cup at me. 'There's hot milk on the hob, Christy. Fetch yourself a drink and come and talk to us; there's time before we go up to the hospital. I was just going to quiz Judith about the High School idea.'

'Shh…' I looked round anxiously. 'Where's Addy? She mustn't know we're talking about her.'

'We're safe for ten minutes or so,' Judith said, looking intrigued. 'I sent her out earlier with instructions to be on the doorstep of the Public Library when they opened. She promised to be back before quarter-to-eleven, and she won't be late because she's dying to see what's going on up at the hospital. Her latest task is to look into ancient medical practices, and I suggested she should begin with the Egyptians. I imagine we will soon be bored to tears by long lectures about burial rites. Never mind, it all keeps her actively engaged in learning. I just hope she doesn't decide to try embalming something!'

'We'd better warn the cats to lie low,' I laughed, then explained briefly that we could afford to send Addy to the High School for a year, citing our feeling that she ought to learn how to get on with other girls before tackling Oxford.

'What do you think, Judith? Exams or not, she'd be far too young to go away and neither of us has time to chaperone her.'

'An excellent idea,' Judith nodded, smiling. 'I'm sure she'll do well in her exams but as you say the experience can only benefit her. Besides, she would go straight into the Sixth Form and the pupils who stay on at the High School will be serious girls, working towards a career and thus motivated to learn. Addy really is the most intelligent child I have ever taught, but she is also extremely immature so it will do her no harm at all to study with girls who are possibly her equals.'

She drained her cup and collected up her notebook and pencil, making a comical face as she did so. 'You know Addy's still agitating for a classroom down in the cellar of Balmoral Lodge, don't you? I do understand, it would be more of an adventure for her but as I pointed out, it hardly matters for just the two of us when we can work perfectly well in your dining room.'

'It's not as though we have formal meals these days,' Alix agreed and Judith rose.

'I suppose you might want a dinner party someday,' she said, laughing at our horrified faces. 'As for your idea of something to occupy Addy for a second year, why not wait and see? I'm sure you'll think of something; you girls are so resourceful!'

Chapter Two

Sure enough, Adelaide banged into the house by the back door as Alix and I stood prinking in the looking-glass in the front hall and checking the time. We inspected her; you can't trust her to stay neat as she has a lordly disdain for her appearance when she's thinking about something more interesting, such as embalming her ancestors, or probably the rest of her family even though we're still inconveniently alive.

'We must make an effort for Henry's birthday; fancy never having had a party. It's a pity we shan't be able to ice and decorate his birthday cake properly, Christy,' Alix remarked as we puffed up the hill the back way through the park belonging to Groom Hall.

'I'll bake it first thing tomorrow but I'm afraid it'll be a very plain one, sugar's in such short supply. I suppose we might be able to spare just enough to sprinkle on the top, Henry won't mind, you know he's not one to make a fuss.'

I turned to make sure Addy was still with us. She has a tendency to wander off if she's bored but today's visit to the Hall was something new so sure enough, even though she was lagging behind, at least she was heading in the right direction. 'I hope at least one lodger arrives today,' I said. 'Next door is quite ready to be filled from top to bottom with guests and Addy picked some blossom earlier so their drawing room looks quite festive.

'As for Henry's birthday, it'll be quite an event for us to have a tea party and I know he's pleased that we're making an effort for his cousins. If we have any lodgers by then we'll just have to manage somehow.'

Henry had shyly introduced us to his much older cousins. He was enjoying his work and Mr Makepeace seemed happy with his progress while Miss Bertha, who was as shy as Henry, had begun to take an interest in us.

'Too much interest,' groaned Alix, when I mentioned this. 'No, I don't mean that exactly; Miss Bertha is a darling, but I wish her friend Miss Diplock hadn't started to interfere. It's kindly meant, I suppose, but she's awfully overbearing.'

'She treats us as a charity project, as though we're her pets.' Addy had overheard us, and she stopped for a moment to look around. 'Isn't the park lovely at the moment, there are still primroses in bloom. Remind me to pick some bluebells on the way home. Yes,' she went on. 'Miss Bertha is kind and thoughtful, but Miss Diplock thinks we're three dear little kittens and she alternates between telling us what to do and being embarrassingly open-handed with presents. Buying our friendship, that's what she's doing.'

'Well, it's not working, and you didn't mind the other day when she sent round a box of chocolates for Granny's birthday. Once we're busy with the new lodgers,' I said hopefully, 'we'll have an excuse to cut her short – politely please, Addy. Let's hope the novelty wears off and she'll find something else to lavish attention on.'

'She already has,' Alix looked guilty. 'I mentioned it to Granny, but I haven't had time to tell you two. Miss Diplock caught me when I ran down to the station just after breakfast to pick up Mother's parcel of books. She wants to rope us in to help with the May Day celebrations in town on Friday afternoon.'

'It'll be May Day on Wednesday, actually, in case you hadn't noticed,' objected Addy, the family pedant.

'The maypole and so forth ought to be on the Saturday,' explained Alix with a patient sigh. Arguing with our sister is usually an exercise in exasperation and is quite pointless. 'Otherwise most people would be at work. This year it's on Friday afternoon instead because there's a big memorial service at the Priory on Saturday. You can't have the mourners making their way through a church fête on the green outside. Friday's not ideal but Miss Diplock says there are going to be stalls selling things: flowers, cakes, that kind of thing, and they want to attract as many visitors as possible.'

'What does she want us to do?' I was full of foreboding. Miss Bertha's friend might think of us as pets, but I was convinced she would be cracking the whip. I wondered how we could avoid this without hurting nice Miss Bertha's feelings though I wasn't too worried about offending her friend, a loud, interfering sort of woman.

When Henry had diffidently introduced us to his cousins at Easter, we had liked them very much. Mr Edgar Makepeace was a kind, quiet man and I could see that Henry would look just like him in about forty years: stockily built, still with a full head of fair hair turning silver, and a quizzical, twinkling smile. Miss Bertha looked much the same, but she was as shy as Henry. However, she made an effort with us because Henry's own nice nature and singular lack of family apart from themselves had appealed to her from the start. I suspected that she was secretly fascinated by the Fyttleton family – as Henry is for some reason – and wanted to be friends.

Miss Portia Diplock was another matter. Apparently she lived in a small house in the middle of town, and Miss Bertha confided that her friend had been forced to draw in her horns when first her father, two years ago, and then more recently her brother, were found to have left their affairs in disarray. She still likes to play Lady Bountiful however and is the scourge of local working parties as well as sitting on the committees of most charitable and social groups. Even the Mayor is reported to have called her a meddling harpy – to her face! She and Miss Bertha have known each other since their schooldays when Portia was Head Girl and Bertha in the kindergarten. It seemed to us that Miss Diplock still expected to be in charge, but that Bertha Makepeace had long since learned how to slip quietly away whenever her friend started to lay down the law. Unfortunately for us, Miss Diplock seemed to think she could bully us instead.

Alix was about to reply but we had reached the kitchen garden of Groom Hall and Sister Wisden was waving to us from the back door.

'Good girls,' she beamed, shooing us into the main hall which doubles as sitting room and reception area when the convalescent officers are in residence. 'I hope you've brought aprons. These books are dusty!'

Several large boxes stood in front of a new bookcase against one wall and Sister Wisden whisked away, promising to send in some coffee to sweeten the task.

'She's such an improvement on her predecessor.' I knelt down to wrestle with the first box. 'We'd never have been offered coffee by Matron.'

'Sister Wisden works harder than anyone,' Alix agreed. 'She makes us work too, but you don't mind because she does it so nicely. Now, what have you got in there?'

'It looks like boys' books,' I waved a copy of The Coral Island at her. 'They'll go down well. 'Oh dear,' I drew back, disappointed. 'There's Children of the New Forest but that seems to be it. The rest are religious books.'

'Mind if I borrow the New Forest one?'

A tall, very fair officer had come up behind us and stood there, leaning on a stick. He smiled and said, 'I haven't read it for years, but I ought to learn a bit about the area now I'm living here. The New Forest isn't far away, is it?'

We scrambled to our feet and stared at him, Alix and I conscious of our already dusty aprons, though not Adelaide who rarely notices trivia like untidy hair or grubby clothes.

I handed over the book after giving it a hasty wipe with a duster. Addy was openly curious.

'Why will you be living here?'

Alix went red with embarrassment and gave her a surreptitious pinch. 'Hush, Addy, don't forget this is a hospital for wounded officers.'

'Oh, yes,' Addy gave the new arrival a searching stare. 'I suppose you're one of the new patients. Do you mind telling me about your wound?' She brushed aside the hushing that I added to Alix's protests and pointed to his leg. 'I hope to be a doctor one day so I need to know things like that.'

I thought he winced but as he took her measure, his expression lightened.

'Of course, you do, I quite understand,' he said solemnly while smiling reassuringly to quell Alix's misgivings. 'I lost my foot,' he told Addy, an impish twinkle lighting up his face. 'It was last year but I'm quite recovered now and I have a splendid new false foot.'

'But how did you lose it?' She is irrepressible when she is on a quest for information. It's a character trait that, admirable in itself, can be wearing in the extreme for her family as we trail along in her wake apologising to her affronted victims. Like Mother, Addy rarely notices if she upsets people. They are both single-minded and lack the social graces they were raised with, though Alix and I haven't yet quite despaired of our young sister.

He raised an eyebrow as he glanced at each of us in turn then he said, completely straight-faced, 'I was big game hunting in Africa last September and a passing lion suddenly fancied a snack.'

I was about to frown at him because I could see that Addy believed every word, but to my astonishment, Alix started to giggle.

We all stared at her: Addy full of affronted dignity and I with amazement because it's well-known in the family that Alix, who for years thought 'custard' was a rude word, rarely sees a joke unless it bites her on the nose. The wounded officer who had turned to go, looked suddenly dazed as he looked at Alix; she really is very pretty. Meanwhile, Alix laughed so hard that she had to wipe away the tears.

'That sounds most unfortunate,' I said feebly, thinking somebody had better make some comment. 'I hope the lion suffered no ill effects?'

That wasn't at all what I had meant to say but the officer nodded appreciatively. 'None at all at the time, that I could see,' he said, still solemnly. 'Sadly, however, it died of indigestion on the following day.'

At that moment Sister Wisden arrived, carrying a tray.

'Here we are,' she said, nodding to the tall officer. 'Biscuits as well, Cook is feeling generous today. I spotted you heading in this direction, Doctor, so I've brought you a cup of coffee too.'

'Doctor?' Addy said it for us as we looked at him curiously.

'Yes,' Sister Wisden smiled. 'May I introduce Acting-Captain Dr Fergus Munro? These are the Miss Fyttletons, Doctor. Miss Alexandra, one of our stalwart volunteers, and her sisters, Miss Christabel and Miss Adelaide who are helping today to sort out these books.'

'You don't have a wooden leg after all.' Addy was disappointed and I despaired of her. It seems unlikely that she'll ever learn to be tactful and that won't be much help if her dream is fulfilled and she becomes a doctor. She'll need at least a modicum of diplomacy surely.

'No, he doesn't.' Sister turned to go. 'Has he told you how he lost his foot?' She smiled and continued without waiting for an answer. 'Such a strange, sad occurrence, coming face to face with a hungry polar bear like that, wasn't it?'

We stared accusingly at Dr Munro who sipped his coffee and looked unabashed as he held out the plate of biscuits to Alix first. She blushed and he still had that dazzled expression, but he said nothing.

Addy had not caught up with events, so now she frowned at him even more fiercely.

'How could you go big game hunting in the middle of a war?' she demanded. 'And what on earth was a polar bear doing in Africa?'

The new doctor didn't answer but grinned tantalisingly before turning to Alix.

'Can you spare me half an hour or so, Miss Fyttleton? To show me round the hospital?'

While Alix reddened and stammered, I caught his eye and turned to my sister.

'Of course, you can,' I said briskly. 'Addy and I can easily sort out the books but you're the only one who knows all about how the hospital works.'

That won me an approving nod from Dr Munro. 'Alix,' I suggested, 'why don't you give Dr Munro the grand tour, gardens and park and all, and then help Sister Wisden prepare for the new officers. In fact, you might as well stay up here till your usual finishing time, even though you're not officially on duty today. I'm sure someone will find you something for luncheon.'

That brought more blushes from my sister but to my surprise the doctor patted my shoulder.

'Good girl,' he said as he walked off with Alix.

'What did you do that for?' grumbled Addy. 'I wanted to ask him so many questions and now you've got rid of him.'

Her eyes brightened and I saw that the doctor, who was waiting for Alix to fetch her hat, was heading back towards us.

'I made a mistake,' he said solemnly, looking at Addy. 'It wasn't a lion, or a polar bear that did for me. I had foot rot.'

If he had hoped to be forgiven for teasing her, he was to be sorely disappointed.

'You're just being silly,' she sniffed. 'And anyway, you mean trench foot. Foot rot is what sheep get.'

'Baaa!' he said with a wicked gleam in his eyes as he laughed and went after Alix.

That was when we recognised that Fergus Munro was not a run-of-the-mill physician. Little did we know that we would soon be confronted with a sudden death and that the new doctor would play a prominent part in our lives.

Addy sulked a bit after he'd gone so I enjoyed sorting through the books in peace, until she interrupted the silence,

'He didn't sound at all Scottish, did he? Not like the postmaster.'

'Neither does Granny,' I pointed out. 'And she was born and brought up in Aberdeenshire. It all depends. Besides, just because he has a Scottish name probably means his family originally came from Scotland.'

She tossed her head, dismissing such a feeble idea. 'I don't think Dr Munro ought to make jokes about having his foot amputated.' She sounded self-righteous as she delved into a box. 'It trivialises what he and the others have gone through.'

'It's his wound,' I said. 'Besides, they nearly all make jokes and tell funny stories about being at the Front, you know that. It's the way they cope.'

'Henry doesn't make jokes,' she pouted.

'Not very often, that's true, though he's starting to relax now he knows us,' I admitted. 'But Henry is quiet and serious, and I don't think his father sounds like a man who liked a joke. Don't forget Bertie laughed about everything.'

Addy went quiet, and I knew she was thinking, as I was, about our darling brother, Alix's twin, the eldest, best and dearest of us all, whose merry laughter was silenced after a shell took him almost six months ago. Addy stopped dusting to touch my hand briefly. Living without Bertie has been the hardest thing we have ever had to learn and I don't believe we will ever get over it. Even when I'm an old, old woman I think my eyes will still fill with tears when I think of him: forever young and beloved, going off so gaily to war.

'Alix was a bit odd, wasn't she?'

I'd been thinking the same myself and was impressed that Addy, who only notices things that interest her personally, should have spotted something unusual in our elder sister. Addy is such a strange mixture; she's so clever, by far the most intelligent person I've ever met and having lived with Grandpapa, a brilliant former Oxford scholar, that's saying a lot. On the other hand, she often seems to have no common sense at all and appears to be far younger and sillier than her actual age. Yet again, she will turn to and helpfully tackle domestic tasks as a matter of course – if it occurs to her. No wonder Alix and I, Granny too, are sometimes at a complete loss as to how to help her grow up.

'You know what she's like with boys, as a rule,' Addy said. 'I'm sure she uses Mother's books as gospel, on how to flirt. You know, 'La, Sir, pray spare my blushes'. That sort of thing.'

I bit my lip and tried not to laugh. Nothing offends her so

much as older people (particularly her sisters) finding her amusing. She thought about it for a moment.

'The trouble is that none of us has the slightest idea how to behave around young men.'

It was true, but I had never expected Addy to recognise that. After all, she is only fifteen and any time she can spare from her books is spent in the pursuit of someone kind enough – or foolish enough – to let her have a go at surgery (on joints of meat, I hasten to explain), to further her ambition to become a doctor.

Alix is extremely pretty and charming and although she went to a few parties in town last autumn, all of that stopped abruptly when we had the telegram about Bertie in November and since then the only young men she's encountered have been wounded. Not that Alix would be put off by a wound, or even – she insists – a missing limb, because she would love to be married. At least, that's what she says, but personally I think she'd just like to have an adoring suitor on hand at the moment and a little less in the way of a struggle to make ends meet. Besides, marriage, as far as I've observed the state, seems to be hard work and we have quite enough of that already.

But – but Dr Munro had looked spellbound – and so had my sister Alix...

'It's all right for you,' Addy said idly as she burrowed into another of the boxes. 'Henry really likes you and you didn't even have to try.'

I felt my face get hot and I mumbled something, but she had lost interest. Henry Makepeace has become part of our family and yes, Addy is right. He's comfortable with us all, in fact I think he loves the whole family, but he's my particular friend. I hastily tucked that thought out of sight for a later inspection and went on with checking the books.

The boxes slowly emptied though a lot of them were far too dull to offer to any young man, wounded or not. Some of the books of sermons dating from the 1830s would be enough to send you to sleep so I did put a few on the bottom shelf in case anyone needed a cure for insomnia. Luckily, the last box yielded treasure in the shape of some Henty books for boys, at least two dozen Mrs Henry Wood mysteries and quite a few romances by Florence Barclay and Ethel M Dell. These looked similar to the ones Mother writes, featuring masterful men and soppy heroines. They weren't as good as hers though. I scanned through a couple and conceded that although we find Mother's books saccharine in the extreme, she does have a talent for writing sickly sweet novels, the income from which keeps our heads above water. And please God let her continue to do so, I thought piously.

I looked at the clock on the grim black marble mantelpiece in the hall and saw that it was almost time for lunch for the staff, so we hastily arranged the books in alphabetical order. I looked in vain for Alix but found an orderly instead and told him we were going home.

'Tell Sister Wisden that the books we've left in the boxes can go to the book stall at the May Day revels on Friday,' I told him. 'I've stuck a label on them.'

When we arrived home our maid, Bella, waylaid me in the hall. She doesn't usually work at the weekend but the invalid aunt who lived with Bella's family had died on Monday. Yesterday, Friday, had been the funeral so her two nieces had been needed at home. Although I'd protested that it was really not necessary Bella had insisted they would make up the time today, Saturday.

'A lady called, Miss Christy,' she said now. 'She asked for her ladyship, but she was white-washing the cellar, so I just said she wasn't at home. The lady said she'd call tomorrow, in the evening, and would like to talk to you, if her ladyship was still otherwise engaged. She hoped you wouldn't mind it being a Sunday as it's the only time she'll have spare.'

'Just a moment, Bella,' I called her back. 'Why was her ladyship whitewashing the cellar?'

'Because she and Mr Jerrold both agreed it would be a good idea, Miss Christy.' Bella looked surprised at my question, but I was still none the wiser.

'Is Mr – er – Jerrold still down there?'

'Yes, miss. He called on her ladyship yesterday and this morning he came in early, by the cellar door. You wouldn't have noticed, I expect, because he didn't knock the hole in the wall until you left and he's been hard at it all morning. I just took them both a cup of cocoa. They've made a fine old mess and I tried to get her ladyship to let me clean up, but she said it's not finished yet and she shooed me away.'

That sounded like Granny but – a hole in the wall? I made for the cellar stairs.

Bella was right. I could see that there certainly was a fine old mess which included dust, mortar, rubble, a pile of bricks and yes, there was a door-shaped hole in the wall between our cellar and the one in Balmoral Lodge. I could also see that Granny and a stout middle-aged man had everything under control and Granny did seem to be doing a bit of tidying up as they went. They both turned to look at me as I came down the narrow stairs.

'Ah, Christy,' Granny turned to her companion and waved a (luckily empty) dustpan in his direction. 'Watch where you put your feet. You remember Mr Jerrold? He was the plumber who put our bathroom in a few years ago. He is kindly going to install a lavatory and basin in each cellar, ours and next-door.'

'Oh?' I've often thought that only someone who knows my grandmother really well can read her expressions accurately. I greeted Mr Jerrold warmly; always keep on the good side of tradesmen is one of Granny's own maxims and watching her now I thought she looked slightly ill at ease. When she continued in an airy kind of way, I knew she was wondering whether she had bitten off more than she could chew, though she certainly would never admit it.

'We now have a door through to the Balmoral Lodge cellar,' she explained. 'For emergencies and for ease of maintenance,' she added with a challenging stare.

'What a good idea, just what we need,' I said brightly, taking the wind out of her sails. 'You seem to be doing a splendid job. Is that why you've started whitewashing the cellar? In case of emergencies?'

'It's this way, Miss,' the plumber was eager to join in. 'There were these two coal bins, yours and next-door's, each with a hatch outside where the coal would come in, and the door opening indoors here, to shovel it into a scuttle. Now you've got the new coal bunkers outside and handier for the kitchen, you don't need these little rooms. There's good head height and being side-by-side, we thought, her ladyship and me, that they'd be right handy for the drains, being underneath the – er – conveniences you already have upstairs.'

Granny was following our conversation with a gleam in her eye as she watched me try to escape without offending the plumber, but like all experts everywhere (and all men, whether expert or not, come to that) he was intent on explaining his work. Every washer, every screw, every saw cut, minutely and at length.

'You see, Miss, what with the – er- convenience in the bathroom, and the one in the hall above us – and just the same in both houses too – it's possible to get a good flow. Aye, that's what you need, you see, a real good flow. The downpipe is handy so all I have to do is plumb in the new – er – appliances with outlets to the existing drain, and Bob's your uncle.'

'Indeed he is.' I nodded enthusiastically and although I was intrigued as to where the new – er – appliances had come from and wondered how much they had cost, I decided to make my escape. 'Well done, both of you, I'll leave you to it. Do carry on.'

Upstairs, I caught up with our senior maid.

'What on earth made her ladyship think of doing such a thing?' I made a face. 'The lady who called, Bella. What was she like? Might she be a relative of one of the patients that are due up at the Hall? Wanting a room?'

'She said not,' Bella replied. 'I did ask, but she says it's really you she needs to talk to.' I groaned and Bella chuckled in fellow feeling and hurried to reassure me. 'She seemed quite nice, Miss Christy, and our Penny said her clothes was ever so smart.'

She was about to go downstairs when I remembered something.

'How is your mother, Bella? Is there anything we can do to help?'

Bella's father had died four weeks earlier and we had all felt horribly guilty for thinking that his wife was well rid of him! Everyone knew he drank and neglected his family, and some of us suspected that he beat her, and possibly his daughters too, though they stayed loyally silent. He had been seen stumbling, the worse for wear, down an alley in town late one night and nobody was surprised when his body was fished out downriver the next day. His sister, as mild and patient as he had been obstreperous, had lived with the family for the last few months ever since her health began to fail and now that she too had died, I wondered how they would all manage.

Before we took up our new career as proprietors of a most superior guesthouse for female relatives of patients at Groom Hall, Bella had come to us three days a week. When her other employer retrenched and let her go, she had been glad to come to us for each weekday, reserving the weekend to help at home. This was a gamble on our part, but the lodgers would bring extra work and, we hoped, extra income. So far, and my fingers are very tightly crossed when I say this, the gamble seems to be paying off.

Penny, Bella's little sister, left school not long ago. She is only thirteen and came to help us with the lodgers' breakfast and dinner, while helping her mother to care for the invalid aunt during the rest of the day. She loves silks and satins and beautiful things and at the moment she thinks she would like to become a lady's maid – not something we are ever likely to need or be able to afford. However, one of our earliest guests had shown Penny the rudiments of a lady's maid's duties and after a couple of weeks Penny had even been allowed to help arrange the lady's elaborate hair style.

'Mum's all right, thank you, Miss Christy,' Bella lowered her voice and looked over her shoulder but there was nobody to hear. 'I know you won't tell but she's got a job now.'

'Really? That's good news,' I said. 'Doing what?'

'She does our house in the morning and leaves tea ready for all of us,' explained Bella. 'Then at twelve o'clock she goes off to The White Horse and helps in the kitchen there till after six. They've been real nice about letting her have time off this week now poor Aunty's died, but I don't mind telling you, Miss Christy, it'll make Mum's life a lot easier without either of them, Dad or Aunty. Our Mum's as happy as a sandboy but we don't say too much because people might think it looked bad, with our Dad not long gone and Aunty only buried yesterday.'

'I quite understand,' I agreed, squeezing her hand. 'Now, as to this lady visitor, it's a pity she's not a lodger, Penny could have practised on her. Oh well, I suppose we'll find out soon enough.'

Bella hesitated and slid a nervous glance at me.

'What is it?' I prayed she wasn't going to tell me she had found a better situation. We simply can't do without her, but it seemed that was not the problem.

'I – I – can I have a word about our Penny sometime, Miss Christy?'

Before I could say anything, Bella rushed on. 'Penny's the baby, you see. There's six years between her and Niggle and I'm a year older than he is. There's a gap where two little ones died and – well, Mum and me, - we want Penny to have a chance. That's why we're so pleased she's learning a lot by being here.' She looked flustered but seemed reassured by my interest. 'The thing is, we don't know best how to help her, and I thought maybe you could advise us?'

'Of course we will,' I nodded. 'I'll talk to Lady Elspeth and perhaps Miss Evershed and see what they suggest.'

Addy wandered into the kitchen and made herself a jam sandwich then settled down in the garden to do the reading Judith had given her. I realised it was long past my own lunch time, so I went to consult Granny who was looking thoughtfully round the two adjoining cellars. The plumber was contentedly opening up a packet of sandwiches while keeping up a running commentary on his activities. He looked up hopefully when I reached the bottom stair, but I gave him a bright smile and whisked Granny away for luncheon. I am certainly not foolish enough to engage in conversation with a man who wants to instruct me in exhaustive detail about his favourite pastime which, luckily for him, is also his occupation.

'You should have waited till we came home,' I scolded my grandmother. 'Addy and I could have done the white-washing. Whatever made you decide to do it today?'

'Because Addy hasn't stopped pestering me to let her turn the cellar into a classroom,' Granny frowned. 'When Mr Jerrold came knocking yesterday, I thought it would be a good opportunity to tidy up both cellars anyway while we have some money in hand. You never know when something might come in useful.'

'Come and have a cup of tea and a rest, I'm starving so I'll find us some bread and cheese. Has Mother been asking for me, while we were out?' I added apprehensively.

'You're quite safe,' Granny twinkled. 'I took her a bite to eat and she barely noticed I was there. She's well away just now.' She glanced round the kitchen. 'No Alix?'

'She thought she might as well stay up at the Hall and help. There's a lot to do, with the new patients arriving this afternoon, and when we left, she was showing the new doctor round.'

'And was he wearing a kilt?' Granny's voice was dry, but she smiled as our eyes met.

'Of course not,' I giggled. 'He doesn't have red hair either; he's fair-haired, much fairer even than Henry. He's young and his name is Fergus Munro and he's certainly an improvement on Dr Pemberton, but then – who wouldn't be?'

'I suppose I should draw up a proper timetable for Adelaide's studies,' Judith sat down to eat her bread and cheese with us in the kitchen. As a rule, the lodgers are expected to find lunch in the town, but Judith's situation is different. The relative she had been visiting at the Hall has now departed but rather than go home to her parents' house in Oxford to convalesce after her accident, she decided to stay on with us and to everyone's satisfaction is now a firm friend of the family.

'We have been working together whenever I've felt up to it,' she added, 'But I'm much fitter now so we ought to have more structure. The suggestion was that Addy and I should turn next-door's cellar into a classroom, wasn't it? Do we have to?' Granny and I just looked at Judith and she laughed. 'Oh dear, what a silly question. I suppose we must at least give it a try. Is there anything I can do to help get it ready, Lady Elspeth?'

'You could be thinking about what books you'll need, I suppose,' Granny sounded doubtful then she brightened and turned to me. 'You didn't look round the corner into the cellar next door, Christy. I'm rather pleased with Mr Jerrold's work; he's turning out to be a great help.'

I hoped I didn't look too apprehensive because once in a while Granny, usually the most serene and sensible of women, is side-tracked into an ambitious flight that clearly shows where Addy gets it from.

'Yes,' she nodded now and passed me the dish of apple chutney. 'As I said earlier, he called in yesterday and mentioned he had some bathroom ware at a low price and wondered if it would be of any use to us. He didn't want much for it, so I engaged him. I must have forgotten to mention it last night.'

She caught my eye, but I smiled sweetly and made encouraging noises, so she frowned suspiciously and continued.

'Mr Jerrold says he can make a useful screen from some wood he says he has to hand. I thought it best to ask no questions; it's to partition off the new lavatory in your schoolroom, Judith, keeping the domestic and academic worlds safely separate. We don't need a screen in our own cellar, and he says it won't take him too long. He's fitting the doorframe between the two houses now. He can turn his hand to most jobs as well as plumbing, so he had a good look round yesterday when he called in. He did some measuring then and today he knocked the hole through to fit a door he already had in his yard. Meanwhile, you girls can be looking for some chairs and a table.'

'Granny?' I asked, pouring us out another cup of tea, an extravagance as tea is rationed, but everyone deserves a treat now and then. 'Alix says she told you about Miss Diplock wanting us to help out at the May Day celebrations on Friday. Have you any idea what she expects from us?'

'Miss Diplock has issued instructions that you are all to report for duty at the green in front of the Priory at eight-thirty on Friday morning,' Granny said drily, holding up her hand at my cry of protest. 'No need to make so much noise, Christy. I sent a note to the lady informing her that you girls are all busy about your household duties in the morning but that you and Addy at least, would probably be able to help out during the afternoon, though I made no promises. Whether Alix can take the time from the hospital is up to her.'

I was sure Alix would be there, as would Addy and I, no matter what we said now. There's not a lot of entertainment available in Ramalley at the best of times, although interestingly the War Effort has meant an increase in concerts and bazaars, and even though you see the same things on sale at each Bring and Buy stall and the same people bringing and buying, it's a harmless excitement that leavens our working weeks.

Granny knows this too. 'Miss Diplock also wanted to rope you in to help during the week, but I told her quite strongly that you would not be available. As for the Friday itself, it won't hurt you to help on a stall,' she said in a bracing tone. 'You'll be going to the Fair anyway.'

Chapter Three

There was a ring at the front door of Balmoral Lodge. I had finished my sandwich and made a face and went to answer it. I did a quick check to tidy my hair in the looking-glass in the hall before slipping through the connecting door, formerly two coat cupboards back to back. Incidentally, Mother has no idea of this opening; she is the least observant of women which suits us very well.

First impressions are so important, and I hoped my plain blue blouse and sensible navy skirt would pass muster. I don't hold out any hope of being admired as elegant because I am not, but I do hope that new lodgers see me as sensible and competent. My hair is pinned up in a low bun on my neck which should indicate that I'm over eighteen and have reached the age of discretion.

'How do you do? I am Miss Myrtle Preston,' briskly announced the youngish, brownish, thinnish woman on the doorstep. 'My brother is due to be transferred to Groom Hall today and I understand from Sister Wisden that you have a room to let?'

'Do come in, Miss Preston,' I shook her hand and smiled at her, partly out of common politeness but mostly, I fear, out of a mercenary satisfaction at the thought of the rent money she would shortly hand over. 'I am Christabel Fyttleton. My grandmother, Lady Elspeth, is engaged at present but you'll meet her shortly. Do come into the drawing room.' I hoped she had not noticed my comprehensive stare at her clothes and bearing. It is important to gauge whether a potential paying guest looks prosperous enough to afford the high cost of staying in a house run by a lady of title, not to mention her daughter, the eminent authoress of painstakingly detailed but quite unreadably dull biographies of early heroines of women's suffrage. It is probably better not to mention her rather less literary but highly profitable short romantic novels under the pseudonym, Mabel de Rochforde.

Actually, the rent we charge is exorbitant, but we do offer congenial surroundings, comfortable beds and meals that are as good as rationing and ingenuity – and a spot of quiet poaching – can contrive. Our greatest asset though, is that people are prepared to pay, for the reasons above, and even more because there is nowhere else in easy walking distance of Groom Hall. However, we do have an arrangement with Sister Wisden and if she judges that an officer's relative is in straitened circumstances, she will send a coded note down to us so that we can adjust the rent. This hasn't happened very often as most of the relatives, fortunately for us, seem to be plump in the pocket.

Miss Preston was plainly dressed in a woollen houndstooth coat and skirt of impeccable quality, worn with a blue jumper and a sensible felt hat. Her capacious leather handbag was handsome too, with what looked like a real gold clasp, so I hoped for the best.

'My brother has been awarded the Military Cross for bravery,' she told me proudly. 'He is Major Montagu Preston and at this very moment he should be arriving at Groom Hall hospital to convalesce from wounds received in battle.'

Miss Preston had returned my appraisal equally thoroughly and apparently found my appearance and that of the drawing room acceptable. 'I am booked into The White Horse for tonight and tomorrow, but I wanted to take a look at the hospital today, before my brother arrives,' she remarked. 'It seems very satisfactory and I understand that as the patients will be tired after their journey and will need to be settled in, there will be no visiting today.'

She glanced round the room. 'I must say,' she added, 'that it is a convenience to find accommodation so close to the hospital. Sister Wisden says she cannot praise too highly the service you offer at Balmoral Lodge.'

I nodded gratefully and reminded myself to do something

nice for Sister. I don't know quite what though, she probably won't want any more kittens, which is a pity as we currently have several of them at different stages from adolescent to two blindly mewing furry dumplings currently occupying a basket in the broom cupboard which their mother has designated a maternity ward. Needless to say that particular cat, a tortoiseshell with a large white patch on her throat, has a royal name too. Even Bertie had protested that Addy's choice of Edith Swan Neck, after King Harold's hand-fasted wife, was a bit much, but she's always known as Swanny anyway.

Not only that but Matilda, mother of our two older kittens, is looking alarmingly plump and more so every passing day. I made a mental note to send an urgent summons to our occasional gardener, Niggle (it's a long story; his mother had only seen the name written down) who is brother to Bella and Penny. We've never dared ask how he used to keep down the kitten population before he was called up, and we certainly will not enquire now he has been discharged from the army. We know in theory what happens but like most people, we prefer to turn a blind eye and be complete hypocrites.

Under the previous regime at Groom Hall relatives of the patients had to trail round Ramalley in search of accommodation, very often finding nothing to suit. One of Sister Wisden's reforms is to make sure relatives are given a list of hotels and guest houses in town, even before the patients leave the big military hospital at Netley. This means that sometimes we have had mothers, sisters or wives move into Balmoral Lodge even before their wounded menfolk have been transferred here.

Perhaps Sister would enjoy some lemon biscuits made from a secret recipe known only to Granny's mother's old cook and passed down to Granny as a wedding present? Pulling myself together I handed our new guest a card with our rules and mealtimes and steeled myself to ask for a week's rent in advance. Three guineas! Per person! I still find it astonishing that so far not one single paying guest has quibbled at this enormous amount though I did once reduce it slightly, by half a guinea, when two ladies shared a room. In this case I needn't have worried, Miss Preston seemed unfazed and handed over the money with a smile.

'I'll show you your room,' I said. We try to keep the former morning room for guests who can't manage the stairs and I noticed that Miss Preston was walking with a slight limp.

'Heavens no,' she cried when I explained. 'I strained a muscle a few days ago playing hockey. I play in goal for the Berkshire County Ladies' First XI,' she said proudly. 'I ran to stop a ball and saved the match but twisted my leg under me when I fell. No need to worry about the stairs, the exercise will be good for me.' To illustrate her point she galloped after me, though I noticed she was wincing a little when we entered the biggest front bedroom.

'Now that will come in useful.' She dropped her outdoor coat on to the bed and pointed to the cupboard in the alcove. 'I like to keep a small store of food by me, in case I feel hungry. That cupboard will do nicely. I don't suppose…' She cast a glance round. 'No, I didn't think so. I had hoped you might have a gas ring so that I can brew up a cup of cocoa if I need one.'

'But Miss Preston,' I protested. 'We'll be happy to make you a cup of cocoa if you want one. During the morning guests are welcome to make coffee or cocoa here in the Balmoral Lodge kitchen if they wish, though many ladies prefer to explore the tea shops in town. We do offer afternoon tea here as an extra, but in any case, the staff at Groom Hall always have tea and cake or a biscuit for visitors in the afternoon when the patients have theirs.'

'I'm sure,' she said doubtfully. 'However, I'm accustomed to making myself a snack if I feel peckish at any time of the day or night although, of course, it's different in someone else's home. Would it be possible for me to use the gas stove in the kitchen? I would be using my own supplies, of course. No need to worry about your rations being depleted.'

As she spoke, she was unpacking a large Gladstone bag and stowing the contents into the cupboard. I watched wide-eyed as the shelves were filled with tins, packets and paper bags of tea, café-au-lait, cocoa, biscuits, a large cake tin (containing cake) and a tin of that dried milk you can buy.

'There,' she said with satisfaction as she added her own cup-and-saucer and a tin-opener to the hoard. 'That will keep the hunger pangs at bay for a day or so.'

I wiped the amazement off my face as she turned to smile at me with satisfaction. Without her coat she was as thin as a rake, so where on earth would she put all that food? It must be all that hockey-playing; and how did she usually cope with all the shortages in wartime?

'Once the patients arrive, you may find the walk up to the Hall and back too much for your sore leg, Miss Preston. I can book the station pony trap for you, if you would like,' I suggested, mentally groaning at yet more outlay, the trap fare. I was greatly cheered when she nodded briskly and picked up her coat and bag.

'Thank you, Miss Christabel, I have beaten you to it!' I was amused at her triumphant smile. 'The trap will call for me a little before three every day next week and will bring me back down the hill after five, when visiting time comes to an end. The charge will, of course, be a private matter between the driver and myself and I can offer a lift to any other guests you may have.' She glanced at the clock. 'And now I must be going. The pony trap is waiting at the end of the road so I shall make my way back into town. If we are agreed, I believe I shall do very nicely here, so I hope to move in on Monday afternoon if that is convenient.'

It was. She had already filled her cupboard, after all, and even more importantly, she had paid her rent in advance and would cost us nothing for the next two days, so we parted on excellent terms. My heart was light when I looked into Granny's room to deposit the rent money in her top drawer pending my next visit to the bank. Other young women of my age would probably be excited by the thought of parties or new frocks rather than the comforting jingle of coins or the rustle of banknotes, let alone the immense reassurance of having a healthy bank balance – but I'm incurably practical.

Accounts that balance give me a warm, satisfying glow.

I had not had time to broach the subject of Penny's future to Granny or Judith but I did manage to snatch some time to myself to go over what I'd written so far of Mulberry Boys March to War. It was a suitably patriotic tale of deceit, daring and dastardly deeds, this time set in a camp 'somewhere in France' but my heart wasn't in it. I hoped for a couple more female relatives of the Groom Hall officers to present themselves as possible lodgers before the end of the day, so I couldn't allow myself to disappear completely into the toils and tribulations of the former sixth form boys of my fictitious Mulberry College. Besides, I needed to persuade Henry to tell me about being in camp which won't be easy as he dislikes talking about his time in France altogether. I sighed, wondering whether Dr Munro might be more forthcoming but decided he wouldn't. Perhaps I should visit the hospital and buttonhole one of the patients; surely one of them would be helpful?

I threw down my pencil. I was finding it harder and harder to keep up with my various jobs: coping with Mother and typing her outpourings in the morning, helping Granny with the cooking and household duties, dealing with the lodgers and, of course, being the only person the hens would tolerate. The hens! Heavens above, something else to fret about. Was it tomorrow or Monday that the point-of-lay newcomers were due to arrive?

My most recent book, St Wulfstan's Under Fire, had been written in record time and I'd sent it off to the editor of Brave Boys' Yarns, a weekly magazine that has now taken all my adventure serials and paid me handsomely. In addition, these same yarns, each suitably re-edited, have subsequently been taken by Mother's own publisher and are now being issued as short books for young men at the Front. The Brave Boys' editor prefers pure and wholesome tales of noble boys and their derring-do so I hope he never comes across the books because they contain a few mild oaths and jokes that might shock him. He and Mother's publisher correspond with the apparently middle-aged Miss C M Fyttleton who acts as agent to Lt Crombie, but if either of them ever discovers that the author is actually a girl of eighteen I imagine they'll each have a fit. However, Bertie had made sure his sisters weren't silly, fluffy girls who would have the vapours at an occasional 'Damn' or 'Confound it' – or swoon at the mention of young men playing poker. Cards, by the way, are referred to by the magazine editor as 'the Devil's prayer book' which seems a little harsh, not to mention rather exciting. I'd have thought the average young man at the Front might find that idea quite attractive, acquainted as they are over there with plenty of evidence of the Devil's much more vicious handiwork.

Sure enough, forty-five minutes later, another candidate arrived for interview, though in this case I think the couple at the door believed they were interviewing me. How little they knew. Ramalley is full, hardly a room to let, or even a bed, and although the hotel and lodging-house keepers pull long faces about the War, they secretly rejoice (though decorously and behind closed doors) because business has never been so flourishing. Also, guests no longer dare to complain about their meals because everything can be put down to, 'Don't you know there's a War on?'

'Canon and Mrs Camperdown,' announced the gentleman importantly, removing his hat and putting a foot in the door.

I gave them my professional smile and invited them in, he a rotund, jolly-looking person on the face of it, prosperous, silver-haired, apple-cheeked and rosy; she, less round, less rosy, dark-haired and certainly not very jolly. Peeking at them from the upstairs window as they came down the front path I hadn't been sure whether the male half of the pair was a husband or a brother, but even at a cursory glance he had that air of entitlement that usually wreathes a man who considers himself lord above all, particularly above women. Even more so, as I saw from his expression when he saw me, when it comes to a very young woman.

He was a husband, it seemed, and I wondered why he was here. So I asked him, jumping in just as he arranged himself in front of the fireplace – why do men do that? There was no fire, just some fir cones Addy and I had gathered a while ago. He spread his ample legs wide apart, hands behind his back, and stood there clearly monarch of all he surveyed.

'How do you do, Mrs Camperdown,' I ignored him as I addressed the lady and indicated a cosy corner. 'Do sit down, you'll find that chair very comfortable.'

Her timid glance at her spouse spoke volumes so I took a deep breath and turned to him.

'I gather you have spoken to Sister Wisden up at Groom Hall? That means one of the patients must be a relative, I do hope you have hopeful news of him?'

'I telephoned the hospital,' he grunted. 'The woman in charge recommended your lodgings.' I saw his wife shiver slightly.

'Thank you, Mr Camperdown,' I interrupted him. 'I'll make sure your wife's stay with us is as comfortable as possible. I'll take the first week's rent at once, if you please. Three guineas, in advance.'

It was a familiar litany by now and I was intrigued to see the plump, rosy face turn puce and swell up so that the stiff clerical collar dug into his fleshy neck. His mouth, I now noticed, had nothing jolly about it, being a small, straight, tight line.

'I shall, of course, be staying with my wife,' he barked, clearly certain of his power to persuade – or intimidate. 'It is not fitting that a husband and wife should be separated in their conjugal bliss. And three guineas,' he added crossly, 'is far too much. I shall pay a guinea each and be done with it.'

'No, Mr Camperdown, you will not,' I corrected him, employing Mother's haughty stare and Granny's firm tone. 'Sister Wisden will have told you our terms and made it quite clear that we do not accept gentlemen as guests at any price; and three guineas is the charge. Now, if that is not acceptable to you, I shall be glad to direct you to the station where you will be able to catch a train to Southampton or Winchester, for you will find no other lodgings available in Ramalley.'

I went to the drawing room door and waited. Mrs

Camperdown looked at me beseechingly and, out of her husband's sight I winked briefly, to her evident surprise and confusion.

He was still on his high horse and he glared at me, glowering as he had to accept defeat. 'Be that as it may, I wish to choose the room my wife will occupy. I must make sure it is suitable for her station in life.'

'Of course,' I returned his glare with a haughty one of my own. 'Perhaps you would prefer my grandmother, Lady Elspeth Gillespie, to conduct Mrs Camperdown to her room? She could then decide whether your wife is a suitable guest for our establishment.'

Mrs Camperdown looked as though she wanted to faint but didn't dare, not while her overbearing Canon was in the room. He gobbled open-mouthed at my rudeness but said nothing, so I smiled charmingly at his wife and led her towards the stairs.

'Here.' He sulked along behind us but wasn't giving up easily. 'This room will do.' He was pointing to the former morning room, so I barred the way.

'Oh no,' I said sweetly. 'We reserve that room for guests who cannot cope with the stairs. I'm sure your wife will be perfectly happy in one of our other rooms. This way, please.'

I opened the door to the smaller of the two front bedrooms, the larger one being taken already by Miss Preston. I ushered timid Mrs Camperdown inside and pointed out the cream walls (painted by Alix, Addy and me), the rose-patterned curtains (rescued from a box in the cellar of Balmoral Lodge, where the former owner had hoarded them), and the comfortable single bed with its brand-new mattress. We do have a second bed that can be put in that room if two ladies wish to share, but the Canon didn't need to know that.

'Is it your son who will be a patient at the hospital?' I asked gently, and the lady nodded, her eyes filling with tears. 'They're very kind,' I assured her. 'He's in good hands.'

'Mrs Camperdown and I do not eat the flesh of the cow or of the pig, nor do we countenance the flesh of the rabbit. The flesh of the female sheep is acceptable, though not of the male, so she must be provided with a suitable diet,' barked my unwelcome visitor. You've just made that up, I thought, watching the smug smirk on his red face. Nobody would be so stupid, though it struck me that, in the remote chance that it was true, he'd find his diet difficult to achieve in this time of strict rationing; but of course he's a man so catering would not be his concern. I nodded and as I did so, I caught a tiny shake of the head from his wife, behind his back.

'Never fear, Mr Camperdown,' I said heartily, (I could see it annoyed him that I was not cowed or impressed). 'We endeavour to cater fully for all our guests' needs. Now...'

I nudged him out of the room but took care to block the stairs in case he had some idea of escaping without paying his wife's rent. 'I'll take the three guineas now.'

Short of pushing me down the stairs he had little choice, so he rummaged in his pocket and handed me five ten shilling notes, two half-crowns, a florin, three shillings, four sixpences and a shillings' worth of coppers counting them triumphantly into my hand. 'I'll have a receipt for that,' he demanded.

'Of course,' I smiled, knowing he had expected to confound me. 'And thank you so much for giving me change, it always comes in useful. Do come with me. I can see that Mrs Camperdown is exhausted so we should leave her to have a really good rest. I know that there is no visiting today, but if you like to call here at about half-past-two tomorrow, you can escort your wife up to Groom Hall to see your son. When you settle into your own lodgings, do send a boy with a message to let her know the address.'

It occurred to me that once Miss Preston moved in, I was sure the Camperdowns could come to an arrangement about sharing the pony trap but I was equally sure that Miss Preston was more than competent to sort that out herself.

'Now, Canon. Let me find my receipt book.' Our business was soon concluded and before he could recover, he found himself on the front steps staring at the door as I closed it.

'Phew!' I leaned against the solid mahogany, hoping it wouldn't occur to him to break the door down in a rage, but silence reigned so I ran into our own kitchen and found Granny on her own. 'I've been speaking so primly it's as though I'd swallowed a book of etiquette and I've been rude to a clergyman! Not that he noticed, he was too busy being important and disgruntled.'

I explained what had happened and took tea and a scone and bramble jelly upstairs to our newest guest who had taken off her depressing grey coat and laid her even more depressing grey felt hat on the dressing-table.

'You shouldn't have bothered,' she protested when she saw what I carried, but I just laughed at her and made her sit down again while I set the tray on a small side table.

'Drink that, Mrs Camperdown,' I urged. 'You'll feel much better for it, then you can have a proper rest. I'll look in on you and let you know when dinner will be ready. It's hard not to worry, isn't it, but I trust you'll have good news of your son.'

'You're so kind,' she nodded. 'Peter's only nineteen. He has a shrapnel wound in his stomach. They say he's making a good recovery but that he'll always have a delicate constitution. I can't wait to have him safely home.' She put out a hand and I squeezed it gently. 'My – my husband doesn't like to be overlooked,' she murmured. 'He does love Peter but I'm not sure how he'll take to having to make way for an invalid when he has always been used to being given the first consideration. This room... It will be a haven for me for the next few weeks and perhaps Aldwyn – my husband – will be more accommodating when it's time for Peter to leave hospital.'

'I'm sure everything will work out happily,' I told her, and after I had brought up the baggage that her husband had been far too important to deal with, I urged her to lie down. 'Perhaps Canon Camperdown will feel able to go home once he sees you settled. He must have plenty to do in – I don't think you mentioned where you come from?'

'Salisbury,' she replied, her eyes lighting up. 'He is a Residential Canon of the Cathedral and yes, you are quite right. I must remind him how very much the Dean relies on him at every turn. And please don't worry about my meals, I'll be happy to eat whatever I'm given. My husband doesn't realise how difficult it is to run a household these days.'

We exchanged satisfied smiles and I drew the curtains before leaving her comfortably tucked up for a nap.

The sky was overcast, and rain threatened in the distance, so I pulled the Balmoral Lodge windows shut and went upstairs in our own house to shut the windows there. Addy's door was open and when I looked in, I found Penny, our very young maid, curled up in a chair and entirely engrossed in a story, Goblin Island, that she had obviously found on Addy's bookshelf. She had no idea I was there. I thought of Bella's request and wondered how we could help; perhaps this was a clue? It seemed so unjust that a child of barely thirteen should have to go out to work, although to be fair, Penny wasn't faced with the prospect of working in a satanic mill like the girls in Mrs Gaskell's books or the poor waifs in Dickens. I thought of Addy, only two years older, the cherished baby of our family and, I hoped, destined to embark on a medical career if her present ambitions succeeded.

Penny must have sensed my presence for she leaped out of the chair, dropping the book. She scrabbled to pick it up and smoothed down the pages as she held it out to me, looking terrified.

'It's all right, Penny,' I tried to assure her. 'I'm not surprised you like that book, it's very exciting, isn't it? Do you like reading?' She nodded timidly as she stood there shivering, and I put an arm round her shoulders. 'Look, would you like to borrow it? You can take it home and when you bring it back you can borrow another one. We've got lots of stories for girls and they're great fun.'

'I won't hurt it, Miss Christy,' she whispered, hugging the book to her chest.

'Of course you won't, I know that,' I said, as she scuttled towards the door. 'Tell me, Penny, what do you like to do besides reading?'

'I like sewing, Miss Christy. My aunty that's just died

taught me a lot; she used to be a dressmaker and she showed me. I really like it. That nice lady that stayed here, she gave me lots of sewing tips too. About trimming hats as well.'

Very shyly, she held out a handkerchief. 'I made this, Miss Christy and I'm making another one for…' She stammered to a halt. 'My aunty taught me to do embroidery and when she knew she was dying she gave me her machine and all her sewing materials and told my mum she thought I had promise.'

'You do have promise, Penny. It's lovely,' I told her, and so it was; an unusual but charming design, beautifully worked. I wondered again how we could help her. However, it was time to think about dinner for our new lodger and to be prepared for anyone else to arrive.

I walked into the kitchen, surprised to see Alix storm in from the scullery, having slammed the back door behind her.

'Honestly,' she grumbled. 'How can anyone as nice as Miss Makepeace have a friend like frightful Portia Diplock?'

She shook her umbrella over the sink and stomped back into the scullery to hang up her wet coat and hat.

'What has she done now?' Addy had arrived, with Judith in the background.

'Oh, she arrived just as I was leaving and sniffed at me, saying she wondered I was any use if I kept such short hours, like a lady of leisure. I snapped and said Sister Wisden knew all about it and besides, I'd been at the Hall in the morning too and that Saturday is not my usual time, but she ignored that. She sneered at me, saying that she's not afraid of hard work or long hours! Apparently, she has a wealth of experience of nursing in a senior position which will prove invaluable, so she has decided to volunteer at the hospital. She says she was in South Africa during the Boer War.

'It was embarrassing because it was clear to everyone that she knew me and they all heard her, but Sister Wisden smiled at me, so I felt better. She, Sister Wisden, was allocating beds to the new officers who have arrived, so she brushed Miss Diplock aside like a tiresome mosquito, with a brusque 'Thank you, but we are not looking for more staff at present.'

'What happened?'

'Fergus, that is…Captain Munro, was very polite and told her it was kind but as she could see they were very busy at that moment and perhaps she would come back one day next week and discuss it over a cup of coffee. I could see Sister Wisden glaring at him, but I think he winked at her because she suddenly stopped frowning. One of the orderlies ushered her out of the house by the front door and I sneaked out via the kitchen garden. Fergus…Captain Munro… said if she turns up again he'll have her washing bedpans! He wanted to see me home, but I showed him the short cut and said I'd be all right.'

She blushed as she headed upstairs to go and change, adding over her shoulder, 'I told him he'd be welcome to drop in and have a cup of tea any time he felt like some company.'

Addy, Judith, Granny and I all stared after her, then looked at each other. Granny raised an eyebrow, Judith smiled, Addy whistled, and I opened my mouth then thought better of saying anything and shut it again firmly.

Chapter Four

Saturday, 27th April, evening

Mrs Camperdown proved to be an exemplary guest who appreciated her comfortable surroundings and was happy to relax in the drawing room when she came downstairs after her refreshing nap.

Granny looked in briefly to say, 'How do you do' and later I introduced Alix and Addy and hoped Mrs Camperdown wouldn't mind her solitary dinner.

'My dear,' she beamed. 'I feel as though I've discovered an oasis of peace! I have a busy life at home and there is always someone who needs my attention, so to be waited on so kindly and every comfort attended to, is luxury indeed.' She held up a book. 'Nobody can raise an eyebrow and look affronted or hurt if I read novels while I eat and that, believe me, is a real luxury.'

Having encountered her complaining Canon I could readily believe it, so Penny proudly served her with the same toad-in-the-hole followed by stewed prunes and custard, which we were having ourselves, as we try to cater for both households at once. I'd been lucky at the butcher's two days earlier when he put a finger to his lips and handed me a wrapped parcel, which turned out to be sausages. The ration had risen to a scrag end of lamb too and Granny had already turned that into a hotpot as well as shepherd's pie which would mean tomorrow's luncheon and dinner were catered for. Shopping in wartime is an art form and one in which we are becoming increasingly proficient, seeking out bargains and wheedling treats from our favourite shopkeepers, all of whom hold Granny in awe and respect, affection too. Not just because they're impressed by her title, though I know they like to boast about their noble customer, but because they all have instances of her kindness to their families at one time or another.

Sunday, 28th April, morning

It would be Henry's twenty-first birthday on Wednesday – May Day – and some time ago I had promised him a cake. Since then Addy had insisted he must have a party too so, as I have already explained, we had invited his cousins in town to come to tea today, rather than on a weekday. This meant setting the round tea table that stands in the bay window of the drawing room and not eating in the kitchen as we do when it's just us. Accordingly, before breakfast I asked Addy, who was for once in a compliant frame of mind, to help choose a recipe while I inspected the larder to look for hidden treasure, just in case I had somehow missed a secret store of groceries. Not surprisingly the answer was no and all I found was the poor-quality flour that we have to put up with at present.

Addy was delighted to have a hand in the cake making as she is very fond of Henry. It's not that he's taken the place of Bertie because nobody could do ever that, but it's very pleasant to have a young man about the house once more and we knew that Henry, who was Bertie's friend, had his seal of approval.

'Date cake, seed cake or gingerbread?' I asked as I consulted the wartime cookery leaflet given to us by Henry's Cousin Bertha. These recipes contain suggestions for baking without the usual ingredients; those are in short supply now that rationing has really begun to bite. Alix had made us laugh by saying that instead of being titled Plain Cakes & Scones the recipes should rather be How to Make Cakes with Mud, Sawdust and Prayer.

'Do we have any dates?' Addy asked.

'I've been hoarding them for Henry's cake,' I said. 'The dates will mean we don't need to use all our precious sugar to sweeten it, though it does need treacle, which we do actually have.'

Date cake it was, and just as well there was no argument as I'd been up for ages and had already boiled up the stoned and chopped dates, the dripping, the mixed spice and the salt, but we find life runs on a more even keel if Addy believes that she makes the decisions. Now, reading out the recipe, she was intrigued that even the date stones had to be tied up in a bit of muslin and boiled. For once she didn't make a fuss when she learned I'd already done that too.

'It says it's to extract every possible bit of sugar,' she informed me. 'Think how economical we'll all be after the war having learned this kind of thing! We could set up a cookery school for people with very little money.'

I wondered how, in that case, they would be able to pay for their tuition but bit my tongue rather than respond sharply. Sometimes you just have to pray that Addy's wild schemes will die a natural death, like the plan to breed ravens to protect her from school bullies or setting up a pheasant hatchery to breed birds for the table, using birds enticed from the Groom Hall park. (We did jump on that idea; one thing we definitely don't want is yet another set of birds eating their heads off because we can't bear the idea of killing them). I won't go into detail about the decision to build a motor car from old bits of metal which had been the brainchild of a local boy who had, for a while, been Addy's collaborator. Luckily, their plans were cut short when the boy was sent to boarding school and his father summoned the rag and bone man to dispose of the untidy heap of scrap.

After breakfast I added the cooled mixture to the dry ingredients and put the cake into the oven, along with some large potatoes to make use of the heat, as well as a couple of bricks to be later wrapped in old towels. These were to air the beds next door at Balmoral Lodge so they would be fresh for the lodgers who, I prayed, would arrive soon, eager to hand over their rent money. You never know, we might have another lodger or two by dinner time this evening so at least there will be a bit less work, with potatoes that just need reheating.

Sure enough I had just escaped from Mother's room – I don't do her typing at the weekend but she had caught me when I was opening the upstairs windows – when I heard a ring at Balmoral Lodge's front door. A very small female figure bundled up in a bulky coat, with anxious dark eyes peering out from under slanting black brows, stood on the step.

'Good morning,' she said, in a high, young voice. 'I have a letter from Sister Wisden at the hospital saying that you have a room available?'

I agreed that this was so and invited her into the drawing room.

'I am Mrs Digby Trellis,' she informed me, rather proudly I thought. 'My husband, Captain Trellis, has just been transferred to Groom Hall and I am looking for accommodation.'

When she divested herself of her outer garments, I was shocked to see that she was expecting – and very soon too, by the size of her even though she seemed very young. I suppose it's not unusual these days; why wouldn't a young couple snatch at happiness when there is no certainty that the groom will survive? For a moment my thoughts strayed to Henry. Suppose he had asked me…oh well, he was safely discharged and would not be returning to the war.

Mrs Trellis should have the downstairs bedroom, I decided, although she showed no sign of weariness even though, as she told me, she had walked up from the station. Nevertheless, I thought she might appreciate not having to climb the stairs all the time.

'Oh, what a - a very large bed,' she said. 'And what a nice room too.'

This is what we like to hear, a guest who is impressed by what we offer and who makes no fuss about paying her rent in advance, which she did quite happily.

'Do you have relatives nearby?' I asked and she stared at me, eyes wide with sudden anxiety. 'I just wondered, because often patients particularly request a transfer to Groom Hall if they have family in the area.'

'My – my husband's cousins live in Hampshire,' she said. 'But they're old. I've never met them.'

It occurred to me that it would be daunting for her to meet unknown elderly people who might be ready to judge her condition, so I nodded and explained the house rules. She said she'd had coffee at the station so would not be going into town to look for lunch.

'I asked them to send my luggage here unless I telephoned to tell them not to,' she explained. 'If that will suit you?'

I nodded and showed her into the drawing room with its comfortable chairs. 'We have one other guest so far,' I said. 'Mrs Camperdown.' I told her about our third guest, Miss Preston, who would be moving in the next day. 'She's going to hire the station trap for the week and says she'll be quite willing to offer lifts too.'

Granny put her head round the door at that moment. She is very shy, but she never neglects to do the polite as she knows our lodgers love to boast that they are the guests of a titled lady, the only child of the late Earl of Inverboyne, no less. Besides, her title is one of the reasons we are able to charge such a high rent, and Granny would never jeopardise that. (Granny and I are far too practical to be proud where money is concerned.)

'Christy,' she said now, after shaking hands with our guest. 'Perhaps Mrs Trellis might enjoy one of your mother's books until it's time for visiting up at the Hall?'

Mrs Trellis had half bobbed a curtsy to Granny before she jerked upright and now she looked slightly alarmed as I left the room to find her a book. Her face brightened when I handed over Mother's most popular romance, Love's Painted Petal.

'Oh,' she squeaked excitedly. 'I've been wanting to read this for an age. I wasn't allow…that is, I never seem to have had the time until now.'

She had her nose buried in the book even as we left the room and when we were back in our own house, I noticed that Granny was looking thoughtful.

'Don't you think she looks very young to be married?' I asked. 'She doesn't look as old as Addy.'

'Hmm,' Granny was non-committal. 'We do hear of a lot of youthful marriages these days, but I agree. I wonder how old the husband is.'

'I'm wondering when her baby is due,' I said. 'I'm not sure we want to find ourselves having to set up a nursery!'

'Get along with you,' Granny laughed at me. 'We'll hope she's not still here when her time comes but even if she is, we'll manage and perhaps Addy can try her hand at midwifery. Now, is everything ready for Henry's party?'

A note had arrived from Canon Camperdown curtly informing his wife that he was now staying with the vicar. Mrs Camperdown looked relieved and took her fellow guest under her wing, suggesting that they should go for a stroll along by the river until it was time to make their way to the hospital. I breathed a sigh of relief. And when she added that, as a treat, they might call in at the tearoom by the bridge before walking up to the Hall for visiting time, I could have hugged her.

'My husband is staying with the vicar,' she told me. 'I was invited to lunch with them, but I said I had a headache and would meet him at the Hall.' She looked demure as I waved them off, happy to think that we might have the birthday party without worrying about the lodgers.

Henry and his Makepeace cousins arrived promptly at four o'clock and after the flurry of greeting, Addy, to my surprise, flung herself at Henry and kissed him on the cheek. She is usually undemonstrative (we all are) but she looked meaningfully at Alix who grinned and held out a hand to him.

'Dear Henry,' she laughed. 'A birthday kiss from me, too.' And she gave him a hug.

When Granny and even Judith followed suit, I felt all eyes on me and coloured furiously.

'Ha-happy birthday, Henry,' I stammered and kissed his cheek, feeling horribly self-conscious. I felt him take a deep breath and he clutched at my hand, then with both of us scarlet and embarrassed I pulled away and hurried to the sideboard.

'Come and open your presents, Henry,' I indicated the cards and parcels. 'Then we can have tea. It's all ready and the kettle should be boiling by now.'

His face lit up with surprise and he beamed. 'I didn't expect presents as well as a party...You're all so kind.'

Granny took his arm. 'Just sit down here, Henry,' she said warmly. 'We always celebrate birthdays in this family and even in wartime we see no reason to change our ways.'

I knew, and so did Granny and my sisters, that it had been a dreadful struggle in January to make Addy's fifteenth birthday very festive, but we had made an effort. Bertie, who had enjoyed parties, and indeed had enjoyed absolutely everything always, had been very present in our minds and hearts that day but we knew he would have laughed to scorn the very notion of letting the day go unmarked because of him, so Addy had her party, small and subdued as it was. I was very conscious of my brother's presence now, and I was briefly, desolately, even more conscious of his absence. When I surreptitiously wiped away a tear, I caught Henry watching me. He smiled slightly and nodded, so I knew he was thinking of his own brother as well as mine. This piercing misery, painful as it is, must be better than the thought that we might someday become inured to the loss of someone so vitally alive, so loved; the sorrow muted to a dull ache and perhaps, sometimes, forgetting altogether that our brother was gone.

'Have you had any presents yet?' Addy demanded, looking suspiciously at Miss Bertha who laughed.

'It's not actually his birthday till Wednesday,' she explained. 'As that's a working day we decided to celebrate properly today and just do all the boring legal business of turning twenty-one on the day itself. We did have a roast fowl for luncheon and an ice pudding, and of course, he's had some presents,' she added. Henry hastened to display a handsome gold hunter on his watch chain.

'It's exactly what I needed,' he explained. 'I had my

service wristwatch, of course, but the wretched strap broke last week and the watch smashed when it fell.'

'The pocket watch belonged to Henry's great-grandfather,' explained Miss Bertha. 'He was a cousin of our grandfather, Edgar's and mine. It gives us both immense pleasure to know that there is still a Makepeace in the family to wear it.'

Henry's cousin Edgar, a quiet man who looked quite as relaxed as Henry does in our shabby but cheerful drawing room, nodded. 'It's an additional cause for satisfaction that the original owner of the watch was called Horace Leopold Makepeace. His initials are engraved inside the case and coincidentally match Henry's own.'

'What does the L stand for?' Alix asked. Like the rest of us, she is very inquisitive but nowhere near as shy, so I was glad she had asked.

'Louis, my French great-great-grandfather,' Henry explained. 'I suppose Father allowed my mother to choose his name. I don't expect he cared having already named my brother, Jonathan William, after himself.'

He caught me sneaking a worried glance at him and smiled to show me that he wasn't dwelling on his difficult childhood or the young, unhappy mother who had escaped to her native Brittany when her sons were babies, dying a year or so later. From what Henry had told me, his late father had been prone to icy rages which could reduce grown men to quivering wrecks. Jonathan – Jonty – had protected his brother but Passchendaele had left Henry all alone, until he met us – and soon afterwards was welcomed into Edgar and Bertha's family.

'Henry, do open your presents!' Addy was practically hopping from one foot to the other. 'I want to see what you've got.'

'Of course, Addy,' Henry said. 'Let's see what this one is.' 'This one' was a handsome Conway Stewart fountain pen from Judith Evershed. She smiled at Henry's stammered thanks.

'Think nothing of it,' she told him. 'A solicitor must look the part and think of the last wills and testaments you'll be drafting with it!'

'All in good time,' Mr Makepeace smiled, admiring the pen.

Granny's present was two pairs of hand-knitted socks and Henry was delighted with the framed photograph of us.

'I'll stand it on my desk,' he promised, glancing at his cousin.

'As long as you don't let such a bevy of beauty distract you,' Mr Makepeace joked.

Addy paid no heed because she was anxiously waiting to present Henry with her own extra present, four ounces of aniseed balls.

'If you keep sucking them long enough they turn white and you get down to the little seed inside,' she informed him and he thanked her earnestly.

'I'll remember, thank you, Addy. They're my favourites, how did you know?'

Alix had done a pen and ink sketch of Groom Hall which he admired very much. 'It looks gloomily magnificent, thank you, Alix. I'll frame it and have it on my bedroom mantelpiece.'

When I handed him my present he hefted the parcel in his hand. 'What can this possibly be?' he beamed and unwrapped a copy of my second book, newly arrived from the publisher.

'Hello? I didn't realise this was out yet. Gun Emplacements on the Cricket Pitch by Lt Jasper Crombie and signed by the author. It looks very handsome, thank you, Christy. Lt Crombie is a clever fellow.'

We served tea on the round table which meant that everyone crammed in the bay window except Granny and Miss Bertha who elected to sit beside the fireplace and be waited on by Alix and me.

To my surprise, Bella appeared carrying the new batch of scones I'd made earlier, accompanied by a shrinking Penny who was clutching a small parcel.

'We just looked in for a minute, Miss Christy,' Bella whispered. 'Penny's got something for Mr Henry, and she didn't like to come on her own.'

When Penny had shown me the handkerchief she had embroidered, she had started to tell me about something else she was making. She stood bashfully silent as I smiled at her and touched Henry's arm.

'Here's another birthday present, Henry.'

It was indeed a handkerchief, beautifully embroidered with his initials.

'My word, Penny,' he said turning it this way and that and holding it up for us all to admire. 'That's really handsome, thank you. Did you do this all by yourself?'

'Bella bought the hanky,' she said bravely, colouring at his praise.

'Our Penny did the embroidery,' put in her elder sister. 'She's got ever so good at it.'

I whispered to Penny that I would save a slice of birthday cake for each of them and they slid out of the room, glad to get away from the limelight.

'That child is coming on a treat,' Granny remarked. 'Can't we do something for her, Christy?'

I didn't want to bore our visitors but Mr and Miss Makepeace both showed an interest, so I said, 'Bella's been asking me for advice about her, Granny, so I said I'd talk to you. Penny loves to sew, of course, but she also loves reading so I've said she can borrow any of our books that she likes. She's only thirteen and I was wondering if she could sometimes sit in on some of your lessons, Judith? To help her – I don't know – perhaps to give her a bit more polish so that she'll have a better chance later?'

Judith, Granny and Miss Bertha plunged into a discussion while everyone else set to and spread their scones with cream from our friendly farmer and jam made by Granny with last year's blackberries from the hospital grounds.

I heard the bell and prayed it wasn't a prospective lodger come to our door by mistake. Not that another lodger wouldn't have been welcome, you understand, but it was an awkward time. A lanky youth beamed at me.

'Good afternoon, Miss Christabel,' he said, vigorously shaking my hand.

'Wilfred? Good heavens,' I said weakly and as he seemed bent on entering the house I stood back. 'Why aren't you away at school in Reading?'

Wilfred is the same boy who was once Addy's henchman-in-chief in the matter of building a car from scrap metal, to name only one of their misadventures.

'I had diphtheria pretty badly last term,' he said, trying to look pale and wan. He is two years older than Addy, with merry brown eyes and a cheerful disposition. I remembered him with a mop of chestnut curls, but he was very close-cropped now. He saw me looking at his head. 'They shaved my hair off,' he said jauntily. 'Mother cried when she saw me but it's growing back quite quickly. The school had to close for weeks,' he explained, not looking at all upset. 'I had to go to Southsea to stay with my old nurse once I was out of quarantine because the doctor said I needed the sea air. I've outgrown my strength so I'm not to go back to school until September.'

'You've certainly grown.' I looked him up and down. 'You must be almost six feet tall!' While Alix is small, fair and slight, Addy and I are both darker and taller but here was Wilfred, whom I remembered as a short skinny boy, looking down at me from quite a height.

At that moment, Addy – eternally inquisitive – put her head round the drawing room door.

'Oh, it's you. I wondered if you'd remember,' she said casually. 'You'd better come in and I'll introduce you to Judith.'

Her air of complete unconcern didn't deceive me for a minute, but this was hardly the time for an interrogation, so I frowned at her through narrowed eyes as the two of them joined the party.

Another surprise awaited me when both Edgar and Bertha greeted our unexpected guest with pleasure, as did Granny, although she too looked sceptical when he explained airily that he'd been just passing.

'Wilfred's father is Mr Seymour, the undertaker – among his many other concerns,' I told Henry as they shook hands.

'Wilfred's at boarding school in Reading so we haven't seen much of him lately.'

'He was at the library yesterday morning,' Addy announced, then with her usual complete disregard of polite customs she turned to Judith Evershed. 'He's not allowed to go back to school all summer,' she said. 'He's supposed to take the same exams as I am so I thought it would be a good idea if he joined your tutorial class because he's missing lessons too.'

As we blinked at this effrontery there was another ring at the front door and as I was nearest I turned to answer it but Alix gave a squeak and turned crimson. 'It's Dr Munro,' she hissed and brushed past me.

Sure enough we had yet another uninvited guest. Or was he? From the sparkle in Alix's eyes and his answering smile, I thought perhaps he had been invited. The same could probably be said of Wilfred Seymour after yesterday's encounter with Addy.

In the hall I could see that Alix was looking anxious, a very unusual state for her, but she's my sister and I love her, despite her many annoying habits, so I greeted our new visitor in a friendly kind of way.

'Do come and join the party, Dr Munro,' I smiled. 'Did Alix tell you we're giving our friend a birthday tea? There's plenty of cake so you're in luck.'

'Thank you.' He shook hands. 'Do call me Fergus, I'm not on duty at the moment.'

After introductions all round Fergus Munro looked searchingly at Henry. 'I know you, don't I? Remind me where it was?'

To my surprise Henry started to laugh. 'All I'll say is – remember le patron's billy goat and the vin ordinaire?'

Provokingly neither of them would explain, not even when they had stopped giggling; I forgave the doctor though. It was such a pleasure to see Henry having fun. They both apologised and Alix led the new doctor to the big chesterfield, then hesitated.

'Sit down, Alix,' I took pity on her. 'You stay and talk to

Dr Munro and everyone. Addy, we're running out of chairs, will you fetch another one from the dining room? I'll make more tea; Henry hasn't cut his birthday cake yet.'

When I looked at Granny, she signalled approval. We both knew that Addy was torn between haranguing Judith about lessons for Wilfred and interrogating the doctor about his war wound; indeed, her head was turning from one to the other in the hope of catching either or both of them in her clutches. We also knew, however, that the prospect of cake would rank even higher.

'I'll help,' offered Wilfred as Addy hurried to collect one of the dining chairs. When it was arranged to her satisfaction, she and Wilfred raced each other to the kitchen, followed by Henry at a more sedate pace carrying the teapot and hot water jug.

I refused to let Addy near the birthday cake and set her to wash up the used plates and take fresh ones back to the drawing room while I made yet another pot of tea. I wondered whether to rescue Henry who was being pumped by Wilfred about life in the trenches, not that he was getting very far from the snatches of conversation I overheard. Henry is very reticent when it comes to war stories, though he did let slip once that he had been mentioned twice in despatches.

'What did you do to get mentioned?' Addy had asked.

'I didn't die,' was his brusque reply and on further questioning he snapped at her. 'Look, Addy... That sort of thing happens all the time if you're still standing when everyone around you is dead. It's nothing to make a fuss of.'

'But you were promoted to captain,' Addy persisted. 'That meant something, didn't it?'

'Dead men's shoes,' he'd said wearily. 'Besides, I got my Blighty ten days later, so it hardly counts.'

He had refused to discuss it any further and even Addy knew better than to nag him today. Now, he looked up gratefully when I addressed him.

'Go and sit down, Henry,' I said. 'Be ready to cut the cake.'

Addy shooed Wilfred and Henry out of the kitchen, then

she peered over my shoulder into the larder, to admire the cake. It did look good, though I say so myself. I'd made one of those snowflake cut-outs: you know, where you fold a piece of paper and cut bits out so it unfolds like a doily. I'd used it as a stencil by sieving sugar over it, making a lacy pattern and now all it needed was the pièce de resistance.

'Got the flowers?' I asked and Addy carefully placed a small silver posy vase on top of the cake and fluffed up the bluebells she had picked earlier.

'Oh, how pretty,' exclaimed Miss Bertha from where she sat chatting companionably with Granny. 'What a delightful picture that makes.'

Henry bit his lip and was clearly very moved as he struggled to thank us all. I tried to imagine a life without birthday treats or kindness from a father, let alone a mother he had never known. Even our own peculiar parents had always loved us, Papa extravagantly so, whether in funds or hiding in the cellar from awkward questions by the law, and Mother in her own absent-minded fashion. For a moment I hated Jonathan Makepeace Senior and yet Henry had grown up to be so lovable. Not for the first time I reflected that Jonty had done a splendid job of being an elder brother and yet again I wished I had known him.

As Henry started to cut the cake and Alix poured out more tea, the drawing room door opened and a slight, fair-haired figure stood on the threshold, looking bewildered. Mother!

I stifled a groan and went to meet her, hoping she would turn tail once she noticed we had company. No such luck, Mother can go for weeks absent-mindedly eating whatever is put in front of her when she's in the throes of creation but there are times, as now, when I swear she can sniff out a biscuit from a hundred paces. She homed in on the tea table and headed towards it, just as there was yet another ring at the front door.

Alix met my panic-stricken gaze and hurried forward.

'Another lodger, do you think?' She patted my arm and pushed me towards the hall. 'I'll hold the fort here, don't you worry.'

Neither of us realised at first that it was our own doorbell that had rung (it has a slightly off key peal) and thus probably didn't herald a candidate for Balmoral Lodge so I was startled, then horrified, to see the solid form of Miss Portia Diplock standing four-square on the front step. Taking advantage of my involuntary gasp, she planted a large foot inside the door. (I say four-square advisedly, she is twice as wide as Mother and is one of those erstwhile large English Rose women who grow blowsy over the years and end up looking like milkmaids.)

'Good afternoon, Christabel,' she said. 'I was passing and thought I would call in to discuss the arrangements for the May Day Fête on Friday.'

She inserted a second foot, followed shortly by the rest of her and held up a hand to her ear.' Hark!' she said. 'I believe I hear dear Bertha's voice. I must just say a brief word.'

With that, she barged uninvited into the drawing room with me trailing miserably in her wake, conscious that everyone looked appalled. Everyone, that is, except Mother who had acquired a plate and was munching her way through scones and cake and staring blankly at the other people around her.

'Bertha, my dear. A word, if I may?' Miss Diplock surged forward and Miss Bertha, unhappily aware that even though she might be able to escape, her brother and Henry were now trapped behind the tea table, held out a limp hand to her erstwhile schoolfriend.

As the unwanted guest began a loud, rambling speech about the number of chairs that must be arranged on the Priory green, how many helpers who would be needed to dress and undress the schoolchildren doing the maypole dance, not to mention supervising them at all times, Granny put down her knitting. She and Miss Bertha had been poring over a pattern and were clearly not happy to be interrupted.

Before anyone could do anything, Mother joined in. She had finished off the last scone and had a greedy eye on the cake intended for Penny and Bella so before she could stretch out a hand, I whisked the plate away.

'I'll just take this into the kitchen,' I said briskly and was waylaid at the door by Alix. 'Don't you dare go and hide,' she threatened. 'You're not to leave us in the lurch.'

I shook my head, dashed into the kitchen, put the cake, plate and all, in a tin and deposited it on a shelf in the larder. I hoped it was out of reach of Bobs the dog (but possibly not out of reach of the cats as Edith Swan Neck has a party piece that consists of lifting the latch of the larder door.) She was nowhere in sight and I couldn't spare the time to look for her, so I hurried back to stand by my beleaguered family.

Mother doesn't have friends; she doesn't cope well with the rest of the human race. What she does have, however, are very occasional fleeting crushes – Schwärmerei I think is the German word – and they are very uncomfortable for the rest of us while they last. And now an unlikely alliance had been struck while I was out of the room, not for more than two minutes, I swear, and as I entered Alix tilted her head towards our difficult parent. She and Miss Diplock were, of all things, discussing clothes.

'My dear!' gushed the latter. 'I am delighted to meet another enthusiast for Artistic Clothing,' and she preened herself, opening her coat to reveal a stout figure clad in a shapeless garment in seaweed green wool that drooped from a yoke embroidered in orange silk art needlework in a kind of swirly wreath.

Mother's dress was a loose grey Merino embroidered in dark pink silk (a hand-me-down from Alix's old lady but with the boning removed from the bodice). Annoyingly, Mother can make a shopping bag look like a Paris fashion.

I caught Alix's eye; like me, she was horrified because she knew what would happen next. Sadly, I could see no way of preventing embarrassment short of tackling Mother to the ground and although Bertie had taught us to play rugby, insisting it would come in handy one day, it's hardly a drawing room accomplishment. Besides, my tactical skills are rusty now.

'Indeed,' Mother said now, looking round at the assembled guests as though seeking praise. 'I have many times written of the evils of tight lacing and corsets for women. I have never found it necessary for myself and I have forbidden my daughters to distort their bodies.'

'Bravo!' Miss Diplock nodded enthusiastically. 'No woman should ever wear those dreadful garments. Indeed, a woman who wears stays can never really be free to reach her true potential.'

Edgar Makepeace, who had escaped from behind the tea table, was sidling past her towards the drawing room door evidently bent on hiding somewhere. He took a hasty step sideways looking hunted as her gaze fell thoughtfully on him.

At that moment Addy leaped up.

'Here, Mother,' she stammered. 'Ha-have some more cake.'

All three of us held our breath but Mother couldn't resist and in the few moments while she was necessarily silenced, Miss Diplock, (whose own bountiful bosom might have been less cumbersome had it been supported by the despised stays) switched to another of her crusades. She started to harangue the company about the need for young women to take part in volunteer activities and to remember our Brave Boys at the Front.

I bristled at that. We needed no reminder from Miss Diplock, when our own brother had been killed and in this very room sat two young men who had both been seriously wounded and were now coping with a lifetime's legacy from the Front. Besides, if the war didn't end soon, I realised Wilfred was only a year away from being called up. I caught Fergus Munro looking at me and tried not to laugh as he raised an eyebrow.

'Very true,' said my mother, swallowing her last crumb and nodding her head in solemn agreement. Mother, who has never in her life taken any notice of anyone else's needs. Certainly not her own children, all of whom she had casually handed over to her mother or – if we were in funds – to a nursemaid. Now it seemed, she was Miss Diplock's dearest friend.

'I despair of my daughters, I do assure you,' she confided

while the rest of the party listened in disbelief, unable to escape. 'I have often deplored their frivolous way of life and wished that they would take a more active part in the life of our country. So many examples,' she proclaimed, getting carried away. 'At their age, Lady Griselda was tearing up her silk petticoats to bandage the wounded and carrying baskets of provisions across the moor to the cave where she had hidden the brave warriors.'

Miss Diplock nodded, looking slightly confused, as well she might, but Alix, Granny and I recognised the signs and tried to hide our despair under bright, social smiles. Mother, as she so often does, had confused real life with that of the characters in her current book and had disappeared into the eighteenth century.

'You are so right, Miss – er – Diptych,' she said, making a brief re-appearance into the present day. 'Alexandra went to a few parties but seems, fortunately, to have abandoned the pursuit of pleasure, though I do not see her taking part in any worthwhile activity. Adelaide, of course, is a pupil at an excellent private school and gives me no cause for alarm; but take Christabel... Apart from half an hour or so occasionally, when she does some typewriting for me, she seems to have no useful occupation. She could be working in munitions, or joining the women's police, but no, I rarely see her undertaking any useful task.'

There was a hiss, a sharp intake of breath from more than one of her listeners but before anyone could speak, Miss Diplock chimed in.

'Oh, my dear, I do so agree. Why, Bertha, for instance... When the South African war broke out I, of course, set sail immediately for Cape Town where I spent quite some time in what, I flatter myself, was a very important post. Bertha, however, refused to go with me and spent the duration of the war safely at home in Ramalley, occupying herself with household duties – her excuse – and attending a few working parties.'

I gave thanks for Judith Evershed's discretion and at any other time might have smiled at the way she was sitting meekly in the bay window, trying to look invisible. It's a miracle that Mother has not so far noticed that Judith is a constant presence in our house, and we hope to keep it that way. More and more since Bertie's death, Mother stays in her room, even for meals. She does make the occasional appearance, as now, but I could see she had begun to look bewildered as she stared at the company. I breathed a sigh of relief because I'd begun to worry that she might suddenly remark now on Judith's presence and make a scene.

Granny had now disentangled herself from her knitting and she reached the two unwelcome guests first.

'Margaret,' she took Mother firmly by the arm and led her into the hall. 'You must be tired. I think you will be more comfortable upstairs. That's right, I'll send up one of the girls with a cup of tea shortly. If you've left any cake, I'll send a slice of that too.'

Mother went like a lamb. Granny is the only person who can handle her when she comes up against real life and real people and I continued the good work by opening the front door.

'Thank you for calling, Miss Diplock,' I said, in a high-handed kind of way while Granny bowed. Alas for our intentions, Miss Diplock had other ideas and when she gave no sign of moving, I followed her outside, made a face at Granny, and ruthlessly shut our front door behind me.

'Let me see you to the gate,' I offered sweetly, taking her arm and guiding her (pulling her, actually) down the front path. To my surprise Mrs Camperdown was just closing next door's gate; I smiled but didn't dare stop to greet her until I had practically pushed Miss Diplock out on to the pavement and firmly shut the gate.

'We've had such a delightful walk down from the hospital,' the canon's wife informed me. 'Mrs Trellis has just gone indoors, she's rather tired and I suggested she should lie down. Isn't it a lovely afternoon!'

'Won't you introduce me?' Miss Diplock had turned back and now loomed large, barking at me while staring at our lodger, who, I was relieved to see had a slight gleam in her eye.

'Mrs Camperdown,' I said meekly. 'May I introduce Miss Diplock who lives in the town?'

To my dismay Portia Diplock immediately began to solicit donations and promises of practical help from our startled guest, so I interrupted her in mid-harangue.

'All our guests will be fully occupied while they are at Balmoral Lodge,' I said. 'Do go indoors, Mrs Camperdown, Miss Diplock was just leaving.' I turned to speed our unwelcome guest on her way. 'Good day, Miss Diplock.'

I hurried round to the back of the house and noticed Mrs Trellis peeping nervously after the departing visitor, before popping back indoors via the Balmoral Lodge kitchen. In our own hall, Granny was still guarding the front door as though Miss Diplock might try to force entry.

'I consider we weathered that very well, Christy, don't you? I watched out of the window and I hope Mrs Camperdown wasn't annoyed.' She didn't wait for a reply but twinkled at me. 'I'll go and hold the fort in the drawing room and calm everyone down while you start thinking about dinner for our two guests. I put the lamb hotpot in the oven on a low heat when I heard Henry and his cousins arrive, so you'll only need to reheat those potatoes and wash some greens. I'll send someone out to help you,' she said over her shoulder as she gave me a little push towards the kitchen.

The someone she sent was Henry and he was very perturbed.

'I know she's your mother, Christy, but she's quite impossible,' he fumed. 'How can she say such things about you?'

'Hush,' I'd put the potatoes to warm through again and was washing up the tea things, so I threw a tea-towel at him and pointed to the cups and saucers on the draining-board. 'Take your wrath out on that, it'll be more useful than complaining about Mother. She is never going to change but don't worry, we're used to her. I hope Miss Diplock doesn't think they're bosom friends now because Mother will have forgotten all about her by the time she was halfway up the stairs.'

'It's so unfair,' he grumbled but obediently started drying as I washed. 'She has no idea how hard you girls work, you especially. And as for that other frightful woman…'

'Henry, stop complaining,' I said sternly and he looked at me in astonishment. 'Mother didn't hurt my feelings, she never does. As I said, we're used to her and we forget how she must sometimes strike outsiders.'

'Am I an outsider?' he interrupted me, an odd expression in his grey eyes.

'Of – of course you're not,' I said, feeling slightly breathless as he dropped his tea-towel on the table and reached out to put his hands on my shoulders. 'You-you're part of our family now.'

'Which part?' he said quietly. 'I don't want to be your brother, Christy.'

He started to pull me towards him, but we heard Addy in the hall. She can tread lightly when she wants to avoid authority but mostly she sounds like a carthorse. With Wilfred Seymour in tow she thundered into the kitchen and Henry released his grip on my shoulders.

'Honestly,' Addy complained. 'Mother is quite impossible; I mean – corsets!'

'What was that about?' Wilfred put in and then blushed as I glanced at him.

'It's all right,' I reassured him and was about to change the subject when Addy, who has little sense of fitness, explained.

'Mother disapproves of corsets, so we've never worn them,' she said frankly and pouted when I shook my head at her. 'That's enough, Addy. Will you and Wilfred please go and collect up any remaining plates.'

I hoped we'd exhausted the topic of women's underwear once Henry and I were left alone in the kitchen. Mother is very slight, almost skinny with an annoying knack of looking well-dressed in whatever she wears. Also, as Alix once pointed out, she might have felt differently about corsets had she ever needed to be held in. It's difficult to realise, looking at her, that she had three children in the space of ten months –

73

that's twins Alix and Bertie in November and me the following September. Not to mention Addy three years later, at which point Mother gave up. (Or perhaps it was Papa who did? For the first time I wondered about my parents. I don't know whether Papa strayed; he was a very good-looking man after all, exceedingly charming too. I doubt it though, his energies always seemed centred on gambling, and not just with money; with chance, with destiny and with life itself. Whatever came along was always full of promise to my father.)

At times we all sigh and wonder whether stays would make us look like the fashion plates in magazines, but we've never yet actually rebelled against Mother's edict; mostly because bouncing bosoms don't seem to run in the family. Addy and I are tall, but I don't think corsets would be a lot of use to us anyway.

Henry is always amused by my tussles with Addy during which I try, and usually fail, to make her behave decently and now he held out his hand to me.

'I'd better see if Bertha and Edgar are ready to leave,' he said but he didn't move. He hesitated for a moment. 'Thank you for my party, Christy.' He leaned forward and gave me a quick kiss on the cheek then blushed and hurried to find his cousins.

Sunday, 28th April, early evening

By half-past six all our visitors had gone home. Next door in Balmoral Lodge, Mrs Camperdown and Mrs Trellis were relaxing in their rooms in readiness for dinner which would be served at seven.

I heard a familiar off-key clang and hurried grumpily to our own front door. 'One day I'll disable that wretched bell,' I muttered but I composed myself and smiled calmly at the tall, elegantly dressed woman who stood there giving me quite as appraising a look as I was giving her.

'Good evening. May I help you?' It would be good if she were to be another paying guest for we still had two more empty rooms next door not counting Judith Evershed's room. She sleeps over there, though she spends much of her time with us. Had this lady, I wondered, come to the wrong door? (The front door of Balmoral Lodge, the other half of our pair of quite large Victorian villas, is right beside that of our own house, Sandringham Lodge, but we cannot risk Mother bumping into the guests.)

'Good evening,' replied the newcomer. 'I believe you must be Miss Christabel Fyttleton? I am Miss Bembridge, Headmistress of the Ramalley High School for Girls. I'd like to discuss the tutorial classes that you will be running here, if I may?'

I stared at that but ushered her into the drawing room. 'Do sit down, Miss Bembridge. I'll fetch Miss Evershed to come and talk to you.'

Judith is supposed to rest in the afternoons but instead of returning to her room in Balmoral Lodge, she often rests on the chaise longue in our kitchen, dozing or chatting to Granny and the rest of us. I found her recovering from the party, with the dog's head on her knee while the rest of him sprawled awkwardly on the floor, a kitten on her lap and another asleep on her shoulder.

When she saw me, she removed the kitten's tail from her face and sat up straight.

'It's a Miss Bembridge,' I said, explaining and shooing the dog away while I helped Judith to tidy herself. 'Come and help me out, do. She seems to think we're running a school!'

I introduced the ladies and we sat down, waiting to hear what it was all about. After a polite preamble, Miss Bembridge got down to business.

'My brother and his wife have recently returned to India,' she explained. 'He is in the Indian Army and they were home on leave during the autumn. When they returned to the East, they left their daughter with me. The idea was that Vera, who is fifteen, should attend the High School. All went according to plan until just before Christmas when Vera had a bad attack of diphtheria during the recent outbreak, though fortunately for me the quarantine period was over by the time school began again in the New Year. The illness, however, has left Vera delicate and the doctor says she is not fit for school. When I heard of your venture, it seemed a perfect solution.'

'Er, Miss Bembridge,' I asked, diffidently. 'May I ask who told you we were thinking of a class?'

'Why, Vera Wakelin's mother, a casual acquaintance of mine. She informed me last week.' Miss Bembridge looked surprised at my question. 'Apparently your sister Adelaide has invited the Wakelin girl to join her when your classes begin. I am not acquainted with Adelaide myself, but I know she is a studious girl and that she and Vera Wakelin were friends when they were at St Mildred's. Is there some difficulty?'

'Oh, not at all.' I vaguely remembered Vera Wakelin as one of the few girls Addy had tolerated at St Mildred's mostly, it must be said, because Vera admired her and never joined in the backbiting that went on there. I could see that Judith was feeling her way and wondering with misgivings, just what else Addy might have arranged.

'It's simply that until this week I have not felt up to doing very much. I am recovering from an accident,' Judith explained.

'Miss Evershed's proposed tutorial group will be very small,' I put in. 'Not more than three or four students at the most. Perhaps your niece would like to call in on – um – Wednesday morning, if you permit? She can meet Adelaide and have a general chat with Miss Evershed who will need to assess their individual requirements.'

Judith took a deep breath. 'I should inform you, Miss Bembridge, that it is very likely that my class will include a youth who has also been ill and who requires tuition to prepare him for his examinations in the summer. Furthermore, it is quite possible that Miss Fyttleton's very young maid may join in some, though not all, classes. We are firmly of the belief that education should be available to all.'

'Do excuse me,' I looked at my watch as Miss Bembridge digested this information – to her credit, she did not seem at all fazed by it. 'I'll leave you to discuss hours and terms with Miss Evershed,' I said, with a gracious smile copied from Granny. 'Our initial thoughts are that classes would be morning only.'

Oh, Addy, I groaned inwardly. What have you started? The idea of a school had been Addy's in the first place and although we had humoured her it seemed quite unnecessary and to tell the truth we had all assumed that, like most of Addy's schemes, it had died the death. All of us apart from Addy, that is. Judith looked amused so I felt I could leave the decision and details safely in her hands, and if it did come to anything at least we had a freshly decorated schoolroom downstairs.

Chapter Five

Monday, 29th April, morning

Just before nine o'clock there was a ring at our front door. I
was halfway down the stairs so I opened it before either of
the maids could get there and discovered Miss Bertha
Makepeace wearing a smile which managed to be both
apprehensive and ingratiating. Behind her was a small,
slightly-built woman of about forty, very handsome and
dressed all in brown: abundant brown hair, large brown eyes,
and a smart brown velvet coat trimmed with fur at the neck.
Dark brown leather gloves, elegant brown button boots, all
topped by a handsome brown velour hat completed this
symphony of autumn colours and suited this far from spring-
like day. This lady looked apprehensive, but unlike Henry's
cousin there was nothing ingratiating about her.

'Miss Makepeace? Do come in,' I was pleased to see her
and showed the two ladies into the drawing room. We all love
the way she's taken Henry to her heart, but I did wonder why
she was here so early. 'Would you like a cup of coffee or
cocoa? It won't take a minute.'

'I won't, thank you, my dear,' she said decidedly. 'I've
come on business. Let me introduce Miss Elsie Acton,
daughter of cousins of my late mother.'

'Elise,' hissed the stranger before giving a rather deep bow
which I returned, though less deeply and less formally.

'Ah, yes. Miss Elise Acton,' Miss Bertha coloured slightly.
I wondered why she was carrying a large, heavy-looking bag.

'You'll think I'm interfering,' she said apologetically. 'I
couldn't help noticing yesterday, dear Christabel, that you are
particularly burdened, what with the paying guests, your own

creative work, helping Lady Elspeth run the two houses, and having to do Mrs Fyttleton's typewriting on top of it.'

I opened my mouth to reassure her, but she held up her hand. 'Just one moment, dear,' she said, as she indicated her companion. 'Miss Acton is an expert at typewriting,' she explained. 'She has worked for many important concerns in London, but the capital no longer suits her and she has removed to Ramalley. I believe she is the ideal answer to lessening the load on your shoulders.'

'That's very kind; of you both,' I murmured, somewhat at a loss. Miss Bertha nodded and I felt a momentary thrill at the thought of liberty, followed swiftly by the sinking of my heart at the idea of the extra expense.

'My proposition is that Miss Acton should come here at nine-thirty each weekday morning and do your mother's typewriting until twelve-thirty. Edgar has given me a spare typewriter from the office and that will free up your own machine. The fee that Miss Acton requires is one guinea per week.'

Bertha Makepeace stared fiercely at me and I realised she was making a 'Hush' face at me. I swallowed the protest I'd been about to make and gazed attentively at her. What was she up to?

'It's not a great deal for a trained secretary, I know, but it would be part-time which would suit Elsie…Elise.' Miss Acton sighed before closing her eyes, apparently in silent prayer. Miss Makepeace appeared unmoved by her friend's manner and continued. 'If you could offer a cup of coffee and a biscuit mid-morning, that would be very satisfactory.'

I must have looked confused but Miss Acton – Elise – inclined her head and Miss Bertha smiled at us both. She was about to say something else when Miss Acton gazed mournfully at me and laid a gloved hand on her bosom.

'Miss Fyttleton,' she said in a surprisingly deep voice for so slight a frame, reminding me – I can't think why – of my former headmistress's dramatic renderings of passages from Shakespeare. 'I cannot impose upon your kindness without first explaining my situation.'

I started to stammer and Miss Makepeace tutted, but we were overruled.

'You see before you, Miss Christabel, a woman brought low.'

'Goodness!' As responses go it was inadequate but then, how does one react in such circumstances.

'I have held increasingly responsible posts in various London merchant concerns,' Miss Acton began. 'In the fifteen years of my sojourn there I worked hard and last spring, at my most recent post, I became the trusted personal secretary of one of the partners, a newcomer to the firm.'

She paused to dab her eyes with a lace handkerchief. 'He – I shall not name him – became infatuated with me and I with him, but alas, he abandoned me, together with all my hopes. And…' a throbbing note entered her voice. 'He stole my heart.'

Do you know, just for a moment I had a horrid premonition that she might be talking about Papa, but I banished the disturbing idea. We had been informed that Papa had gone down with the Lusitania in May 1915 and whatever the truth about that might be, I was almost certain that he had not been seducing anyone in London last summer. However, Miss Acton had not finished her tale of woe.

'I should have been more restrained, I know, but a heart that is broken knows no boundaries.'

Bertha Makepeace kept her face completely impassive except for winking, very briefly at me, which almost caused me to choke with laughter but unlike our visitor and her broken heart, I did manage to restrain myself.

'What happened?' I was agog. This made a change from the usual wartime woes we are accustomed to hear from our lady lodgers.

'I followed him one day to the Ritz Hotel and found him at luncheon with another woman.' There was a catch in the deep voice. 'I left at once, of course, but not before telling her, and the other patrons, how he had betrayed my trust. That afternoon I knew he had an appointment at the Stock Exchange and there I denounced him as a philanderer in front of all the most important men in London.' Out came the handkerchief once more. 'He is dead now, alas.'

'Yes, well…' Miss Makepeace snatched at the reins and took control of the conversation. 'The upshot, Christabel, is that Elise has no reference and cannot find a suitable new position in London because, of course, the news of her outbursts spread, as did her identity. My idea is that she should assist your mother for at least six months, after which she will have a reference as well as experience in a completely different sphere of employment and in a different part of the country.'

Alix put her head round the door at that point, interrupting Miss Makepeace with an apology. She made an anxious face at me, so I followed her into the dining room.

'Do you need me for anything, Christy? Will it be all right if I go up to the hospital for the morning? I – I more or less promised Fergus, I mean Dr Munro, that I'd help to show him the usual routine now the patients are installed.'

I hid a smile, though she spotted it and grabbed my hand.

'I'd really like…Can you manage…Christy, do you think he likes me?' Her blue eyes were wide with apprehension and I gave her a reassuring hug.

'I do,' I said. 'He couldn't take his eyes off you. Go on, I'm sure Sister Wisden will be glad of a helping hand. And – he's nice, Alix. We can manage here.'

It felt odd, waving my sister off to meet a young man, for that's what was happening. Yes, she would work hard up at Groom Hall, but work wasn't the attraction. I said a quick prayer to whatever deity might have time to pay attention that Alix should not get hurt then I hurried back to Miss Makepeace, wondering what on earth was going on.

'Is your mother at work? Very well, we'll all go upstairs and beard her in her den.' Miss Bertha's plan sounded plausible as long as Mother and Miss Acton could cope with each other, and my heart was beating faster. We could certainly manage to pay the modest amount required, because we had that windfall we don't talk about. (I know we grumble about Mother, but she does earn the lion's share of our combined income with her writing and we do truly appreciate it. Nothing must interfere with that!)

I followed the two women meekly up to Mother's study, outside which Miss Bertha looked enquiringly at me.

'You have a separate office, I believe, Christabel? Is that where you do the typing?'

Obedient to her hint I led the two of them to the box-room and showed Miss Acton ('Call me, Elise, dear') the files and folders, the paper and typewriter ribbons, the pens and ink. At Miss Bertha's suggestion I picked up my own typewriter and removed it to my bedroom while Elise set up the much more efficient-looking relic from the office. I wondered whether Edgar Makepeace had been quite as willing to hand it over as Miss Bertha implied but I could see she was on a crusade to rescue me from drudgery. And quite frankly I was in no mood to stop her.

An unholy glee filled me as I watched the dramatic Elise Acton move the chair and settle herself at the desk, twitching a few of the folders into a neater arrangement. I saw that she was in her element and that, drama queen or not, she did at least seem to know what she was doing. But what would Mother say? And did she – or I, for that matter – have any say in this new arrangement?

It seemed not. Miss Bertha glanced round the office with a satisfied smile and beckoned Miss Acton and me to follow her. I pointed out the bathroom while our leader knocked on the study door and opened it without waiting for a reply.

'Ah, good morning, Mrs Fyttleton,' she ignored Mother's appalled expression. 'Miss Acton is here to take over your typewriting from Christabel.'

My mother stared, and her visitor gave her a soothing smile. 'An author of your stature, dear Mrs Fyttleton, should not have to manage with an amateur amanuensis.' I could see Mother looking blank at that. Considering her own father was a brilliant scholar, she has quite a few gaps in her education.

Bertha regrouped. 'Christabel has done well, of course, but she is very young and has other duties. Here we have Miss Acton who, owing to family circumstances, has had to relinquish her former position as Private Secretary to a prominent London businessman. At last you will have an assistant who is not only efficient but is experienced in working on the most important matters. She is delighted to have this chance, aren't you, Elise?'

'Oh, indeed,' gushed Miss Acton. 'I'm in awe, Mrs Fyttleton. I've read every single one of your books; the Margaret Gillespie ones as well as the Mabel de Rochforde romances. I have a subscription to your publisher, and I take each new book as it is published. If you will allow me to help you with your work, I shall be the happiest of women. It will be an honour and a privilege.'

I stood there, silenced. Miss Bertha concealed a naughty grin behind her handkerchief, and Mother – who for once appeared to be relatively alert and conscious of her surroundings – allowed Elise Acton to pump her hand enthusiastically.

It seemed an opportune moment to escape. 'I'll be downstairs if you need anything, Miss Acton,' I murmured. 'I'll bring you both a drink soon.'

Bertha Makepeace and I made our way downstairs demurely and not until we had reached the safety of the kitchen and shut the door behind us, did we burst out laughing.

'What have you done! Who is that imposing Shakespearian tragedy queen and how can I possibly pay her so little? Her London salary must have been so much higher.'

Granny raised an eyebrow as we both giggled, and she took down cups and saucers.

'I made tea when I heard you go upstairs,' she said calmly. 'I thought you might need it. Do sit down Miss Makepeace. Christabel? Have you seen Alix lately?'

'She's needed up at Groom Hall,' I said briefly and caught Granny's eye. She cocked her head thoughtfully. 'Hmm… perhaps you'd care to explain what's happening in your mother's room, Christy?'

'I think Miss Bertha, I mean Miss Makepeace, should explain,' I said, and our visitor smiled.

'Please do use my name, my dear,' she said. 'We are partners in crime, after all. I was struck yesterday, Lady Elspeth, by how many jobs the girls have, particularly Christabel. It seemed a pity that her own writing should be put aside to service her mother's requirements, not to mention her household duties. I also knew that Miss Acton needed employment outside London to earn a reference. Don't worry, Christabel, Elsie – Elise – has a private income from her family who live in Somerset. She has no financial need to work but as you saw, London has its attractions. And her family do appreciate her far more when she is a long way from home.' She had a mischievous twinkle as she spoke.

'I suppose I oughtn't to tell you, but I will anyway,' she said and hastily explained the situation to Granny. 'When she left London under a cloud last autumn, Elise returned to Bath, but it was awkward for them. Her original departure for London fifteen years ago followed a similar experience with a visiting bishop and as her father is a clergyman (a cousin on my mother's side) it was mortifying for her family. There have been several of these dramas over the years and each time Elise has left her employment with an excellent reference. My brother Edgar suggests that her employers probably mention that her work is exemplary (which it is, apparently) but that they neglect to refer to her unfortunate habit of throwing herself at senior members of staff. That way, the company can be certain of getting rid of her amicably and it's no fault of theirs if she does it again somewhere else.

'This time, however, her mother wrote to me for advice and a plea for me to find her something to do. I had your many tasks in mind, Christabel, even before yesterday's party so I agreed albeit with a few reservations. She has already taken rooms in Ramalley, near the Priory, and her parents are happy to keep up her allowance rather than have her live at home. I believe their curate was beginning to look hunted!'

Granny and I goggled at her. There's no other word for the way we stared.

'Um, this latest philanderer,' I ventured. 'She said he had

died recently. Did she have anything to do with that?'

'What? Murder by a woman scorned. Good heavens no,' Miss Bertha tried not to smile. 'No, he died in a street accident when a brewer's dray crashed into a taxicab.'

She hesitated. 'The man was Reginald Diplock,' she said. 'Yes, Portia's brother, but she has no idea of this. To her he was a paragon of virtue so this must go no further. My brother knew him, of course, and helped to keep his name out of the newspapers, for Portia's sake.' She raised an amused eyebrow. 'Not that Portia would believe a word against him.'

I was shocked but Granny and I promised to guard the secret with our lives. Another query sprang to mind. 'And she didn't – there wasn't a child – was there?'

'What an imagination!' Miss Bertha shook her head. 'No, indeed. I don't believe Elise has any notion of that kind of thing, her love is always intense, cloying, and – and pure.'

Without a word, Granny reached for the oatmeal biscuits cooling on the range and offered the biggest one to Miss Bertha, which meant Granny was pleased about this ingenious solution to my problems. We should be safe enough, I thought. Miss Acton would be hard put to find a suitable object for her affections in our small circle, unless she ventured to visit the hospital and found a middle-aged wounded officer to adore.

I excused myself for a moment while I looked in on our two guests and found both of them reading in the drawing room. Mrs Trellis was engrossed in Mother's novel but Mrs Camperdown nodded pleasantly. Elsewhere, I found Addy and Judith discussing history and geography, with reference to places that Judith had visited and that Addy would like to visit. Bella was at the back door engaging in cheerful banter with the man from the laundry as she handed him our sheets and pillowcases and so forth, with an admonition not to lose anything. Noises from the cellar meant that Mr Jerrold, the plumber, was making headway with Judith's classroom, while Penny had washed up the breakfast things in both houses and was making the lodgers' beds, singing as she did so.

Back in our own kitchen I looked at Bertha with narrowed eyes.

'What makes you think I have writing of my own to do?' I asked and she looked a little guilty.

'I'm afraid my late father let it slip just before he died at Christmas,' she confessed.

'But how did he…?' I paused. Of course, old Mr Makepeace had dealt with the legal side of things when our neighbour died and we took possession of the house next door. I'd asked the old lawyer, rather tentatively, whether there would be any difficulty with banking my earnings in my own name, because I use a nom-de-plume when writing.

'I was sitting with him a few days before he died,' Bertha said with a fond smile. 'He'd never had a day's illness, but everything ran down very quickly. I thought he was asleep, propped up on his pillows, when suddenly he started to chuckle. 'Damned plucky little girls,' he said. You mustn't mind his language, dear, he admired you and your sisters very much. He told me about meeting you all and how you were struggling with grief on top of everything else. 'Bowed down by the shock of their brother's death, but still the eldest works for a tyrannical old woman and spends her spare time helping out at the hospital. The middle one, would you believe, is writing adventure yarns for young fellows at the Front, and making money selling them too, clever girl.' Bertha wiped her eyes and tucked her handkerchief into her sleeve.

I remembered the kind old gentleman who had quietly, and without fuss, agreed with Granny that it would be wise to make sure that Mother had no control over our surprise legacy, the house next door. They had exchanged conspiratorial nods and shaken hands on their decision and Mr Makepeace Senior had made all the arrangements so that everything was safely signed and witnessed. (It's a sad fact that Mother will sign anything put in front of her if you choose the right moment. We're not proud of the way we deceive her on occasion but it's a precautionary measure. She has no common sense and cannot be trusted with money.)

We'd been sorry to hear of the old gentleman's death shortly afterwards and it was heartwarming to learn of his approval.

The next excitement was the arrival of a young lad from the farm up the road. Because Granny is universally admired, we tend to have acquaintances in all walks of life, so I knew him at once when I opened the back door and found him with a hand raised to knock.

'Your pullets, miss,' he said politely as he thrust a basket at me, giving me a smart salute, and disappearing hastily round the side of the house lest I expect him to help. I lifted the basket lid and was immediately greeted by shrieks and lamentations from the four bedraggled birds inside.

'Oh, do be quiet,' I tutted at them. 'You're going to live in an excellent house with plenty of room to peck about and four nice older hens to show you what to do. What more could you want? Besides, if Kaiser Bill's eggs hatch, they'll be your sisters or aunts or cousins, or something. That'll be nice, won't it?'

Attracted by the squawks Addy and Judith ambled out to the garden to see what was up.

'Are there only four of them?' Judith was astonished. 'From the racket I assumed the circus had come to town and you'd invited them all to tea.'

'Apart from the little black one they look a bit scruffy,' Addy sniffed, and so they did. As far as I could tell not one of them belonged to a recognizable breed. Not a Wyandotte among them, but that didn't matter because our four elderly ladies weren't aristocrats either. I thought the white one might be a Leghorn and there were two anonymous-looking brown hens as well as a very small black one.

'You'd look scruffy if you'd been taken away from your home,' I pointed out. 'I expect the little one's a bantam and anyway, it doesn't matter what they look like, as long as they lay a lot of eggs; and look, there's already an egg in the basket. I wonder which of them is responsible? You can help me introduce the new girls to the others.'

Kaiser Bill sat smugly on her messy nest and refused to show any interest in anything but the eggs under her, but Body, our senior hen, complained long and loud about burglars and interlopers and probably pirates too, until she suddenly shut her beak and ignored them. (Bertie had named her John Brown's Body but that's too long a name for everyday use.) The newcomers were soon busy pecking and barging in front of the remaining resident hens, Jasper and Crombie. These two are very meek by nature and used to being bullied so it looked as though they would be resigned to the upheaval. Incidentally, they were named for two of the ghillies who taught Granny her woodland skills and whose names I had adopted for my boys' serials and books.

'Well, they haven't pecked each other to death – yet,' I said, crossing my fingers before I latched the door to the hen run. 'I'm going to leave them to settle. Miss Preston moves in this afternoon, so I've things to do.'

Addy and Judith turned to go indoors so I called after them. 'Don't forget those two girls are coming to see you tomorrow morning, Miss Bembridge's niece and the other one. We need to have a discussion, Judith, about practicalities; this evening, perhaps?' I turned to my sister. 'It's all your fault, Addy, so you'd better start now and practise being amiable to everyone, because you're going to have to make friends with them if this school idea of yours is to work.'

Judith hid a smile as Addy shot me a look of disgust, but I knew she was far too proprietorial about her scheme to let it falter and die.

I looked down the garden and spotted our occasional gardener, Nigel, (the elder brother of our maids Bella and Penny), busily digging in the vegetable plot.

'Morning, Miss Christy,' he greeted me with a friendly, gap-toothed grin. 'I'm planting onions today.'

'So I see,' I said, admiring them and wondering they had come from, but he has his own methods of acquiring seeds and plants and we don't like to enquire too closely.

'I got something for her ladyship,' he added, looking a bit

shifty which, in Niggle (as his mother insists his name is pronounced) is almost his habitual expression. Things do somehow fall into his hands and his sweet nature, combined with the suffering he experienced after being trapped underground in the trenches, makes everyone turn a blind eye.

'That's kind, Niggle,' I told him, wondering aloud if it could be more pheasants like one of his recent offerings. He tapped his nose and said, 'Ask no questions, Miss Christy, I'll bring it in later.'

The grandfather clock in the hall wheezed eleven and I prepared a tray which I took upstairs. I knocked on the study door and was pleasantly surprised to find a busy scene. Miss Acton's typewriting was much faster than mine and she was handing pages to Mother as she worked. Mother still had that dazed look about her, but I could see she was coping; and long may it last. I laid out their elevenses and made my escape; no use alerting Mother to the fact that I was no longer her slave.

Downstairs again I was surprised to find no trace of Granny but supposed she had decided on a shopping expedition. She and I both enjoy looking round the shops in town even though there's precious little to buy and not much money to do so even if we wanted to.

Our next boarder, Miss Preston, was expected after luncheon and after I'd checked that her room was ready I read through another chapter of the Mulberry boys and their adventures. I was finding it hard going and I worried that I might dry up. It's not easy writing books set in the Trenches and I'm running out of ideas. Henry offers suggestions now and then, but I find the whole thing depressing because the facts are far too dreadful to turn them into fiction. I really don't know what to do about it though and I was relieved when this morning's episode flowed from my pen and I realised I was galloping through the wretched book.

At half-past twelve I was hovering in the hall when our new employee came downstairs, dressed in her outdoor clothes. She smiled graciously when I opened the door.

'What an interesting morning,' she said brightly. 'Your mother is a true inspiration, you know.' I blinked at that but summoned up a gratified smile that widened considerably when she said, 'I'll see you in the morning. Good day to you!' Thank goodness she hasn't resigned as I had feared she might.

Although the sun was shining brightly it was quite chilly out in the garden, so I wandered indoors feeling aimless. At this time of day I would normally be busy with Mother's work and it felt very odd – slightly sinful, in fact – not to be working, so after luncheon I made pastry for a pie as well as some jam tarts for tea. There are drawbacks to being the sensible one in a family, even though Alix is certainly not the flibbertigibbet that Mother believes. I take after Granny. She and I have always been in charge of the constant struggle to keep up appearances on a relatively small income. To some people, of course, we are fortunate, because we have not one, but two houses – riches indeed. We are fortunate, of course we are, and we have two housemaids as well, but living up to expectations isn't always easy.

As the daughter of an earl, Granny was brought up to marry well and not to deviate from that aim. Her parents thought it was the least she could do – to marry money and plenty of it – considering they could never forgive her for not being a son and heir. She was left to the care of an elderly governess who taught her to be a lady of title: perfect manners, embroidery, deportment and able, had she not been distressingly bashful, to converse with anyone from royalty downwards. Luckily, in view of her shyness, she also spent much of her time with the housekeeper and head ghillie at the ancestral Scottish castle. They taught her useful skills like cooking, household management, how to set snares and tickle trout; how to gut and cook rabbits and game birds and even to gralloch deer. This last is something we could all do in theory but have not yet needed to attempt, though Addy lives in hope as roe deer are wild in this part of Hampshire. (I might add that she would be distraught if she did find a dead deer as they are such pretty little creatures.)

Granny's greatest talent is adaptability, something she has passed on to her granddaughters but sadly not to her own daughter, who is brilliant, reclusive and stiffly unhappy in the company of other people. This is because Mother takes after Grandpapa, a brilliant scholar who was eminently unsuited to life outside an Oxford college. If only Mother could have lived her life immersed in study and surrounded by the dreaming spires; fortunately her cleverness is supported by our practical attributes and so we all muddle along.

Mind you, even in our small Hampshire town people would not like to think of an aristocrat like Granny as living in very straightened circumstances and they would be shocked if, as Alix and I once threatened to do, we went out as housemaids ourselves being surprisingly well-qualified to do so. However, we have managed to keep up appearances and now, with a nest egg in the bank and the extra income from the lodgers, we are doing very well at present and long may it last. (It hasn't cured me of worrying and penny-pinching though.)

In the scullery I found a bundle of celery wrapped in newspaper and Granny nowhere in sight so, puzzled, I set the jam tarts to cool on the rack. Addy sat down to work on an essay while Judith and I composed a letter which laid out the times for the proposed class as well as a provisional syllabus and a discreet mention of the fees required – as worked out by Judith and me.. Penny was delighted when I asked if she would walk into town to deliver copies of this letter to Mrs Wakelin, Miss Bembridge and Mrs Seymour, Wilfred's mother. I fished in my pocket and gave her the fourpence ha'penny that was all I found.

'Buy yourself a little treat, Penny,' I told her as Judith went to her room next door for a nap. I tiptoed upstairs to listen at Mother's door but there was no sound either from the study or the bedroom, so I hoped she was asleep. She writes at all hours, often through the night; it stops her thinking of Bertie. We all cope in our own ways and hers is to cat-nap in daylight hours.

Still feeling at a loose end, I went in search of Granny and found her down in the cellar again. Her henchman, Mr Jerrold, was switching lights on and off and I was impressed to see he'd fitted another light at the end of the proposed schoolroom.

'Ah, well, Miss Christy,' he told me, pleased with my admiration. 'I'm a jack of all trades, you know. It pays to learn how to do things.'

This is so much my own philosophy that I think I overdid the praise because he marched me off to inspect the new lavatory in Balmoral Lodge.

'You pull the chain, Miss Christy,' he urged. 'Go on, there's a lovely flush and I know you'll be as satisfied as her ladyship is. Go on then…There! What did I tell you? That's as handsome a flush as I've heard.'

'What an excellent flow of water,' I told him, gushing almost as much as the cistern, and so it was. Mr Jerrold showed signs of wanting to instruct me further into the finer points of hydraulic engineering but Granny pointed out to me that it was nearly time for Miss Preston to move in and I should tidy myself in readiness.

Mr Jerrold shook hands with both of us, discreetly palming an envelope that Granny gave him. He assured us of his firm admiration for our whole family and entreated us to call on him at any time if we needed further assistance.

When he finally left, I looked at my watch and realised that Granny had exaggerated. There was a full half hour before our guest was due, so we did a tour of the schoolroom; rather a short tour, of course, because it was completely bare.

'Hmm,' I pursed my lips. 'We need a couple of tables, don't we? A smaller one for Judith and a big one for the girls – and Wilfred. Chairs too.'

When we had opened up next door to paying guests we had stored anything potentially useful in the cellar that now stood empty and the two iron bedsteads bought by our late neighbour when the town asylum closed down were now stored down there. We had kept them during the general upheaval of setting up the guest house but so far they lurked unwanted in the cellar. Baskets of bedlinen – unused but dusty – had been laundered and moved to the airing cupboard next door, and surplus crockery, cutlery, pots and pans were now stored in the kitchen over there.

'There's not much,' I sighed. 'We were quite ruthless when we cleared out the rubbish, though I don't remember any spare tables anyway. These two cane-backed armchairs can go in the schoolroom; with cushions they'll be ideal for quiet reading, but otherwise I'd better go into town tomorrow and see if I can find some bargains.'

I had a sudden thought. 'Do you know anything about some celery in the scullery?'

'Ah,' she looked mysterious. 'That was from Niggle. He was very shifty about it so I didn't ask awkward questions.'

'Yes, I thought it looked forced, as though it came from somebody's greenhouse,' I said. 'We'd better serve it tonight. He did hint earlier about a present for you, but I rather hoped it might be more pheasants, or a couple of ducks or even a shoulder of pork. Still, braised celery will add variety to dinner.'

'Just a moment, Christy,' Granny held out a hand to stop me going back upstairs. 'I called in on Bella's mother this morning and had a long chat with her.'

'About Penny?' I was intrigued. I'd still not had time to catch Bella and here was Granny taking on the job, thank goodness.

'I knew Penny was very much the baby,' Granny nodded. 'It comes as no surprise to hear that Mrs Harper wants to do her best for the child, particularly now her husband is no longer here to put his foot down.'

I looked at her.

'Oh yes,' she sighed. 'He was adamant that what was good enough for him, going out to work at twelve, was good enough for his children – as of course it has to be for most people – but Bella is as eager as her mother that Penny should have a better start. I mentioned the possibility of the child joining some of Judith's classes now that she doesn't have to go home in the afternoon to help with their own housework and reassured Mrs Harper that this would be an extra at no cost to her and would make no difference to Penny's wages.'

'I was worried that she might think we were being patronising,' I suggested, and Granny nodded.

'I don't believe the thought entered her head. Bella has been with us for some time and she knows perfectly well that our means are straitened, sometimes extremely so. If she knows, you can be sure that her mother does too. I put it to Mrs Harper that we are all working together to keep our heads above water and that Penny is such a good child that this is something that we are happy to do. Fortunately, neither she nor I suffer from false pride!'

I wondered. Odd though it sounds, I'm never entirely sure that Granny quite understands the shifts and balances of small town society. She comes from a different generation and from the highest tier of society, regardless of her unorthodox upbringing and she treats everyone in exactly the same way and in return is regarded with admiration, respect and affection. The kindest of women, there is nonetheless always a slight distance from other people and I'm not at all sure she has ever realised that. She was born to it and besides, her title alone would ensure that sense of deference .

Then again, Alix, Bella and I, have a good working relationship, but – I pay Bella's wages. I hope, and am sure, that she knows we appreciate her hard work, but I'm still her employer.

Perhaps Addy and Penny, as modern, Twentieth Century girls, might forge a different kind of friendship?

The afternoon meandered along uneventfully. Miss Preston arrived as expected and moved in, expressing satisfaction yet again at the convenience and comfort she found there. I outdid myself and churned out yet another chapter of the current book and was halfway through another before I realised I was dying for a cup of tea. I could see the end in sight and luckily I now knew where I was going so it was only a matter of buckling down to it and allowing my characters to survive all the hazards they faced. These included all the usual horrors of the war in France (turned into entertainment for my readers, a point that suddenly made me pause though I had no time at the moment to explore that thought), along with jealousy from a superior officer (a staple in my plots!); a letter from an ailing parent who thought she was going down with Spanish flu, as well as a letter from a Best Girl who sounded as though she was having far too much fun with a rival who was home on leave. My plan was to explode a shell close to the superior officer – not enough to kill him but sufficient to get him away from the unit, whereupon he would be discovered to be a spy; to have a follow-up letter, this time from a sister, saying Mother was much recovered – it was just a cold and not to worry; and a scented note from the Best Girl, on pink paper and sealed with a kiss.

'You must be telepathic, Granny,' I exclaimed as I walked into the kitchen to find Granny pouring out tea.

'Hardly.' She raised an eyebrow. 'When are you ever not gasping for tea? And do not even think about setting me up as a telepathic medium to fleece the unwary and contribute to our coffers.'

'Oh, Addy would love that. Think what she could do with ectoplasm!'

I giggled and had barely had time to sit down when there was a knock at the back door, which opened to reveal Wilfred's red head and cheerful grin. He held out a letter to me.

'Good afternoon, Lady Elspeth, Christabel,' he said politely. 'Addy said it would be all right for me to use the back door to save you having to open the front one every time. This is a letter from Mother, Christy.' His eyes danced. 'She says she'll pay you any sum you care to ask if only you'll keep me here all day and not just for the mornings.'

Chapter Six

Monday, 29th April, evening

Judith, Granny and I had planned a council of war for that evening but unfortunately, we were thwarted. To begin with, Bobs the dog escaped after tea and even though Addy and I hunted him through the Groom Hall park the infuriating animal eluded us. Then our paying guests – our bread and butter! – were ready to chat and to be entertained when they had finished their evening meal. This is not usually a hardship, I am always ready to enter into their interests, but it was almost eight o'clock before I managed to leave them to their books, their sewing and their conversation.

Although we tend to go to bed early, there would still have been time to discuss the proposed tutorial classes but Judith was looking weary, so Granny sent her off to bed whereupon Bobs appeared at the back door. He was delighted to see us, but we were less happy as he had clearly found something unpleasant to roll in, and that meant Addy and I had to give the wretched creature a bath.

Tuesday, 30th April, morning

We seem to live in a constant whirl of activity but at least we had no idea at that time that we would soon be faced with a sudden disturbing death that, if not quite on our own doorstep, would unfortunately involve us in a difficult period. As though we hadn't suffered enough complications from an unexplained death only a couple of months earlier!

Mercifully, one of our recent experiments appears to be a success. At nine-thirty precisely I opened the front door to

Miss Elise Acton who greeted me effusively and disappeared upstairs to tackle Mother and her latest outpourings. I hadn't realised how apprehensively I had half-anticipated a polite note of resignation, until my shoulders relaxed, and I breathed a sigh of relief. Thank heavens for Bertha Makepeace and her brilliant idea!

I had sent Wilfred home the previous day with a promise that I would write to his mother but had not had time to do so when a messenger boy arrived bearing similar heartfelt pleas from Mrs Wakelin and Miss Bembridge. Not one of these ladies, it transpired, wished to take responsibility for their respective son, daughter or niece during normal school hours. Not only that, they were each more than happy – desperate in fact – to pay whatever sum we required if only we would accommodate them in this desire. The handsome sum mentioned in the two most recent letters suggested collusion, probably by urgent telephone conversations between the ladies, and I had no difficulty in believing that they had been in touch with Mrs Seymour and that she would be equally open-handed.

A ring at our front door revealed Wilfred Seymour himself who, it appeared, wondered if he could take the dog for a walk. 'I thought it might be helpful,' he explained, oozing sincerity. 'I know how busy you all are.'

'I'll go with you,' Addy volunteered then, as I looked sceptical, 'I promise I'll come home before lunch and do that exercise for Judith.'

I nodded and wrapped two jam tarts and added a couple of oatmeal biscuits for them which she graciously accepted and as soon as they had gone, Granny suggested we snatch the opportunity to discuss the latest developments regarding Judith's proposed class.

Mrs Wakelin had no objection to Penny's occasional presence, having clearly read between the lines of my letter that this was not open to question. Miss Bembridge went one better and congratulated us on our egalitarian outlook. That was one hurdle taken care of and I hoped it would work out well. Granny's title, as ever, probably smoothed away any anxiety on behalf of the parents and guardians who, I knew, would enjoy a little name-dropping about the classes at Lady Elspeth's house.

'One thing is certain,' I declared. 'Judith must not undertake any further teaching. You're not fit,' I said, with a nod in her direction. She made a face but agreed and so did Granny.

'This being so, I do have a rather vague idea as to how we might manage this.' I saw that my grandmother was looking thoughtful. 'You too, Granny?'

'I suspect we are both thinking along the same lines,' Granny said slowly. 'It does seem a pity to turn away what amounts to quite a lot of money for just a few weeks, if we can possibly do this. Let's hear your idea first, Christy.'

'Wilfred and Addy are the least of our worries,' I began. It sounded so unlikely that I blinked at my own statement, but Judith nodded.

'Strange but true,' she said, catching my eye and smiling at my expression. 'I don't need to teach them actual lessons. Addy just needs me to check that she is working at her revision, a guiding hand now and then. Wilfred too, is much brighter than I had expected. I did have a quick word with him about his work and he surprised me by being very sensible too. I believe the two of them will thrive on some healthy competition.'

She turned to me. 'Can you tell me a little about the boy?'

'His father is a prominent local businessman with a finger in many pies and a rumour round town suggests that he may be in line to become mayor in due course. The undertaking business is only one of those pies and came to him through his first wife with whom he had three sons: all fine, upstanding young men who manage his various concerns now that he takes a less active role.

'Wilfred is the son of the second wife. Again, local gossip is our source because it all happened long before we moved to Ramalley. Mr Seymour's eye fell upon a house on the outskirts of town and he was induced not only to buy it, even though the land had all been sold off, but to marry the owner's spinster sister as part of the agreement!'

'Good heavens!' exclaimed Judith. 'Small town life is so much more interesting than I had ever imagined. What happened?'

'Mr Seymour was left with three young sons to bring up and needed someone to manage the house he wished to purchase,' I explained. 'The owner of the house, a retired naval officer, suffered from heart disease and was anxious to establish his sister who was nursing him through his last illness. The tale is that Mrs Seymour was only too glad to accept.'

'She's a very pleasant woman,' put in Granny. 'A good wife, an affectionate stepmother and if she is a trifle anxious about Wilfred, it is put down to his being born when she was over forty.' There was a twinkle in her eye as she glanced at me. 'She has high hopes for her son, which is understandable, but the fact that she considers Addy to be a stabilising influence on him might suggest that she has a good deal to put up with. Wilfred is an extremely lively lad!'

I made cocoa and called the meeting to order. Alix had looked in on us earlier, then disappeared to her attic to try out a new hairstyle and Addy was still out for a walk with Wilfred, though as she really wanted to read about Cretan burial practices Judith thought she would be back in good time.

'If Judith is happy to oversee Addy and Wilfred's revision in the mornings,' I suggested. 'I think we can send them out for walks in the afternoon or let them work quietly together. As to the two Veras... According to Miss Bembridge, her niece is not strong but, in any case, is not remotely interested in anything academic and Mrs Wakelin writes frankly that her daughter is not at all clever, so I wondered about teaching them useful arithmetic and how to write sensible letters? Whatever their station in life may be, whether as wives or daughters at home or professional women, it can only be good for them to acquire practical habits. I'm thinking of how to budget for a meal, or for a party, that kind of useful knowledge. It's helpful to learn to calculate how much cloth you need to make underclothes or curtains and how to alter a dress pattern to fit someone smaller or larger. And what about learning how to write a polite acceptance to an At Home or a reference for a departing cook, perhaps? We can all come up with useful ideas of that kind.'

Granny nodded. 'That's very much along the lines of what I was thinking, Christy. Don't forget some French conversation, Judith. I'm sure you could work that in satisfactorily.'

'Oh, yes,' Judith agreed. 'I see what you mean, Christabel. I can do that in the mornings once Wilfred and Addy are settled, but what about the afternoons? And what about lunch?'

'Cocoa and biscuits are one thing, but we certainly can't provide meals. I'll make it a condition that they must bring their own lunches,' I said, working it out as I spoke. 'Granny? What else did you have in mind?'

'Another condition will require the girls to have outdoor shoes and an apron,' Granny clearly had a plan. 'We'll need to bring Penny in on this, Christy. Until last week she's been helping with dusting and making beds here till lunchtime, eating here and going home to keep her ailing aunt company, after which she returned here to help with tea and dinner.'

I thought I could see where Granny's idea was leading but Judith looked slightly bewildered. Granny gathered her thoughts.

'Now that the aunt has died, I suggest we ask her to have lunch with the two girls, either here or perhaps next door's kitchen would be better, we don't want them underfoot. Addy and Wilfred can eat with them to break the ice as neither is shy; they can then disappear to whatever pursuit Judith has prescribed. This will help the girls get used to the idea and give Penny more social confidence. Learning different points of view will broaden all their minds.'

Judith and I were nodding as Granny outlined her plan and I could tell that she was amused and pleased at the rapt attention we accorded her.

'We must make sure the girls understand that Penny is

here to learn, just as they are,' I put in. 'They mustn't think they can patronise her or treat her differently. For a start, she'll call them by their first names, Addy too, though I suppose I'll have to be Miss Christabel to all of them; that will help, I hope! I know it's unusual, but the war has changed everything, and girls particularly face an entirely different way of life.'

'Meanwhile, you and I, Christy, will teach the three of them how to cook,' said Granny. 'You talked of managing a household budget, so we'll show them how to turn out a meal under wartime restrictions and with a limited budget. What could be more educational and practical, because I intend their efforts to be eaten by the lodgers and ourselves. When we bake, they can take home samples to show off their prowess.'

I sat back and applauded, and Judith joined in with a peal of laughter.

'Lady Elspeth,' she said. 'That amounts to genius! What a Machiavellian mind you must have, to make the parents pay for their daughters to cook your dinner!'

Granny hid a grin as she bowed her acknowledgement.

'I've had an idea about sewing,' I said. 'I like the idea of the girls eating and cooking together. We've made it plain that Penny is part of our scheme – though come to think of it we haven't actually asked her what she wants to do! We must do that, even though we know her mother is agreeable, so I suggest that some of the afternoon classes finish with a sewing session. Penny is exceptionally skilled, and she could help them, perhaps teaching them to embroider too. And we'd pay her for her time out of the exorbitant sum their families are offering!'

'She's a polite, clever child,' Judith said. 'I'm glad there seems to be no objection to her joining the experiment. I'd wondered about that.'

'Mrs Wakelin and Mrs Seymour are Ramalley born and bred and will be aware of the family already,' Granny said. 'Miss Bembridge will have made enquiries you may be sure of that. Naturally enough, there are few secrets in a small

101

town and the father was known to be a disgrace. However there has always been a good deal of sympathy for her mother, who was in good service before her marriage and the aunt was employed at a very respectable dressmaker's in Winchester so Penny's speech and manners will certainly not corrupt our young lady pupils!'

'It begins to sound possible,' remarked Judith. 'Any other suggestions?'

'Gardening!' Granny exclaimed. 'There's a lot of planning and planting to be done at this time of year so on fine afternoons the girls can learn about that and ask Niggle to…'

'I don't think we should involve Niggle,' I frowned. 'The girls might find him odd and the parents probably wouldn't like it. He's a young man after all.'

'I suppose so,' Granny shook her head. 'Oh well, I'm sure we can come up with something and at least you can teach them about hens. Are we agreed that we'll offer domestic economy and husbandry combined with mathematics, English Literature and French conversation? That will surely satisfy the parents and interest the girls as well.' She looked thoughtful. 'I'll have a word with Penny tomorrow morning, her mother will have told her the plan and I'll make sure she's happy with the idea. It's rather unusual and very modern, after all, but I think she'll have enough confidence in us to cope.'

We seemed to have covered a lot of ground and it was still barely nine o'clock, so I took myself off to read in bed, but genius was burning for once and at ten-to-one I laid down my pencil and rubbed my eyes. The wretched Mulberry Boys were finished, thank heavens, only needing a critical read-through and a polish before typing tomorrow.

Wednesday, 1st May, morning

I was in the kitchen when Addy opened the front door and I heard girlish voices as she greeted her proposed classmates and took them to meet their new schoolmistress. For a moment I thought of sneaking upstairs to carry on with my typewriting but I'm far too inquisitive to do that so I put out a plate of biscuits and some glasses of milk as well as coffee for Judith and me. I carried the tray into the drawing room and found two schoolgirls perched awkwardly on the edge of the chesterfield, staring worriedly at Judith. One of them looked even more apprehensive when she glanced at Addy who, I was relieved to note, was looking quite pleasant. Well, at least she wasn't scowling, let's put it that way.

'Tell me, girls,' Judith asked. 'What do you hope to gain by coming to our classes?'

Although we already knew what their families expected of them, very little), Judith wanted to see if the girls had any ideas of their own. She was met with blank looks.

'I mean, do you hope to take exams, like Adelaide? Or is it simply because your parents would like you to stay in school for a while longer?'

The tall, fair-haired girl whom I recognised as Vera Wakelin, a former fellow pupil of Addy's at St Mildred's, heaved an extravagant sigh.

'Not exams, Miss Evershed, I'm not clever like Addy, but Mother says I need to keep up with my French and reading and so on. She says I'm not old enough to be useful at home; you know, with visitors or tennis parties or anything and I'm not clever enough to go to the High School. If it wasn't for the war, she might have sent me to a finishing school in France. When she heard about your class she said it was an answer to a prayer.'

Judith shot a flickering glance at me and I knew we were both thinking that a prayer was an unlikely description of the fall that had nearly taken her life and that currently kept her convalescent in Ramalley, but by the way she kept her face expressionless I knew she was trying not to laugh.

'This class is only intended for the summer months,' she explained. 'I shall be returning to full-time teaching in September, but I suppose we can arrange something to suit us all meanwhile. And what about you, Vera?' She turned to the smaller, dark-haired girl, Miss Bembridge's niece. 'I know you've been ill, and your doctor says you mustn't exert yourself too much, but what sort of thing do you like to do?'

'I like sewing, Miss Evershed,' she whispered. 'And reading. I wasn't clever enough for Aunt Lilian's school even before I was ill. I think she's disappointed in me.'

My eyes met Judith's and she answered briskly but kindly. 'I'm sure that's not true, Vera. Your aunt has been very worried about you and she is only concerned with finding something interesting but not taxing for you to do. Reading and sewing are useful occupations and perhaps we can find one or two other subjects to interest you and Vera. Good gracious!' she exclaimed. 'We'll have to do something about your names. What about Vera B and Vera W? just to stop us all getting in a muddle?'

When I mentioned that Wilfred Seymour would be joining them their eyes opened wide but there was no giggling, which was a relief. They had already heard about him and besides, Vera W knew him from various social functions in the town while Vera B was a shy mouse who apparently had no opinions on anything. I hoped we could make her feel comfortable and I had an inkling of a way to help her.

'Wilfred has exams soon so he will be sharing Adelaide's studies,' Judith told the two girls. 'This will entail a lot of reading, and writing essays, so I'm sure we can manage to combine that as well as some reading, sewing and French conversation for you girls as well as some practical work. I suggest that you come here at nine-thirty on Friday morning until half-past twelve; bring your lunch with you and then you can all go together to the May Day celebrations at the Priory. That will give us all time to become acquainted and we can begin the class properly on Monday.'

At a nod from Judith, Addy went to find Penny, whisked her out of the lodgers' kitchen and took off her apron before bringing her into our drawing room to meet her classmates. She was very shy but I was pleased to see that the other girls were friendly and when Judith showed them some of Penny's embroidery Vera B was frankly envious.

'I wish I could do work like that,' she sighed and brightened up when Penny diffidently offered to help. It looked promising and while Addy wandered off to the dining room to work on a maths problem, I suggested that the other three might discuss which books they liked to read and whether they could think of anything else that they would like to try. I had already typed out a list of topics that we proposed to explore so Judith and I composed a letter which laid out our planned timetable for the proposed class, as well as details of the introductory meeting on Friday. Half an hour later our two newest recruits set off for home clutching their letters and Penny went back to her dusting. I heard her singing later so I assumed she was feeling happy about the proposed arrangements.

Mother must have been on her best behaviour because Miss Acton was still smiling when she came downstairs at half-past twelve.

'Your mother is such an inspiring woman,' she enthused as I opened the door. 'I feel privileged to know her.'

'We are so grateful to you,' I gushed quite as fulsomely in return. 'It's such a relief to know that Mother is in safe hands and that you appreciate her talents.'

And so it was, I reflected as I waved goodbye and turned to see all three of our lady lodgers who were dressed for an outing and just closing their own front door behind them.

'We are going to walk into town,' explained Mrs Camperdown with a smile. 'Such a beautiful day! It's not early closing day is it? Oh, that's tomorrow? Good. We'll have plenty of time to explore. I suggest we have lunch at the White Horse, do a spot of shopping, then go on to Groom Hall afterwards.'

Despite Mrs Trellis's advanced pregnancy, she seemed happy about the ten-or-fifteen-minute walk, as did Miss Preston. I knew that Mrs Camperdown was a gentle, motherly woman when liberated from her controlling Canon and that she had taken to our youngest guest; Miss Preston was restless, full of nervous energy, so I was pleased to see them all getting on well together.

For more than thirty minutes I struggled to come up with a plot for my next book. This was unusual, I normally have a fund of ideas but as I've said before it's getting more and more difficult to cope with writing ripping yarns set against the background of the never-ending terrible news from the war. When a sudden shaft of sunlight danced across my writing pad, I threw down my pencil and went to look for Addy. To my surprise she really was finishing off the essay she had promised Judith and as I looked into the dining room, she blotted her work and looked inquiringly at me.

'I'm going to post Henry's birthday card through the Makepeaces' letter box,' I said on an impulse. 'Do you want to walk into town with me? We'll have lunch out, my treat.'

She looked suspicious but the lure of lunch in town was too enticing and within ten minutes we were heading towards the bridge.

'We don't do this often enough,' I declared as we walked briskly along the Ram Alley, as the main road is known because that's where the sheep were driven to market in the past. 'Do something just for fun,' I explained as Addy looked puzzled. 'I know we're on an errand of sorts but usually we only go into town for shopping or business. To go out to lunch or tea for the sake of it is almost unheard of. We should do it more often.'

Granny had nodded when I told her where we were going. 'Very wise, Christy. All work and so on... No, I've no errands for you, unless you spot any bargains, of course.' We exchanged grins, neither of us can resist something being sold off cheaply.

As we walked over the bridge, I explained my dilemma about plots to Addy.

'It's easy,' she said. 'Write books for girls instead. You know about girls and if you do school stories we can all help with ideas.'

'I wonder...' I thought about it and when we reached the tea-shop by the market square I stopped and hugged my sister – much to her surprise. 'I think you've got something there, Addy. I wonder if I could?'

'Of course you can,' Addy said scornfully. 'You don't realise how good your stories are.'

I was surprised, as a family we tend not to go in for lavish praise, but Addy wasn't looking at me.

'You can still have cricket matches,' she said, pointing to a gang of young lads who had set up a wicket, quite unlawfully, on the Priory green. 'So all those details you used for the war books will come in handy and you'd better talk to Miss Preston about hockey and lacrosse while she's here.' She paused, frowned and peered at the cricketers. 'They'll get into trouble with the vicar, playing there. And anyway, what are they doing out of school at this time of day?'

'Half holiday, I expect.' I wasn't interested and pushed her into the tea-room. I could only see one free table and didn't want to share.

We had soup (tinned tomato) and sandwiches with a thin scrape of margarine and not enough cheese. I thought I'd better refrain from criticising out loud, 'Never upset tradespeople' is one of Granny's many maxims, so instead we discussed Addy's idea. It looked surprisingly possible but I wondered what my editors would think.

'Don't forget there are magazines for girls too,' Addy pointed out. 'I'm sure they'd jump at the chance.'

I was touched by her faith in me and I found an old envelope in my bag and jotted down some ideas.

'You have to start with a new girl,' Addy suggested. 'You can still keep to the present day and have the war in the background, which will make it more interesting, but it won't be so upsetting to write. What else?'

'She arrives three weeks after the beginning of term; and says she isn't allowed to play games?' We stared at each other and I added it to my notes.

'Everyone thinks she's dreadful, a spy perhaps, but she's really a heroine,' Addy said. 'Or an orphan, or a princess, or something and she saves the most hateful prefect in a fire.'

'There are an awful lot of stories with plots like that,' I demurred but Addy was adamant.

'Why do you suppose that is? Because it makes a good

107

story and people like that kind of thing. Besides, yours will be better!'

I was touched by her faith in me. Because our impromptu holiday was doing us both good I agreed when Addy said we ought to throw some money into the Font by the Priory and make a wish, so we strolled across the square towards the ancient spring.

On the way I slipped Henry's card into his cousins' letterbox without knocking. I didn't want to interrupt their lunch and we had to get home soon.

'Oh, lord, Christy,' hissed Addy as we emerged from the square and stood at the edge of the green, surveying the ancient grey Priory. 'Quick, pretend you haven't seen her and let's turn back.'

'What? Who? Oh!'

It was Miss Portia Diplock and to our astonishment she collapsed on all fours in the road, and stayed there, bellowing.

'What on earth has happened?' I reached her first and was horrified to see that blood was welling up from a wound on her ankle. I fished my luckily clean handkerchief out of my bag and handed it to her while Addy and I took an elbow each and helped her to the low stone wall that borders the green.

'You'll have a nasty bruise, Miss Diplock,' I said, taking the bloodstained handkerchief and pressing it against the injured leg. 'Sit quietly for a moment, you're shocked. Let Addy brush you down, you're covered in dust. Are you hurt anywhere else? Did you fall? How did this happen?'

Miss Diplock stopped howling and let me gently mop her up. Luckily I had another clean handkerchief (a miracle in itself) so she blew her nose loudly and I was about to send Addy to find help when, of all people, our favourite lodger Mrs Camperdown hastened towards us from the direction of the Priory.

'I saw her fall,' she exclaimed, as she reached us. 'Can I help? She simply dropped to the ground, is it her heart?'

At the same time, Miss Preston loped across the green.

'I've been doing a little shopping in the Home and Colonial Stores and had just started across the road when I saw the lady tumble down. Did she faint?'

The third member of their party, Mrs Trellis, hurried across from the direction of The White Horse to see what was happening. 'Has she had a fit?' she asked, wide-eyed.

'A fit? Miss Diplock was recovering rapidly and she scowled at our youngest lodger. 'I didn't faint, either,' she glowered at Miss Preston. 'I was struck down. Somebody shot at me!'

Chapter Seven

Everyone gasped and I bent to examine Miss Diplock's injury.

'I'm quite sure it wasn't a shot,' I said gently probing the spot. 'There's a bruise forming already on the shin, just above the ankle, but the skin is only broken in one place and the bleeding has already stopped. It's not a bullet wound.'

'It was probably this,' Addy had been ferreting around and was holding up a cricket ball. 'This was not far away and those boys have all run off. I should think one of them hit a six and caught you by mistake so they've escaped before we could catch them. I bet it hurt!'

The injured victim shuddered when Addy held the ball out for her inspection and I hastily intervened.

'Do you think you can walk, Miss Diplock? Addy and I can help you home so you can rest.'

She mumbled crossly but allowed me to help her stand. I glanced at our lady lodgers. 'Don't worry,' I said. 'Miss Diplock lives down at the end of Paradise Row; it's not far and Addy and I can manage.'

Lydia Trellis looked curiously at the injured woman but turned back towards the White Horse. 'I'm hungry,' she announced as she headed to the hotel.

'I was always hungry at that stage,' smiled Mrs Camperdown. 'We took rather a long time looking at the shops, especially in Bracewell's hat department. If you're sure we can't help?' She nodded when I assured her that we could manage.

Miss Diplock lived in a pretty Georgian house at the junction of Paradise Row, one of the rabbit warren of very old streets surrounding the Priory, and the former cattle market. This had flourished in the Middle Ages until the area rose in gentility, when the market was moved to the outskirts of town. I knew from Henry's cousin Bertha that the Diplock family home had been substantial and surrounded by many acres but that successive owners had made bad investments so that when Miss Diplock's father had gambled on the Stock Exchange and lost almost everything, the estate had to be sold a couple of years ago to pay off his debts.

Luckily for Miss Diplock her present home and small but regular income had come directly to her from her mother's family so she was not left without support when her brother died last year.

'Goodness!' Addy exclaimed as an elderly maid opened the door to us. 'You can hardly move for all the furniture.'

I pinched her arm and she subsided in a sulk, but I sympathised. The small drawing room and the hall were so full of large mahogany sideboards, tables, chairs, bookcases and whatnots that navigating a passage towards an equally large chaise-longue was quite a hazard.

I explained to the maid about the accident and she produced a decanter of sherry and a glass, pouring it for her mistress, though not, I noticed, offering anything to me. After a second glass 'for your nerves, ma'am' Miss Diplock seemed calmer and the servant disappeared, muttering about lunch being spoiled.

I was just about to say that we would leave her in peace when Addy, who had been impertinently poking around by the fireplace, suddenly dislodged something and exclaimed, 'Whatever is this, Miss Diplock?'

'This' was a strange grey furry mat in front of the fire. It seemed to have something like a head, of all peculiar things, rather like a small grubby tiger skin rug without the stripes.

'What's that?' Miss Diplock sat up, looking invigorated, and to our surprise she burst out laughing.

'That, Adelaide,' she said impressively, 'is one of the Brothers Grimm!'

We stared and she laughed again, suddenly human and quite unlike the bugbear we had made of her.

'My father fought in the Crimean War, you know,' she began. 'A few years later he and my mother were on their honeymoon in Paris when he was accosted by a familiar figure, his sergeant during the war. It turned out that he had deserted and later married a Frenchwoman but had fallen on hard times after she left him and he was now reduced to selling his greatest treasures. Would my father take pity on him?'

'What were his treasures?' Addy was agog with interest.

'Two fireside rugs,' said Miss Diplock, impressively. She laughed again. 'The sergeant's story was that he had picked up two very large dogs, Alsatians they were, after the battle of Sevastapol and had made guard dogs of them. A year or so after he settled in France both dogs died – he didn't tell Father how – and he had them stuffed because, he said, he couldn't bear to be without them.'

'I'm not surprised his wife left him,' I murmured but Addy was fascinated.

'There's only one by the fire,' she pointed out. 'What happened to the other one?'

'Father was quite sure he was being cheated,' Miss Diplock chuckled. 'But he was amused by the rugs and bought them, much to my mother's disgust. When my brother and I were small we christened them the Brothers Grimm, but unfortunately the other one was devoured by moths.'

'I think it's lovely,' sighed Addy. She can be quite ghoulish sometimes. 'Look, Christy, the body is flat, like a rug, but his head is stuffed to be lifelike. Just look at his glass eyes and teeth!' She gazed in admiration at the horrid thing. 'I expect it's your dearest treasure now, isn't it, Miss Diplock?'

To my surprise, Miss Diplock's expression softened, then she smiled. 'Of course it is, Adelaide.'

As we left Miss Diplock in the capable hands of her maid, Addy heaved a sigh.

'What's the matter?'

'I didn't want her to be nice,' she grumbled. 'It was much easier when we didn't like her because of all her meddling and bullying. Now I can't hate her, because she laughed and because I just love the Brother Grimm.'

I didn't bother to say something improving about not hating people; I knew exactly what she meant, so we walked back towards the square in companionable silence.

'There's no sign of those boys who were playing cricket,' I said thoughtfully. 'I expect they ran off the moment they realised Miss Diplock had been hurt…' I stopped short but luckily Addy didn't pick up on my hesitation, then I mentally shook myself.

For heaven's sake, I scolded inwardly. Just because there really had been a murder at Groom Hall, even if only Alix and Granny and I know about it, I mustn't start seeing death and disaster behind every bush. Besides, if not an ill-aimed cricket ball, what was I thinking? That one of our respectable lady lodgers had taken a dislike to Portia Diplock and thrown a stone at her? Because there had been nobody else in sight, or rather within throwing distance. Surely a misplaced cricket stroke was the only logical answer?

'Oh, there's Wilfred,' Addy exclaimed and so there was.

'Good afternoon, Christy, Addy,' said Wilfred with an ingratiating smile. 'Do you want to go for a walk, Addy? Is it all right if she comes with me, Christy? I'll see her home in plenty of time for tea.'

My sister looked torn between indignation at the thought that she should need his protection, and a slight anxiety in case I might refuse permission. I nodded and they set off towards the Priory. Knowing Addy, I thought she was still bent on making a wish in the Font; she hates to give up on a plan. Also knowing her, I was pretty sure Wilfred would be expected to provide a coin to throw. Addy is usually penniless.

I set off round the shops to look for bargains for Granny and was rewarded when the grocer, another ardent admirer of my grandmother, beckoned me furtively to the back of the shop and tucked a bag of sugar and one of flour into my shopping basket. He reluctantly took the money I offered, knowing that Granny would insist on it – 'something still edible but in spoiled packaging is acceptable' is what she would say, rather than take money from the shopkeeper by accepting something he could sell at the full price. He shrugged but as I left the shop he hastened after me.

'I know her ladyship has scruples,' he said shyly, 'and I admire her for it. However, I do hope she will be kind enough to accept a bluebag for the washing, with my compliments? We have several in stock so one won't be missed.'

'How very kind,' I reassured him. 'That's just what we need; my grandmother mentioned only on Monday when the washing was on the line, that it's almost impossible to find bluebags. They do make the sheets white.'

It is extremely convenient to have a grandmother who is so popular with the local tradesmen and you only have to look at her to see where Alix gets her good looks from. Speaking of whom…I glanced across the Square and saw my sister walking towards The Copper Kettle, the nicest of the teashops in town, and where Addy and I had lunched earlier – and she was not alone. Beside her was the tall, uniformed figure of Acting Captain Dr Fergus Munro and as I watched, the doctor held the door open and in they went.

Well, well! I was torn, what with being glad that Alix seemed to be so happy, and with a melancholy sense of change looming. We're content enough as we are, aren't we? I felt guilty for being selfish because I was pleased for Alix and praying things would go well for her, so I sighed and walked briskly away lest they should notice me and feel they ought to invite me to join them.

'Slow down, Christy,' said a familiar voice and Henry held out a hand to stop me cannoning into him. 'Where are you off to in such a hurry?'

Suddenly my mood lifted, and when Henry suggested we should stop for a cup of tea, I hastily turned him away from the Copper Kettle in favour of the Violet Tearoom; not quite so elegant but still much better than the market café which was rumoured to reuse the tealeaves which were, in any case, said to be the sweepings from the tea warehouse floor.

'I got your card,' Henry explained. 'Thank you. I loved Addy's drawing though I'm not sure why she though a wolf was suitable? Is it meant to be me?'

'For pity's sake don't say that to her,' I urged. 'It's not a wolf, it's meant to be Bobs!' (Bobs is our dog, a mixed breed of uncertain parentage. His mother was certainly one of those really big poodles but his father is unknown but believed to be at least part retriever. Or, as our brother had remarked when he brought home a curly-haired brown puppy, the dog's father might well have been a Shetland pony, to judge by the size of his feet.)

'I had to drop off some letters at the post office,' Henry explained. 'But Cousin Edgar laughed at your card and said if I bumped into you he had no objection to me taking you out to afternoon tea.'

Although I had little time to spare, Henry insisted I must at least have a cup of tea and a cake with him, and I was interested to note that the teashop was serving rock cakes. How is it that every teashop in town manages to make the cakes taste as though they are made from actual rocks? Perhaps I have a lighter hand with cakes and pastry than I thought, because my efforts are never so solid.

It was lovely to have half an hour just to be with Henry, he really is my best friend and I'm so glad we have adopted him into our family. Thinking this, I felt myself go bright red when I remembered what he had said at his party – 'I don't want to be your brother, Christy' – and I was covered with confusion. It was probably time, I thought, that I should head for home so I blew my nose to hide my blushes and stood up.

'Tomorrow afternoon,' I told him, after thanking him for the treat, 'we're going up to Groom Hall for tea. It won't seem the same without you there.'

'I don't know,' he smiled and took my hand as we stood on the pavement. 'I heard yesterday that a chap from my unit has been sent to the Hall. He won't walk again poor devil – shrapnel wound – and I'd like to see him. I might get leave to drop in tomorrow, if Cousin Edgar is in a good mood.'

'Your Cousin Edgar is always in a good mood, from what I've seen,' I laughed as we said goodbye.

As I walked past the baker's shop his wife was standing in

the doorway, enjoying the sunshine.

'Oh, Miss Christy,' she greeted me with a delighted smile and I wondered what I had done to deserve it. 'I'm so glad to see you. My husband's put a little parcel under the counter for her ladyship and I was going to send the boy to deliver it, but if you wouldn't mind…'

'How very kind,' I said, wondering…

'It's just a few sponge cakes that have gone a bit stale,' she said diffidently. 'I know her ladyship is a great one for sensible cooking, and now you've got all those ladies to feed as well, we wondered if she could use them? If you don't think she'd be offended?'

'Of course she won't, she'll be delighted,' I said, meaning it. 'We could have trifle, couldn't we? Our guests will be truly impressed.'

It wasn't till I reached home that I remembered I hadn't told Henry about our encounter with Miss Diplock. I thought his cousin would like to know, as they were old friends.

The recollection made me wonder again how on earth she had been injured. The boys playing cricket was clearly the most logical explanation but still that ridiculous notion persisted – had someone deliberately targeted the overbearing lady? And if so, who. Why, unfortunately, was not hard to understand; Miss Diplock had alienated so many of her fellow townsfolk with her meddling and bullying, though throwing stones (or cricket balls?) at her seemed rather drastic. I think I've spent too long writing penny dreadfuls for young men so that my imagination runs riot at the slightest provocation.

It also occurred to me that to score such a hit deliberately one would need to be a very good shot and although Miss Preston was athletic, I could hardly see Mrs Camperdown or Lydia Trellis in the role.

Dislike her or not, nobody would seriously contemplate injuring a respectable (however unpopular) elderly woman just because she was annoying.

Would they?

Chapter Eight

Thursday, 2nd May 1918

At half-past twelve I waved goodbye to Miss Acton who, to my endless astonishment, remained happy and enthusiastic while doing Mother's typewriting. Even if she resigns next week I'll always be grateful for the respite I've enjoyed. Of course I pop my head into Mother's room every day but I take care not to linger in case she remembers an urgent task that only I can fulfil.

I felt unsettled uncertain about the way my life was going at the moment. I mean, how on earth had we taken on a school, of all things. As though we hadn't enough to do, now I'd have to plan some suitable activities to justify the generous amount of money the local ladies were prepared to pay. We're overburdened and yet it all seems irrelevant compared to the never ending carnage just across the Channel not more than a couple of hundred miles, as the crow flies, from where we live.

I'm also finding it difficult to reconcile our very domestic lives with what other girls of my age are doing. Is Mother right after all? Should I train to be a nurse, a VAD? Or perhaps go and work at a munitions factory? Or even a telephone operator in France, which sounded adventurous.

I took a cup of cocoa and some bread and butter into the garden and sat on the bench, enjoying the sunshine as I ate my lunch. There was no point fretting about doing something different for the war effort. I knew that perfectly well. Somebody had to run the guest house and it had been my own idea in the first place. Besides, I can't leave Granny to bear the whole burden of managing the two houses as well as the family.

I abandoned the fleeting gloom and surveyed the hens instead. There had been some unusual developments recently and the elderly hens seemed to have made friends with three of the new point-of-lay birds. They were all huddled in a corner just outside the chicken run and staring at the run's sole occupant, the small black Bantam, .

'They're all scared of her,' Alix, also carrying her lunch, sat down beside me and looked approvingly at the fierce little hen. 'Well done, Bad Fairy, you're not going to let them bully you, are you?'

'They won't get a chance, she's far too aggressive, and I told you not to name them,' I grumbled. 'Anyway, what are you doing home at this time?' While her old lady is away Alix has been spending the mornings up at the hospital where Sister Wisden usually finds her some lunch. I carefully haven't mentioned that or asked how she's getting on with Dr Munro; she'll tell me in her own good time and besides, we've all been pretty busy.

'I've come home to change,' she said. 'I'm not going to an official tea party in my usual working blouse and skirt. I'm planning to wear the pink silk I wore to the wedding last month and pray the weather stays fine so I don't need a coat. You're going to wear your blue frock, aren't you?' She peered anxiously at me and I reassured her.

'Of course I am. How often do we have an opportunity to dress up? Or something so elegant to wear.' I had a sudden qualm. 'We'll have to make sure Addy's decently dressed. You know what she's like.'

Alix giggled. 'As long as she doesn't take it into her head to wear a disguise. Remember when she and Wilfred went carol singing in town? Granny was appalled to see them standing outside The White Horse with a begging bowl in front of them. I think the makeshift habits they'd made from blankets made it worse, even though they protested the disguise was intended to make them unrecognisable. Addy was most aggrieved at Granny's reaction, remember? She claimed they'd worn it to be considerate of the family's feelings.'

'Why they thought a pair of short, skinny monks would be begging in Ramalley I can't imagine,' I smiled at the memory. 'Everyone laughed at them but still put money in the hat. I think Granny found the laughter worse than their actual cheek! Mind you, they weren't very old then so I'm crossing my fingers that Wilfred, at least, is grown-up enough to think twice now.'

A squabble broke out in the hen run as the bantam defended it from the meek hen who had put her head round the open door.

'Why do you let her get away with it, you silly birds?' Alix shook her finger at them. 'You outnumber her and every single one of you is twice as big as she is.'

'Most of the others seem to have made friends, thank heavens,' I said, nodding towards three of our four original ageing prima donnas, who were accompanied by the three more docile new birds and all now poking their beaks into well-loved nooks and crannies. Kaiser Bill, of course, still brooded possessively on her nest, pretending to peck at all comers. 'Alix, I really wish you hadn't named them.'

'Poor old Christy,' Alix grinned guiltily at me. 'Flora and Nora and Mrs Archibald, you mean. I'm sorry; you can't even blame Addy this time.'

I had despairingly issued instructions about naming the new hens, knowing what the result would be, and I'd been ignored, just as I'd expected. It hadn't even been Addy who had slipped up, but Alix who had carelessly remarked, 'The little black one looks like the bad fairy at Sleeping Beauty's christening, doesn't she? Beady-eyed and sinister, the way she's watching them.'

And that was it, Bad Fairy had a name and Granny had laughed, which was no help at all, so that meant the other three newcomers had to have names too.

I'd protested, of course, arguing without hope of success that a hen with a name was never going to end up on our dinner table and while they had laughed again, they and I knew it was true. Roast chicken was off the menu unless

Bobs the dog brought home another contraband bird.

Granny had joined in, contributing Flora and Nora as names for the two brown hens, saying they reminded her of two maiden ladies who had lived in the village near her childhood home, a bleak and comfortless castle in Aberdeenshire. Mrs Archibald had been Judith Evershed's offering. 'There was a mistress just like her when I was at school,' she had explained. 'Mrs Archibald, a plump, white-haired widow, who pretended to be nice but really looked down her nose as though we were worms. Just like the hen. In fact, if you fluffed her feathers up on her head and tied a fussy bow of ribbon under the hen's beak, the likeness would be uncanny.'

First thing in the morning I had moistened some of the baker's offering of stale cake with a mixture of warmed honey and water as a kind of syrup. While this cooled down I'd made custard because the new hens were at least paying for their keep already and laying eggs, while milk arrives courtesy of our friends at the farm. A big bowl for our own pudding now sat in our larder, alongside some elegant small glass dishes of the mixture, intended to impress our guests.

We were still mostly offering only two courses for dinner and had not received any complaints so far; tonight, for anyone who still felt hungry (Miss Preston, always!) I'd made biscuits from the rest of the stale cakes crumbled with margarine and using honey instead of sugar. I'd made a big batch but could spare one or two each as an after dinner treat.

'That looks quite tempting,' Addy sounded surprised. 'What are we having for the first course?'

'Resurrection pie, and you needn't start groaning,' I snapped. 'It's a superior version! Very nutritious. Leftover sausages, some bacon, whatever vegetables needed using up, and fried onions, the not quite gone-off ones that Granny found hiding in the rack. It's a much tastier mix than the usual ancient remains and I've done individual pies for each of the lodgers with a bigger one for all of us.'

Something rather nice happened when the ladies next door were getting ready to stroll up to the Hall – they've abandoned Miss Preston's idea of hiring the station trap, unless the weather turns unpleasant. I was surprised but pleased when Mrs Camperdown knocked on the door connecting the two houses and buttonholed Judith.

'Won't you walk up with us this afternoon, Miss Evershed?' Judith was startled and opened her mouth to say something.

'Please don't refuse, my dear,' Mrs Camperdown said kindly. 'I know you are recovering from an illness but I do assure you that we walk very slowly, taking in the flowers and trees and admiring the view! I'm persuaded that it would do you a world of good and give us a pleasant new companion. Besides,' she added cunningly. 'I'm eager to introduce new horizons to my son. You know that he is beginning to take an interest in the world and you are so knowledgeable and so well-travelled that I'm sure your stories would give him great pleasure.'

Who could refuse such a request? Not Judith, certainly. She is as kind as she is clever and I could see from the light in her eyes that the idea appealed to her. She hurried upstairs to change her blouse and put on her hat while Mrs Camperdown and I smiled at each other in a conspiratorial kind of way. It was just the diversion that Judith needed; I wasn't sure how the tutorial classes would go. She might enjoy them, she had once told me that she thirsted to teach, but I was worried that she might rather be driven to despair by the two Veras and their complete lack of interest in schoolwork.

'Let me look at you, Addy,' demanded Alix as the three of us met at the back door. We two elders had checked our reflections in the looking glass in the hall but usually one or both of us has to make sure our sister is tidy. 'Goodness, you look very nice!'

Addy scowled at our surprised faces and headed down the garden to the back gate. She did look attractive though, in pale green linen with her hair in a tidy plait under a smart straw hat, and Alix and I raised our eyebrows as we hurried after her.

'She's growing up,' I whispered hopefully.

'Ye-es,' Alix looked sceptical then stifled a giggle as Addy, looking far from ladylike, stomped ahead of us. 'Perhaps not quite yet?'

I was looking forward to seeing the menfolk belonging to our lodgers. Mrs Camperdown's son was going to take a lot of coddling and home comforts from the sound of it and I wondered how his difficult father would take that.

Reading my mind, something we both very often do, Alix said, 'Peter Camperdown is improving, but whenever his father visits he looks a different boy. With his mother and with encouragement from the staff, he's making real progress and can eat light meals with enjoyment, as well as walking quite well.'

'I wondered about the Canon,' I nodded. 'Does he scold the boy?'

'All the time,' she sighed. 'Sister Wisden and Fergus – I mean Dr Munro – have told us all to keep an eye on what's going on. Scolding is not helpful for his recovery.'

'Never mind,' I consoled her. 'Judith will protect him; she's not frightened of any blustering man. Remember her dreadful brother-in-law? What about the other menfolk? You said the other day that Captain Trellis is a lot older than his wife?'

'Yes, but he seems a pleasant man, very quiet and shy and utterly besotted with her.'

'What about her though? She's so very young.' I was concerned because Lydia Trellis struck me as being not much older than Addy.

'Oh, she seems fond of him,' Alix said. 'They seem happy enough and he's delighted about the baby.'

'What about Major Preston?' I ran my eye down a mental list of our lodgers. 'Is he like his sister? She seems satisfied with his condition, from what she's said.'

'He's exactly like her,' giggled Alix. 'Didn't I tell you? Oh, well, I suppose it's only Thursday, so it hasn't been very long though it seems like ages. The only difference is that Major Preston is as stout as his sister is thin, though they

122

both eat like horses. He is a few years younger and she dotes on him. I suppose they are alike in other ways, they're both very athletic. He's always happy to talk about his sporting triumphs, how he got his Blue at Cambridge for rugby and would have got one for fencing too if he hadn't joined up. He's very jolly and likes a good joke, but he's kind and not insensitive, so we've put his bed next to Peter's. He helps take the edge off Canon Camperdown's nasty temper.'

Addy had slowed down now and was trying not let us know that she was listening. I'd been watching her as we trudged up the hill towards the plank bridge over the muddy ditch that was grandly called the ha-ha. She had grown up in the last few months, though probably it took the eye of faith, or perhaps love, to discern it. Losing our brother had changed our lives and we all had moments of dreadful sadness when we thought of him. Only this morning, shortly after breakfast, I had discovered Addy down in the cellar where she was supposed to be arranging books and stationery for Judith, sobbing fit to break her heart.

'Oh, sweetheart,' I'd said, hugging her tight. We didn't speak, because I knew, of course I knew. If she'd had a tiff with Wilfred or an ache anywhere we'd have heard all about it but if she was quiet it was serious. I could only hold her and mingle my own tears with hers because there was nothing to say. Bertie was gone and with him the promise of his whole future, and that was unbearable because he would have enjoyed it so much and enriched our own lives, always. After a while I mopped us both up and shared one of the cake crumb biscuits with her, though I didn't let her see where I'd hidden the tin because that would be plain foolish.

Watching her now as she walked purposefully up the hill, I remembered the way she had thrown herself into helping with the guest house idea when we had embarked on it a couple of months ago. There had been sulks and grumbles occasionally, of course, but mostly Addy had been helpful and sensible too, sometimes. I'd been right though, for a girl whose nose is almost constantly in a book and who shows considerable academic promise, well beyond her years, my little sister really was growing up. It was just that she didn't realise it yet.

The garden at Groom Hall was looking lovely even though where there had been several men before the war, there was now just one elderly gardener who had the doubtful blessing of Niggle's assistance three days a week. The tulips were doing well and the may blossom looked as spring-like as ever, so cheered by the beauty surrounding us, I straightened my shoulders and followed the other two. Alix was also looking lovely, and no wonder, because we were met at the door by Dr Munro himself.

He smiled and greeted us but before we could say anything more Addy launched into what was evidently (to us) a prepared interrogation.

'Dr Munro,' she said, frowning at him. 'I wanted to ask you something.'

'Go ahead,' he said solemnly but I could see that he found her extremely amusing.

'Do you have any Viking blood?' She was perfectly serious and even Alix and I were bewildered at this. 'I mean, how is it that you're so fair? With such pale hair, I mean?'

'Adelaide!' I remonstrated. 'That's none of your business, don't ask impertinent questions.'

'It's all right,' Fergus Munro had a mischievous gleam in his eye, not that Addy noticed, of course. 'It's no secret that a thousand years ago a handsome blond Viking was washed up on the shore, the only survivor when his long ship hit the rocks near my ancestors' family home in Scotland. Naturally, he married the laird's only child, a daughter. Heroes often did that, of course. Legend has it that his wife was descended from a Selkie, a seal woman, which is why I'm fair like the Viking and charming like the enchanting wife,' he claimed modestly.

'You're just being silly,' sniffed Addy, stalking past him and into the large hall that was used as a sitting room for the patients.

Fergus smiled at Alix and me as we rather shyly followed her indoors. 'Don't give me away to Addy, but there's a grain of truth in the Viking story! I take after my father's mother who was Swedish and very fair, as is my Dad and my elder brother, but not my sisters to their eternal annoyance.'

Groom Hall is appropriately known to us as Gloom Hall because it is built in a forbidding grey granite with a purplish slate roof and there is also a profusion of black marble indoors in mantelpieces, statuary and the awkward proportions that generally encourage you to feel downhearted. Today, however, the main hall was looking almost handsome with vases of bluebells, daffodils and other spring flowers on every surface. The room was alive and bustling with patients looking cheerful, nursing staff and volunteers busily meeting and greeting, and family and friends visibly encouraged by these signs of improved health and spirits in their loved ones.

I summoned up the appropriate smile for a landlady meeting her guests at a social event and approached Miss Preston whose companion was so like her that he must have been her brother.

'Miss Christabel!' Our lodger was radiant as well she might be with a plate full of sandwiches and cake at her side. 'Do let me introduce my brother, Major Montagu Preston. Monty, this is Miss Christabel Fyttleton, of whom I have so often spoken.'

I was happy to have my hand clasped warmly and shaken heartily by the rotund gentleman who was also, I observed, guarding a laden plate, though his enthusiasm took me aback.

'I say!' exclaimed the gallant officer. 'This is a jolly surprise! I am so happy to meet you. How do you do, Miss Christabel? Myrtle has not stopped singing your praises; she says you never fail to produce excellent meals. It's wonderful that so young a lady should be such an accomplished housekeeper. How do you manage, in these days of rationing?'

'Sheer ingenuity, Major,' I smiled. Was he taking notice, as they say? My domestic gifts had certainly won his admiration and I thought he was looking at me in a particular way, perhaps assessing my personal attributes? Without undue haste I gently disengaged my hand from his and moved on, making sure I went to the other side of the next bed where Mrs Camperdown, looking anxious, was gazing adoringly at a pale, slightly-built young man who, clad in a dressing gown was lying on the bedcover and leaning back against his pillows. He was painfully young, barely out of school, and listening to his mother, who was fussing over him while radiating pride and devotion.

'Christabel,' she spotted me and beckoned. 'Peter, this is Miss Christabel, you already know her elder sister who volunteers here.'

The boy blushed a fiery red and glanced across the room to where Alix was laughing with the doctor. Poor lad, I could see devotion, even adoration, in his face but of course he had no chance with my sister. I caught his mother's eye and we both smiled and sighed.

We chatted easily together and the boy's bashful air dissipated, until I felt a sudden chill. Mrs Camperdown stopped in mid-sentence and Peter hastily closed his eyes, as though trying to escape. Canon Camperdown approached the bedside and stood there, looking for all the world like a clergyman in one of those rustic cottagey landscapes – you know, church, thatched cottage, humble tenant and rosy-cheeked, benevolent vicar. There are usually a few exceptionally clean hens and sheep too, not that the Canon would tolerate such untidiness; I imagine sheep would be banished to the fold and hens to the coop. Nor did the likeness extend to his small, cold eyes as he recognised me.

'Ah, Miss – er – harrumph,' he grunted. 'It would have been a gracious act had you allowed me to stay at your boarding house instead of having to force myself on the hospitality of the local vicar.'

I opened my eyes wide at this but I'm hardened to rudeness now so I smiled politely. 'Perhaps you and the vicar should regard your time together as a trial sent from heaven, instead of purgatory? Besides, a gentleman such as yourself, used to the stimulating company of great men would have found an otherwise all-female household most restricting,

I'm sure, Canon. We women, you know, seldom discuss matters other than the price of – of muslin – and other domestic inanities and it is a house rule that everyone must retire to bed by nine o'clock. Before that, most of our guests enjoy knitting and – er – embroidery and other feminine pursuits.' (Muslins? Where on earth had that come from? Ah, Jane Austen, of course.)

Peter Camperdown had looked horrified at my opening remark and as I continued, his eyes opened wider still. He slid a startled glance at his mother who, despite the stiffness brought about by her husband's presence was, I could see, trying not to laugh. She bent her head.

'Indeed, my dear,' she told him meekly. 'Miss Christabel has the right of it. We women are sadly without the resources you have yourself in abundance.'

To my surprise the Canon, who had clearly dismissed my opening gambit, now preened himself and as he was settling down to lap up more about his superior intellect I nodded sweetly, then I twinkled at Peter – who was afflicted with a sudden cough – then I moved on.

As I turned aside I found Judith Evershed looking hesitant. I had looked for her earlier and found her chatting to Sister Wisden. Now, I seized her hand.

'You're just the person we need, Judith. Here…' I nodded to Peter Camperdown. 'Miss Evershed will be able to tell you all about her visit to France before the war. If you recall we had just begun to discuss our hopes for foreign travel in the future.'

I gave Judith a nudge and Mrs Camperdown picked up the baton, enthusing about 'dear Miss Evershed' and her interesting tales. I composed my face to look solemn as the canon grunted and walked away to harangue some other unfortunate patient, leaving his wife and son to discuss the frivolous side of visiting France.

'You're quite as bad as Addy,' a familiar voice murmured in my ear. 'Except that she can't help it and you do it deliberately!'

'Henry!' My heart leaped and as we shook hands I saw a

gleam in his eyes that showed me he was just as pleased to see me.

'Come and meet my friend, Minton,' he said, leading me to an officer in a wheelchair by the fireplace. Frank Minton was, I learned, about ten years older than Henry and they had been together for much of their time in the trenches.

'Frank even followed me to the field hospital,' Henry laughed and his friend nodded solemnly.

'I did,' he agreed. 'Couldn't let this fellow get ahead of me, we'd shared some stirring times. Remember when the CO shot a rabbit, Henry? Wasn't he in a bate!'

'Why?' They were both amused when I looked puzzled. 'I'd have thought he'd be pleased. My brother wrote that the men were always glad of something extra to add to the pot.'

'He was pleased,' Henry explained. 'Even more so when he bagged a second one. Trouble was a mangy vixen appeared from nowhere and stole both of them before he could get to them. It was quite something to see her carry both rabbits in her mouth as she ran off.'

It was good to see Henry so happy and animated, usually he's quiet and rather serious. That's partly because he is quiet and thoughtful by nature but also, from what he's told us of his father, he was always wary of a scolding. His confidence has increased since he met us and has been welcomed by his elderly cousins. His friend was watching him too and he nodded briefly as our eyes met.

'It's good to see the boy looking so much better,' Frank told me. 'He was a sorry sight when they carted him off to Blighty leaving me to my pick of all the pretty nurses.'

'There's no justice,' Henry teased. 'And you got your majority. Promotion and pretty girls while lounging around in bed like a lord, I ask you!' I saw his expression as he glanced at the wheelchair and I remembered what he'd told me. Frank Minton had been paralysed when a piece of shrapnel severed his spinal cord and would never walk again.

I looked for our third lodger and saw Lydia Trellis staring out of the window. I could see no sign of a likely husband, so I turned to Major Minton.

'Can you point out Captain Trellis,' I asked. 'His wife is staying at our guesthouse and I've not met him.'

An odd expression flickered across his face but he made no comment, apart from indicating the far corner of the room. 'That's him, sitting beside the end bed,' he said.

'But…' I tried not to stare, then glanced back at Henry's friend who made a wry face.

'I know,' he nodded. 'Bit of a surprise, aren't they? Talk about May and December. He's a decent enough sort of fellow, you know. Bit of a stick in the mud but he did his bit. Wangled himself into the Pay Corps – I gather he's an accountant or something – but managed to get his foot run over by a tank, or so the story goes.'

'That's not exactly true,' Henry remonstrated. 'The poor fellow collapsed with a perforated appendix, right in the path of an oncoming tank. He was lucky not to be killed but escaped with a broken bone or two. The appendix was more severe and has left him much weakened, hence his Blighty.'

'I didn't realise he was so much older than Mrs Trellis,' I murmured, peering discreetly at the captain, then I spotted Alix carrying a tray of used crockery out to the kitchen so I nodded to Henry and his friend and caught up with my sister.

'You didn't you tell me Captain Trellis was so old?'

'I did, just now on the way up through the park,' she said indignantly. 'I definitely told you he was a lot older than she is, though I haven't really seen much of him. He spends most of his time in the conservatory, reading horridly serious-looking books and making lots of notes. Sister Wisden told me not to bother him. He's quite shy and likes his own company, she says.'

'What happens when Lydia – his wife – visits? Does he talk to her? Or stay tucked out of sight?' Alix had said something about Lydia's husband being older but not so much older. 'He looks at least fifty,' I complained.

'Not that much,' Alix stared across the room. 'He's only just forty, I believe. It's the spectacles and general weediness that makes him look more. And of course he talks to her, he's besotted with her and can't take his eyes off her. Look at him now.'

She was right, he was watching Lydia as she moved over to sit beside him and even from the other side of the room I could see his face light up. I remembered my conversation with Granny when we had speculated about Lydia's age. She was so very young, had she married him for security? I felt ashamed at the momentary distaste I felt. I knew nothing about her but she had told me she had no family so perhaps being an older man's darling had seemed a sensible way to go. Who was I to judge, constantly worried about finances but secure in the love of my family and with an income that, although erratic, had never yet failed us? A young girl alone might well feel that a balding, middle-aged accountant who adored her was a far better prospect than a life of struggle.

I gave up, it was none of my business anyway so I caught up with Addy and marched her round the room, introducing ourselves and making polite conversation. They were all pleasant men who seemed to appreciate the attention but that was probably because they didn't realise that Addy's avid interest in their wounds and the treatment thereof was a preamble to asking if she could examine them. After she had minutely cross-questioned one poor man about his operation, I pulled her to one side.

'You simply mustn't badger the patients,' I scolded. 'Haven't they suffered enough? Look, Alix is sitting with Henry and his friend. I expect Dr Munro is somewhere about too. Let's go and have tea with them now we've done our duty. Why don't you go and find Judith? She'll be glad of a rest.'

She sulked but collected Judith who did look a bit weary but smiled as Henry pulled out a chair for her. To my surprise it turned out that Major Minton thought he remembered meeting Judith when he was up at Oxford.

'Heavens,' she said, startled. 'I'm surprised! I was insufferably pleased with myself in those days, and full of ill-considered opinions. I'm afraid I was far too arrogant to pay attention to male undergraduates. What a dreadful girl I must have been!'

'Not at all, we were a rackety lot,' he smiled at her and then turned to greet Addy, as I motioned to her to sit beside him. I'd first glanced at Henry, who raised an eyebrow and nodded, which clearly meant that his friend would cheerfully cope with anything Addy came out with, and so he did. On my way to fetch a cup of tea I bumped into Dr Munro who said the tray he was carrying had tea for Alix and me too, as well as some fairy cakes.

I thanked him nicely, nodded approvingly at Alix for having such a helpful admirer and chuckled when she blushed, obviously having understood my meaning. Sitting quietly in that ugly room, surrounded by friends and family and trying hard to ignore my constant worrying, I felt very much at home. Dr Munro moved his chair between and mine and Alix's and sat down and to my surprise handed me the promised cup of tea and two fairy cakes on a plate.

'Doctor's orders,' he said kindly. 'You can afford to take ten minutes off duty, Christabel – and you must.' He spoke seriously. 'Alix tells me you're the mainspring of the family and that she worries that you will overstretch yourself. I think you are a sensible girl and will listen to your doctor!'

I was very touched and I ducked my head to hide the sudden tears that welled up but from that moment I lost my usual shyness with newcomers and Fergus Munro was admitted into my circle of trust.

Later, as I sipped my tea I heard the tail end of an earnest conversation and saw that Judith was listening with a concealed smile.

'You'd be surprised at the wear and tear on saws and chisels and other cutting tools,' said Frank Minton to an open-mouthed Addy. 'Oh yes, cutting into bone day after day, week after week, is hard work, you need good strong muscles. Is that the kind of medicine you'd like to go in for?'

So she had already confided her ardent hopes to him? I was pleased, Addy takes time to get to know strangers and if she trusted Major Minton practically on sight it meant he was very sound. She's a good judge of character, look how quickly she took to Henry.

'Buckets, too,' he said, all innocence but I saw a smile flicker across his face when she was reaching for another sandwich. 'What? It's battlefield surgery, use your imagination, Miss Adelaide.'

She blushed and I was even more impressed. It's rare for her to accept any kind of reproof without a long and ferocious argument.

However, she had no chance to say anything because a familiar, and most unwelcome voice rang out,

'Good heavens, it's Mr Camperdown, isn't it? I hardly recognised you without that beard of yours, and you're wearing glasses too. I gather you've moved on from that unfortunate parish, the one with all the scandal. Very wise of you, I must say.'

Portia Diplock had planted herself in the doorway from the entrance hall and as I looked round the room I saw several people shrink back from her piercing gaze. Nobody seemed pleased to see her.

Chapter Nine

Canon Camperdown's eyes bulged in his furious purple face as he glared at her, unable – for once – to speak. His wife and son looked terrified but I saw Peter reach out for his mother's hand. Alix was right, he really is a nice boy.

Major and Miss Preston looked haughtily down their identical noses, clearly appalled at such behaviour and Sister Wisden bore down on the intruder, looking much more starched than usual.

Miss Diplock paid no attention to the ripples of unease and strode round the room, rather nimbly dodging the senior nurse until she arrived at Captain Trellis's bed.

'Ah!' she boomed, standing in front of him. 'Digby Trellis, I presume? Yes?' She acknowledged his nervous nod and carried on. 'I'm glad to make your acquaintance,' she informed him. 'I heard this morning that a Captain Trellis was here at the Hall and wondered that I had not heard from you. You are my heir, after all!'

She looked him over, not appearing much impressed. 'However, as you are here in the hospital I suppose you may be excused for not writing to me. I have spent far too much of my valuable time today looking through the family bible and I am satisfied that you are my great-aunt Minerva Diplock's grandson. She married a Trellis quite late in life, and a poor specimen he was too. I shall inform my solicitor at once of your whereabouts.

'How do you do, Cousin Digby?'

She reached for his hand and pumped it vigorously up and down. Apart from blinking rather frequently, the captain seemed pleased at this attention and the two were soon deep in ancestor worship.

Just as I wondered what Mrs Trellis would do, her husband took charge of the conversation.

'This is my wife, Lydia,' beamed Captain Trellis proudly. 'I'm delighted to inform you that we expect a happy event in the near future. Lydia, my dear, this is my cousin, Miss Portia Diplock. Doesn't she resemble the photograph of my mother? The one I showed you?'

Watching the scene enthralled from the other side of the room I could see that Lydia was biting her lip and looking worried. I remembered that the lady lodgers had encountered Miss Diplock at their front gate only yesterday morning; but no, Lydia had hurried indoors, hadn't she? I had assumed a call of nature at the time but now I remembered she had stared at the other woman from across the market square but made no effort to help her. Again, I'd thought she probably felt there were enough of us already but if she had recognised Miss Diplock by her resemblance to a photograph, perhaps she had been too nervous to introduce herself. Her apprehensive expression made me felt sorry for her so I smiled encouragement and she nodded nervously before approaching her husband and his new-found relative.

'Your wife?' Miss Diplock looked frankly disbelieving but Lydia stared bravely back at her. 'Well, well, I am delighted to hear about the impending event, Cousin Digby. There are no other Diplocks as far as I know, so your child will be particularly welcome. The line will continue…' She paused, subjecting Lydia to an intimidating scrutiny. 'I hope we can depend upon you to produce a male child?'

'Cousin Digby' appeared delighted at this mark of favour and Lydia swallowed the retort that only too clearly hovered on her lips, murmuring platitudes instead. As I watched she made a clear effort to smile and set herself to charm the older woman.

Good luck with that, I muttered to myself. I suppose it will be worth buttering her up after all particularly if Captain Trellis is her heir. Miss Diplock, presumably in a rare moment of diplomacy, had quite obviously – to an interested observer – (me), bitten back the comment about Lydia's youth that must have hovered on the tip of her tongue. It looked as though she must intend to accept them as family. And what of them? According to Henry's cousin Bertha, the Diplock menfolk had run the larger property into ruin but just how prosperous was Lydia's wounded hero? A small, pleasant house in a bustling market town might suit him very well, particularly if there might be even a small fund attached. Though the prospect of having Portia Diplock also attached was far from attractive. I was quite sure that arrangement would never work and in any case, I wasn't sure I could see Lydia as one of the local middle-class ladies, presiding over bazaars and doling out alms to the poor, but you never know.

Addy passed me on her way to the cake table. She shot an appraising glance at Captain Trellis who was standing up to let Lydia have his chair.

'He's frightfully weedy, isn't he?' she said dispassionately. 'Still, I suppose he's better than nothing, or at least Lydia must think so. Pity he's got Queen Anne legs.'

She trailed away and I took another look at Captain Trellis. Is this something only my family say? Legs that bend outwards and turn in at the ankle? On reflection it might be some flight of fancy of Papa's. He used to say that he was glad none of his daughters had Queen Anne Legs because they reminded him of his grandmother, though he would never be drawn further as to how in the world he could possibly have seen the old lady's legs! It probably was one of his jokes, but it had become a family legend. However, Adelaide was right, Captain Trellis was bandy-legged and his ankles definitely turned in, as far as I could see.

I thought I had better be a good guest and make polite conversation again so I took another circuit of the hall, chatting shyly to the patients and staff and escaping towards the table where Addy was still interrogating Major Minton. As I reached them he burst out laughing and patted her hand.

'You're a gem, Miss Adelaide,' he chuckled. 'However, a tea party isn't the place for discussing the effects of mustard gas. Catch me another day when we're not surrounded by more delicately-minded souls.'

At that moment Miss Diplock joined us and there was a shuffling of chairs when it was clear that she intended to sit down.

'Christabel,' she fixed me with a determined eye. 'I have put you and your sisters down to take part in the Maypole dance and the country dancing tomorrow afternoon. I know you will be happy to oblige.'

'That won't be possible, Miss Diplock,' I replied, equally firmly. 'We are needed at home so our visit to the May Day Revels will have to be brief.'

'But…that is most unsatisfactory,' she frowned. 'I have counted on you. The frocks are charming and I shall appear myself in a splendid costume fitting to the occasion.'

What could she possibly mean? Surely she wasn't planning to be the Queen of the May? I opened my mouth but,

'What a pity I'm no longer able to dance,' Fergus Munro astonished us all by addressing her. 'Before I was wounded I had a go at Morris dancing and it was capital fun. Sadly, my dancing days are over now.' A shadow crossed his face and I saw Alix edge more closely towards him.

'You? A man? Morris dancing? Impossible,' cried Miss Diplock.

'Not at all,' he said, easily. 'A year or so ago I was at a camp in France where a team of dancers from London arrived, bent on teaching folk dancing to the men, because it offers interest and exercise, both always in short supply in the camps. In any case, village Morris dancers are always men. It used not to be considered at all suitable for women.'

'Well, I have never heard of that,' she said shortly then turned her attention to us. 'I'm disappointed in you, Christabel. I know that your circumstances are reduced these days, but I am persuaded that Lady Elspeth would expect you to do your patriotic duty; noblesse oblige, after all.'

Before I could rise to the bait, Addy burst out, 'You make us sound like the Distressed Gentlewomen's charity, but that's nonsense. Our circumstances aren't reduced at all.

They've always been reduced – and Granny expects us to use our own judgement and common sense.'

Fortunately at that moment, Sister Wisden rose, clapped her hands and announced that visiting was over.

'Thank you so much for coming, everyone,' she said, firmly moving us all towards the main entrance. 'We hope to have another tea party soon and a few more guests from town too.'

'Promise you'll come and see me again, Addy?' Major Minton solemnly shook hands with her and she was evidently gratified. 'You've cheered me up no end and as a reward I'll tell you all about a very messy field operation where I had to assist. It was touch and go! Now run along like a good girl, I'll see you soon.'

Alix, Henry and I opened our eyes at this but the major winked at us and waved us off.

'I'll walk down with you,' Henry said. 'I shan't see you all for a day or two, did I tell you? Edgar has business in Birmingham so I'm to represent him there and while I'm in the Midlands I have matters to discuss with my manager at our own family works. I'll miss the maypole dancing,' he said not looking at all sorry. 'I'll be back on Saturday morning, so you can tell me all about it then. Now I'd better hurry. It was good of Edgar to give me time off and I can't outstay my leave of absence.'

Chapter Ten

Thursday evening

After our busy afternoon, both households settled down to a surprisingly peaceful evening. Looking in on our lodgers I found all three drinking coffee (from Miss Preston's secret store) and gossiping which struck me as a very good sign. I do like people to get on together and besides, it makes running the guest house so much easier.

In our own house peace also reigned. Granny reported that Mother had dozed all afternoon and was now in full 'genius burning' mood, her pen galloping across the page and unaware of the outside world. Which is just how we like it.

Addy and Judith were talking about the encounter with Major Minton and I noted that both of them had been very taken with him. Addy saw in him the promise of a far more informative ally than Fergus or Henry, though I was quite sure that the major would divulge no more than he felt suitable to her years. As I said before, he seemed eminently trustworthy. Judith too, and that was interesting, had found him good company and when I looked in on the pair of them, she asked me what I knew about him.

'Very little, I'm afraid, except that he and Henry seem to have served together for most of Henry's time in France. And that he's ten years older and Henry admires him immensely.'

'What about his injury?'

'I understand that it's permanent, unfortunately,' I told her. 'He's very brave and I gather he has no family, so we must all do what we can for him. He will certainly appreciate some visits from you, Judith. He clearly longs for good, intelligent conversation in the same way that young Lt Camperdown aches to be distracted by tales of foreign places. I wonder,' I had a sudden thought. 'Perhaps Major Minton could be persuaded to settle in Ramalley as he has no other ties?'

I was reading in bed later on when Alix slipped into my room. I had left it up to her, no point in forcing her confidence.

'I think I'm in love,' she exclaimed as she snuggled down beside me, making me shriek when she rubbed her icy feet up and down my leg.

'I think so too,' I agreed, after we'd squabbled about her manners!

'How can I know if it's real, Christy? I've wanted to be in love for such an age, you know I have. Is this another of my make-believe games?'

'It's nothing like that, silly,' I hugged her. 'Has he said anything?'

'Not really, but he has a smile just for me, when our eyes meet, even if he's doing something serious.'

'I think…' I spoke slowly, wanting to get it right. 'I think he has strong feelings but doesn't want to hurry you. He can see that although we have lots of responsibility, we're all actually very young for our ages. Why don't you get to know him slowly? You've plenty of time, it's not as though he's a patient and likely to be sent miles away. He's here for the rest of the war at least; don't forget he's recuperating too and it's not an onerous appointment. You'll have ample time to discover if it really is love!'

After she had scurried away to her attic I lay back in the dark and thought about a brief conversation Addy and I had had after supper. She had waylaid me in the garden as I shut the hens away, checking up on Kaiser Bill to see whether she had obliged with a chick or two. Of course she hadn't, the last thing on earth that hen will do is anything obliging.

'It's funny, isn't it, Christy?' Addy said idly. 'We've each got a follower now.'

'What? Don't be so vulgar,' I was startled. 'And anyway, what on earth do you mean?'

She stared. 'You've got Henry. Alix has Fergus and I've

got Wilfred, of course.'

'What? You're fifteen, Addy, don't be ridiculous.' (I glossed over what she had said about Henry and Fergus, this wasn't the time to think about that)

'I don't see why it's ridiculous. I think it would be a good idea.'

'What does Wilfred think about it?' I couldn't believe I was engaging her in conversation about such a thing but I knew she would insist on telling me anyway. When Addy has a bee in her bonnet, everyone is expected to listen – and possibly answer questions at a later date.

'I haven't told him yet. He won't mind though and of course I have to go to Oxford first and qualify as a doctor and he wants to study to be a chartered accountant.'

I was distracted by this, as well as amused that Wilfred's future was now laid out for him. 'That sounds sensible. He should talk to Captain Trellis about accountancy training, but what about the undertaking business? Won't his father expect him to take over?

'Of course not. You know Mr Seymour branched out long ago into other businesses. The undertaking is just one of them and none of the brothers will be involved with it. Anyway, Wilfred has decided he's going to study and make enough money to buy land and go in for building houses. He says everyone needs somewhere to live.'

'What does his mother say to that?' (I have met her over the years, most recently at a dull lecture in town last year and she seemed very pleasant. Quiet but friendly.)

Addy shrugged. 'She never says much but she doesn't really like the undertaking business and Wilfred says she's pleased that his father isn't so involved in it now.'

Well! I had a great deal to think about but of course I didn't think at all. Instead I slept soundly all night and woke up to hear the dawn chorus and the birds singing their heads off on what promised to be a beautiful morning in early May.

Friday, 3rd May, morning

'The schoolroom is ready for our first class,' Addy announced smugly as she emerged from the cellar stair. 'Penny and I have dusted and arranged the chairs and tables and put out pencils and notepads.'

Oh Lord! Would you believe I had forgotten all about our inaugural school session? I praised them for their foresight and help and was then distracted by the post arriving with two letters addressed to me. One was from my magazine editor and the other, scarily, was from the bank. I took a deep breath and read that one first.

And then I read it again.

Impossible to read it aloud with everyone milling around the kitchen but the gist was that the bank manager would be grateful if I could make time for a brief appointment with him to discuss an unexpected deposit in our account. A deposit? Well, that's never happened before but he added a note to the effect that the deposit was perfectly legal and above board, but that it was something he felt we should go over together.

Luckily nobody noticed that I'd fallen quiet and presumably my face hadn't drained of colour leaving me ashen pale (as countenances – which is what she calls them – do in Mother's books) so I tucked the letter into my pocket and opened the other one. (Incidentally, Mother insists that her heroines have 'rose leaf' complexions which, as Addy pointed out, sounds as though they are green and shiny.)

'Oh, my goodness!' This time I could – and did – shriek with no qualms about discretion. 'Listen to this, everyone! It's from the editor of Brave Boys' Yarns. He says they're starting a magazine for girls and he wonders if I (or Lt Crombie) might have anything suitable. How very opportune! New Girls at St Ethelfleda's School, you have a home to go to!'

'What will you call yourself?' Granny wondered after we had all celebrated with another slice of toast – which is more extravagant than it sounds because we buttered the toast lavishly.

Of course we ran the gamut of silly names, all of which I loftily ignored, until Addy, of all people, said, 'Why don't you say it's Lt Crombie's sister who is writing books for girls and call her something sensible like Beryl? That's a serious, sedate sort of name and it'll impress people. We don't want another soppy name like Mother's Mabel de Rochforde, do we?'

'What will you do with poor Lt Crombie?' asked Judith. 'I hope you're not going to kill him off?'

'Posted overseas,' I explained. 'People will believe that, and I expect they'll accept Miss Beryl Crombie. Writing often runs in families, doesn't it? Look at us: Grandpapa, Mother and me too.' (Not to mention Papa's exceptional talent for fiction, but I kept that to myself.)

'Lt Crombie won't be leaving yet,' I told them. 'The magazine has two serials in hand because I wrote so much when the hospital was closed. I edit those into the books as soon as I reach the last episode and that means the publisher has them ready as well.'

'What's this?' Alix bent to retrieve a slip of paper from the floor. 'Christy! It's a cheque for a guinea.'

I clapped my hand to my mouth. 'It must have fallen out of the envelope. Here, let me finish reading the letter. Yes. I'd forgotten that I sent off a short story last month for the Brave Boys' Yarns Christmas Annual. What a lovely surprise!'

Addy was mulling over the news but it was something else that concerned her. 'I don't think St Ethelfleda is a good name for a school, Christy. Nobody will know how to pronounce it.'

'I only chose her because she's Ramalley's local saint,' I said mildly. 'Would St Mary's be more universally acceptable? I don't mind.' We took a vote and changed the name then and there then I made my escape.

'I'd better get my hat and go into town. I must put this cheque in the bank at once before I lose it again. I'll leave you in charge of your class, Judith, if you're up to it. Addy and Penny will help, I'm sure.'

I escaped before anyone could give me a shopping list and

arrived on the doorstep as the chief clerk went through the impressive performance of opening up and declaring the premises open for business. Soon I was sitting in the manager's office feeling very unsettled. He smiled at me and offered me a chocolate so I felt slightly reassured that whatever he had to tell me definitely wasn't going to be that we had lost all our money.

'I'm sorry to have caused you some perturbation, Miss Christabel,' he nodded, 'but I did feel we should discuss this deposit in person. I know that Lady Elspeth prefers that you are involved with the business decisions,' he added. 'You see, a bank draft has been made out to your name for quite a large sum. In fact, one hundred pounds has been paid in.'

I opened my mouth but no sound emerged and he nodded again, smiling.

'Be assured that the Bank has checked this most carefully and I'm happy to reiterate that the deposit is perfectly respectable. The only information we have is that it comes from a Miss Agatha Trubody, a lady who has an account at one of our London branches. Hence the smooth transfer.'

Perfectly respectable? I took leave to doubt that. Miss Agatha Trubody does not exist but is an alias of our allegedly late and strikingly not respectable Papa who was last heard of planning to go to Australia. (That, by the way, is a secret. To the rest of the world Papa sadly drowned when the Lusitania was sunk by enemy action three years ago.)

I thanked the bank manager most politely, indicating that the donor was indeed a friend of the family (how on earth did I keep a straight face?) I took another look, and then another to confirm that the extraordinarily healthy balance of our account did appear to be genuine, and almost skipped all the way home. Only I and Alix and Granny know that Papa, like a perennial bad penny, survived the sinking of the Lusitania and I couldn't wait to whisper this news, except that I probably wouldn't have a chance till much later. Already the town was bustling and busy and I was glad I didn't have to go near the Priory on my way home. Far too much risk of running into Miss Diplock.

Granny was the only person in sight when I slipped quietly through the back door. She raised an eyebrow and I nodded eagerly.

'Tell you later, when we can catch Alix as well. Something extremely interesting to our advantage and, for once, not a problem!'

'Just as well I trust your judgement, Christy,' was all she would say, in her dry way. 'Because that statement sounds unlikely in the extreme.'

I gave her a hug, which she does actually enjoy though she would never admit to it and tuts as she brushes them off. 'What's happening with the school room?' I asked. 'I can't hear any sounds of misery or mayhem – can it possibly be working?'

Reassured that Judith's pupils were all occupied downstairs and that Miss Acton had yet again arrived at her appointed time, apparently still eager to work with Mother, I disappeared up to my room and flung myself into my new story, planning it first as a serial and then, I hoped, to be re-edited as a book, though I'd need to write to the publisher about that.

Carried away with enthusiasm for a new venture and relief that I could now refer generally to the War, as Addy had suggested, without having to go into the dreadful realities of the Western Front, I wrote and wrote and wrote.

Granny herself appeared at half-past twelve with a cup of Camp coffee and a fish paste sandwich.

'You deserve some time to yourself, Christy,' she told me, whisking round the room to tidy up. 'The classroom is working very well; your mother is occupied with Bonnie Prince Charlie; and Miss Acton has not yet found an opportunity to fall any lower. Make the most of it and I'll send Penny up to give you warning when it's time to go to the Revels.'

Just before two o'clock Penny tapped on my door. She was trimly dressed in a plain blouse and skirt, with a straw hat, which was my suggestion for all of us. Not an occasion for silks or smart linens, rather a time to look fresh, competent and respectable. And so we did.

'Her ladyship says it's a good time to go now, Miss Christy,' she said solemnly but her eyes were shining. 'She says the opening ceremony will have finished by the time we get there but you'll still have plenty of chances to look round but you should be able to avoid anyone you don't want to see!'

I had come to a suitable place to stop writing so I jumped up and tidied my hair.

'Just a moment, Penny,' I called as she headed for the stairs. 'Here's a little spending money. The other girls will want to buy ices and drinks, it's a warm day, and they will certainly have money. This is just for you.'

I slipped a florin into her hand and when she looked startled, I smiled. 'Today you're working for me, don't forget, and I know you'll look after them. They'll have more fun without any grown-ups and you have much more sense. But don't say I said so!'

She was pleased and excited and skipped off now to join the others. I sighed, Penny is yet another of life's sensible people, destined to sort out other people's problems. Like me, however, she seems to enjoy it, and so do I really. I just like to grumble.

Granny had been quite right. The usual crowds that you get at the start of these affairs had thinned out by the time I arrived at the Priory as townsfolk scooped up cakes and bread and practical items such as socks and vests, so I was able to amble about at leisure. I scanned the crowd and duly noticed Miss Preston and her brother, the jolly Major, coming away from the cake stall. Of course they were! I knew that Fergus and Sister Wisden had decreed that any patient who felt up to the exercise might attend the jollification, with the proviso that the station trap must be hired for the trip. (Unfortunately, the hospital ambulance had been pressed into use today to take a patient back to the huge hospital at Netley, in Southampton, so it was the trap or walk.)

Elsewhere, Mrs Camperdown and Mrs Trellis were

strolling gently round the green with no sighting, as yet, of the blustering canon. I could relax and just as I wondered what to do next I saw Dr Munro wave to me and point to an empty chair beside him.

'Come and sit down, Christabel,' he told me. 'You always seem to be up and doing, take five minutes to slow down, do. Doctor's orders again,' he added.

After yesterday's comfortable conversation, I no longer felt shy with him, which is really unusual for me, particularly as we have known him for less than a week. (How is that possible?). 'I will in a minute, I promise,' I laughed. 'Let me just – ah, I can see Addy and Wilfred looking suspiciously sedate over by the Font. I suspect Addy's bullying him into letting her make more wishes. She always likes to be sure and the more coins they throw, even if they're only farthings, the more the gods will be propitiated.

'And there's Judith, Miss Evershed. Good, she's going into the tea tent so at least she'll sit down for a while. She's not strong yet. Oh,' I exclaimed. 'How nice for them.'

Fergus looked startled and followed my gaze.

'She's fetching tea for herself and Major Minton. How delightful that they've chummed up.'

'Are you matchmaking, by any chance, Christabel?' he teased.

'Of course not,' I said primly. 'But they are both lonely and they have Oxford in common. Besides, a friend is always good to have.'

I craned my neck and felt slightly anxious.

'Now what's the matter?' Fergus was watching me.

'I can't see Alix,' I confessed. 'She came down from the hospital didn't she?'

'Of course she did, I walked down with her. She's talking to that lady right over there by the West door of the Priory. The vicar's wife, isn't it? She's quite safe, Christy.'

'Is she though?' I was startled. Where on earth had that come from? I ploughed on, staring at him. 'You're not to hurt her, Fergus,' I said fiercely.

He smiled. 'You know I won't do that, don't you?'

I did know. Fergus was like Henry: patently decent, honourable and kind. I'd been amused by him when we first met and taken aback when the attraction between him and Alix was so immediate, so obvious, and so strong but now I felt safe with him. Believe me, with a father like ours, it seems strange to trust any man. There's Henry, of course, but he is very young. Fergus is … a grown-up. What an absurdly childish thing to say, even inside my own head! But how comforting.

'You carry such a lot of weight on your shoulders, don't you, Christy?' He was still looking thoughtfully at me. 'Too much for a girl of your age.'

'I don't think so,' I was surprised. 'Certainly not more than a lot of other girls. We have a roof over our heads, two roofs in fact, and we have enough to live on so we never have to go hungry. We also have Granny to hold the family together and that means everything.

'I'm very busy, I grant you,' I warmed to my subject as he listened gravely. 'But so are we all, even Addy who is revising hard for her exams. Don't be misled by this last week. I have more time on my hands because Miss Acton is doing Mother's typewriting and Alix has been having a holiday from her old lady. Next week she'll be run off her feet attending to old Mrs Redfern's whims; it's then that the afternoons at Groom Hall are more of a rest than a chore.'

At that moment Wilfred and Addy hove in sight again. She looked pleased with herself so I deduced that she and Wilfred had come to an agreement about how much the gods would expect in the way of farthings to make wishes come true. I watched as she said something and he nodded, whereupon they walked off in the direction of the sweet stall. Fergus was grinning.

'You're so good with her,' I said as we both watched them squabbling on their way.

'She reminds me all the time of my sister Phoebe,' he said very quietly.

'Your sister?' He had mentioned a brother and two sisters but Alix said he didn't talk about them much.

'Phoebe was the youngest.' He sighed and shifted his position. 'There are – were – four of us; my brother Jamie is thirty-three and helps Dad run the place, it's more of a big farm than an estate though we do have a park and a lake! He's married with two small boys and then there's Emily, two years younger, who is horse mad and married to the local vet. I'm next, at twenty-seven and Phoebe came just over two years after me.'

'What happened to her?' I whispered.

'She trained as a VAD,' he said, staring blankly at the grey stone tower of the priory. 'She served in Mesopotamia and died of typhoid two years ago, on a hospital ship that was on its way home. She had saved countless lives but nobody could save her. She was the darling of the family.' He bowed his head. 'It broke my mother's heart and she died a few months later.'

My eyes filled. The grief in his voice brought back my own desolation at Bertie's death and I squeezed his hand.

'I must go,' he stood up abruptly. 'I see the trap has returned and I promised to relieve Sister Wisden so she can come to the Revels.'

'Go and find Alix,' I whispered. 'Take her back with you. And – Fergus? Tell her about Phoebe and let her talk about Bertie, our brother. It will help you both.'

I watched him limp purposefully towards the Priory door where Alix was still trapped by the vicar's wife who is kind but garrulous. He skilfully detached my sister and I saw them clamber into the trap, with several other patients and staff who had clearly had enough excitement for one day.

Feeling aimless I thought perhaps I should find Judith's pupils and as I made my way across the green there was a great fanfare. Well, I say fanfare and that was clearly what it was meant to be, but it was actually a long, wheezy chord on an accordion accompanied by some hopeful toots on a boy scout's bugle. I had no time to wonder what was happening because a procession of young girls came skipping hand-in-hand from behind the tea tent, heading towards the maypole.

Knowing Granny's strict views on noblesse oblige I

followed the throng, prepared to represent the family and applaud enthusiastically. The girls at least seemed pleased to be the centre of attention so I gathered that Miss Diplock had not bullied them too severely. Or perhaps it was only the Fyttleton girls she thought of as grist to her mill?

I was sure I remembered some suggestion that she might have made herself special costume and was relieved to note that she was not parading as Queen of the May. That honour went to one of the older girls, identifiable by her larger wreath of flowers. Miss Diplock was certainly vivid, resplendent in a colourful smocked cotton dress with a bright floral pattern that that resembled our old drawing room curtains and seemed somehow far too girlish for a stout lady well into middle age. Oh dear, what a horrid thing to think, but she did look like mutton dressed as lamb. Mercifully, she had contented herself with a simple muslin cap.

I moved closer to the dancing and mingled with a familiar group. The Priory green is laid out with elegant herringbone brick paths in a vain attempt to make people keep off the grass and Mrs Camperdown and Lydia Trellis were standing on the path at the outside edge of the grass where the maypole had been raised, off to the town side of the green. There are benches set at intervals along this perimeter path which in turn has a slightly raised edge that looks decorative and stops bicycle riders from taking a short cut. I saw Major Preston sitting on one of the benches while he and his sister, to my surprise, were talking to Bertha and Edgar Makepeace. Chance acquainted perhaps?

Lydia looked hot and tired and I thought she should have been sitting on the bench with the major. However, she was eagerly watching the dancing and trying to see what was going on, though her view was restricted by the throng in front of her. Distracted, as the dancing commenced, she mopped her scarlet face with a handkerchief and with help from Mrs Camperdown briefly removed her hat. I could understand why, her hair is like heavy black silk, very slippery and very difficult to keep in place. We Fyttleton girls all have curly – but not unmanageably curly – hair which is easy enough to control but I imagined Lydia's hair, though beautiful, would be a trial in everyday life

The accordion player pumped away and some schoolchildren sang raggedly in tune with the tumpty-tumpty-tum beat and everyone appeared to be having fun. Apart, that is, from anyone who came under Portia Diplock's eagle eye. She cantered round the circle, bellowing encouragement, instructions and trenchant criticisms in an unending stream, and pushing the spectators out of the way in order to take hold of some poor girl's shoulder and turn her in the opposite direction. This happened several times, each with a larger audience gathered round – presumably hoping to hear someone other than themselves get into trouble.

It all happened so quickly. Almost in the blink of an eye.

I squinted over my shoulder at the Priory clock tower to check the time and as I did so a scream rang out. Followed by more cries and panicky wailing. To my horror I saw that Lydia had fallen on to the grass and was gasping for breath; not an easy task when you realised that Portia Diplock was lying partly across the path and partly across her! Around them lay a tangle of maypole dancers who seemed to have fallen like dominoes, though how on earth that could have happened, I had no idea.

The crowd rushed forward and then receded as, to my relief, sensible Mrs Camperdown, with the help of the wiry Miss Preston, unceremoniously heaved Portia, no lightweight, off the very slightly-built young mother-to-be. Although my instinct was to rush forward and help, I left the others to deal with the accident. I had a more urgent task and craning my neck I was relieved to spot Wilfred. I beckoned and he ran over.

'Wilfred,' I hissed. 'Get Addy and Penny and the other two girls and take them into town. Look after them, buy them ices or something and get them straight home. With any luck they won't have seen anything.' He is a competent boy and I added, 'Now, Wilfred. Get them away from here at once and don't take any nonsense from Addy.'

My most pressing responsibility dealt with I could turn to the melée in front of me. My first emotion was exasperation. Why on earth was that irritating woman just lying there, getting under everyone's feet? Mrs Trellis's case was far more worrying. To the side I could see that Judith Evershed had joined Mrs Camperdown, one of them coaxing her to take deep breaths and drink some water and the other hastily pinning up that lovely waterfall of hair out of the way and replacing the hat on top.

If only Fergus hadn't gone back to the hospital. I could see that the trap had not yet returned bringing with it Sister Wisden and some of her well-trained staff. Instead a very elderly man hobbled to the scene and I recognised him as a retired doctor. He was certainly over eighty, according to local gossip, and looked very frail but not, it seemed, too doddery to recognise whether someone was dead or alive.

Why he glared at me, I have no idea, but glare he did, as I stared, horrified, at Portia Diplock as she sprawled on the grass at my feet.

How could she possibly be dead?

When the doctor pronounced that life was extinct I was aware that the crowd who moments, ago had been wide-eyed and pressing forward agog to hear his diagnosis, had as though by some mystical force retreated to a safe distance. It felt unreal, as though the three of us were left alone in the circle: the doctor, the dead body, and me.

It had all been going so well, I thought in a dull sort of way. We had weathered the winter, at first paralysed by grief at my brother's death but gradually we had managed to cope with sorrow, with our perennial lack of funds, and with wartime restrictions until we had forged a new kind of life. With the arrival of spring we had begun to feel hopeful, even to be happy now and then…

'Well? Did you hear me, young woman?' The elderly doctor was barking at me and I blinked. 'I asked if you could furnish me with the name and address of this poor soul.'

And that's the trouble with being the sensible one –

everyone always steps back and expects you to deal with any difficulties.

Even a dead body...

Chapter Eleven

Saturday, 4th May, early morning

I opened my eyes, stared groggily at the day, and discovered that Addy was fast asleep in my bed with me. I rolled over and found Alix carefully carrying a tray of tea which she put on the bedside table and then put her finger to her lips.

'I've brought some of those cake crumb biscuits you made,' she murmured. 'Early breakfast!'

As though summoned by magic, Addy sat up. 'Breakfast?'

Alix scrambled back into bed and we sat there, saying nothing but so glad to be together. I could have cried and might very well later on when it has all sunk in, but just now I felt safe, and loved and – goodness! –accompanied not only by sisters but by five assorted cats and kittens.

'Do you want to talk about it?' Alix pushed a second biscuit into my hand and wonder of wonders Addy barely looked envious, so I shared it with her, of course.

'It's all one huge, horrible muddle,' I muttered. 'I know I kept going but I don't remember much, even how on earth I ended up in my own bed.'

'That's easy enough,' said Alix. 'Sister Wisden arrived and thrust all of the lodgers into the trap and sent them home, but you refused to go, saying Granny would deal with them. Judith told me what happened. That doddery old Dr Salt was bullying you and making you help him with Miss Diplock, examining her, looking at her injuries, checking whether she was really dead. Judith thinks he believed you were a nurse and that's why he pressed you into service but she says she and Miss Bertha got you away in the end though the doctor kept barking orders at you. Henry's Cousin Edgar read him the riot act about involving a minor in such a way. You were an awful mess and we cleaned you up before we tucked you into bed.' She gave me a quick hug. 'Don't worry, Bella washed your blouse and sponged down your skirt and she's managed to get all the blood out, though you might not want....'

She broke off, looking pale. 'I can't believe...never mind, that's not for now.'

'Miss Preston was helpful,' put in Addy. 'She organised all the maypole dancers and made them pick themselves up and go to the tea tent to be seen to; then she made them go home.'

'What do you mean?' I plucked fretfully at the sleeve of her nightgown. 'You weren't there, surely? I was relying on Wilfred to get you and the other girls out of the way.'

'He did, don't worry.' Alix frowned at Addy. 'As I said, Judith saw it all and she told us. And you needn't be anxious about her either. Sister Wisden sent urgently for Fergus and the rest of the staff, which is why I was there later on. Judith was taken home and put to bed with a sedative after a light supper.'

'Wilfred whisked us away from the Priory before we realised anything was wrong.' Addy looked slightly disgruntled. 'He said it was all getting too crowded and that you'd told him to buy us all ices so naturally we went with him.'

'Naturally.'

She narrowed her eyes suspiciously but carried on. 'Luckily Vera Wakelin's elder sister was at home and she said she would look after both Veras, as her parents were at the fête and so was Vera Bembridge's aunt. They weren't scared, Christy, just interested.'

I heaved a very long sigh. Let's hope their families see it that way too. Though on reflection, I don't believe anyone could possibly blame us.

'When it was just me and Penny, Wilfred stopped at the little sweet shop on the bridge and bought us bulls'-eyes,' Addy explained. 'He says they're very comforting and take so long to finish that all your troubles disappear by the time you get to the end.'

Alix caught my eye but all she said was, 'That's very true.'

I knew there was more to talk over but neither of us wanted to involve our little sister. She had enjoyed the novelty of the morning class (I must talk to Judith about that if ever life returns to normal). She and the other girls had clearly made friends and Penny was already an integral part of the group. As for Wilfred, he had proved himself kind and resourceful and was probably now a Fyttleton family fixture.

I stirred and at once three kittens moved like lightning to attach themselves to me. Even old Matilda, mother-cat-to-be and bulgier than ever, had a gleam of interest in her golden eye. I looked at my clock.

'Oh, Lord,' I groaned artistically, avoiding Alix's startled gaze. 'It's Saturday and no Bella and Penny. The animals need feeding, the hens must be seen to, and there's always the lodgers' breakfasts. I'm not sure I can cope with it all today.'

Alix opened her mouth but Addy rushed to reply.

'I'll get dressed straightaway,' she said eagerly. 'I can do the animals and the hens if Alix starts the breakfasts. Granny will be stirring too, so why don't you stay in bed for once, Christy?'

'Good idea,' Alix nodded, giving me a gentle push so that I lay back on my pillows. Mind you, it didn't take much theatrical ability to make me look apprehensive about the day ahead.

'You get started, Addy' Alix added. 'That will be an enormous help and I'll catch up when I'm dressed. Breakfast is easy today; Granny mixed a big jug of pancake batter last night and we actually have a lemon, though we'll have to be sparing with that. If they want more to eat they can have toast.'

'Has she gone?' I struggled back into a sitting position.

'Yes, she's fired up with virtue and helpfulness. Now, what do you remember after that silly old doctor?'

'Lydia?' I had a sudden panic and Alix squeezed my hand.

'Lydia has been thoroughly examined by both Fergus and

Sister Wisden. She was naturally shaken but no physical harm seems to have been done. She had a light supper and dear Mrs Camperdown insisted on sleeping with her in case she had nightmares or worse.'

'What do they think happened to Miss Diplock?'

'Dr Salt has diagnosed a heart attack. She was quite old and very stout and prancing about the green like a fat old pony. He said she was asking for trouble and that's more or less what he put when he signed the death certificate.'

'But there was an awful lot of blood,' I remembered. 'You're sure Lydia…?'

'Certainly not Lydia,' Alix told me firmly. 'She was squashed which must have been awfully frightening but she wasn't actually scraped or cut, so there was no blood, more shock and bruising. Miss Diplock's case was a bit different. Don't forget she was wearing that very unsuitable thin cotton dress and besides, we know she didn't approve of wearing corsets so she had very little protection for her chest and back against crashing on to a rough brick path, and Dr Salt said she had multiple abrasions. He says the onset of the heart attack must have caused her to fall, and that death would have occurred soon after she hit the ground or at that moment.'

'What does Fergus say?'

'Dr Salt thanked him and the Groom Hall staff for their valuable efforts in aiding the maypole dancers and distressed spectators but insisted that no further medical assistance, or opinion, was required.' Alix's tone was dry and she shrugged. 'Fergus can only comply. A heart attack looks the likely culprit and it's all true about her being extremely over-excited.'

'We'd better get dressed,' I sighed. 'I predict a very busy day.'

First however, I gave her an edited version of my visit to the bank. She immediately recognised the name of our alleged benefactor.

'Trubody?' her eyebrows disappeared under her fair curls. 'But that's…Hmm…and the bank said it's all above board?'

'Apparently,' I said as I shrugged myself into my everyday blouse and skirt and twisted my hair up into a neat bun. Today promised a lot of hard work with no opportunity to be ladies of leisure. 'We must catch Granny on her own and let her know this latest development but the bank seem quite satisfied so I don't think we need consider it urgent.'

I was wrong about no Bella or Penny. Both were hard at work when I finally made my way downstairs.

'Of course we came,' said Bella, firmly. 'You'll need help with the ladies next door and depend on it, you'll find yourselves busy with visitors. They'll all want to know what happened and they know you and Miss Alix were there.'

I must still have been suffering from exhaustion because Bella's kindness made me want to cry, but I sat down in our kitchen and let Penny serve me with two pancakes with lemon and sugar, as well as a cup of tea.

'I know it was all horrid later on, Miss Christy,' whispered Penny when we were briefly alone. 'But I had a lovely time yesterday, with the young ladies – the girls I mean. They like the same books as me and we're going to read one together. And I'm going to teach them really neat hemming to start with. They know a bit but I can help them. And I didn't spend the money you gave me, because Mr – um – Wilfred bought us ices.'

'Keep it, Penny,' I folded her fingers over the coin that she tried to hand back to me. 'You were a great help yesterday. Let's call it a bonus!'

For the second day running the post brought me an unexpected communication. Fortunately only Alix and I were still in the kitchen when we heard the letter box rattle and she picked up the post and sorted it.

'One for you from Nantwich,' she said, puzzled, as she handed it to me.

'Isn't that in Cheshire? Do you know anyone there?'

'Nobody, as far as I know,' I said thoughtfully as I slit the envelope. 'I don't recognise the handwriting either.' There was no note but inside was another envelope, addressed in a flowing, flamboyant handwriting that was instantly recognisable to a Fyttleton daughter.

'Ah,' Alix sat down slowly. 'From Miss Trubody, I presume?'

I reluctantly slit that envelope too. I was tempted to put it on the fire without reading except that the circumstances were unusual. This time, quite unprecedentedly, money had come in, instead of the usual way. The letter deserved inspection at least.

'Shall I read it?' Alix watched me as I just sat there, holding it as though it might explode. Silently, I passed it over to her.

'My dear young ladies, I thought I would pen a line to let you know that I am well and have settled into my new home. I have a share in a small tea shop and we are doing a roaring trade, so do not worry about me.

'This morning a customer left her umbrella behind in the shop and a gentleman handed it in to me, remarking on the lady's carelessness. He said that he had himself recently encountered one or two other very careless individuals who had also managed to lose valuables. He confided that he, on the other hand, had had a stroke of luck recently and hoped to share some of his good fortune with the poor and needy. He mentioned that he was planning to take up gardening very soon and I applauded this decision, digging is such excellent exercise!

A splendid sunrise this morning reminded me of that charming brooch of your dear mother's – the one with green and blue lights in it, and with occasional flashes of fire. Such a lovely piece and such fond memories.

'I trust, dear girls, that you all thrive and prosper, and I will write again soon. Probably,

Yours very sincerely,

Agatha Trubody'

'He must have asked someone to write the envelope for him and post it,' I said, looking wide-eyed at my sister. 'I'm sure we can discount Nantwich as a clue. There's no forwarding address anyway.'

'The tea shop doesn't ring true either but there's a breezy air about the letter that sounds as though he's up to no good. A garden? Papa? and digging?' Alix was puzzled. 'And what on earth is all that about a sunset?'

'Oh, my goodness,' I read the letter again and started to chuckle. 'I know exactly what it means. It's in code, of course it is. You know what Papa is like; I expect he couldn't resist it.

'I'd been wondering whether he could have struck gold to be able to send us that hundred pounds, but he has barely had time to get as far as Australia, it's only seven weeks since I saw him. In fact this letter might mean he has only just gone, because Australia is definitely his destination.

'But Alix, it's not gold; he's talking about opals, which is what that talk of a sunset means. I think he's planning to go out to the opal fields!'

'How in heaven's name do you make that out?'

'I'm more familiar with Papa's fantasies than you are! It's ridiculous, but then so is Papa. First of all, there's a clue in the conversation about the umbrella,' I ticked points off on my fingers. 'Note the remark about the careless individuals who had lost valuables, followed by her customer's stroke of good luck. Knowing Papa as we do, can there be any doubt as to there being a connection?'

'Oh,' Alix whistled softly. 'That hadn't occurred to me; I thought it meant he had stolen an umbrella – which didn't make sense!'

'No, no, of course he didn't, it's just an example of carelessness with property. Papa is talking about far greater stakes. Then there's the remark about sharing with the poor and needy; I'm quite sure that's a hint about the money in the bank and that we are the recipients in question.'

'And the mention of digging is another clue?' She mulled it over, with a wry smile. 'I really cannot see Papa doing any digging, that's not his style at all, but if there are going to be rich pickings – that I can see.'

(Don't think for a moment, by the way, that we condone

anything our errant parent has ever done – apart from accidentally providing us with our recent windfall, and that had only been due to my own quick thinking. I had actually snatched up the money from under his very nose – and only just in time! I have no intention of delving any more deeply into this latest episode. The bank has declared it all above board and that should be good enough for us.)

'It's always a pantomime where Papa's concerned, isn't it?' I sighed heavily. 'Or perhaps a farce is more accurate. All this cloak and dagger nonsense and drama. Oh well,' I met her glance. 'You can't choose your parents, can you, and at least we're lucky enough to have Granny to keep us balanced.'

'Did Mother ever have an opal brooch though?' Alix was still cogitating.

'I don't remember one, but that doesn't mean she didn't,' I grinned. 'We have to tell Granny about this latest caper of his but then we must definitely put him back in his watery grave with the Lusitania.'

Chapter Twelve

Gradually the business of the day took over and Granny told me that Fergus had given Lydia Trellis orders to stay in bed all day. Mrs Camperdown popped her head round our hall door and waylaid me, saying,

'Don't worry about her, Christabel. I'll stay with her until visiting time at the hospital and then I believe Adelaide and Penny have volunteered to keep her company.'

When I stared doubtfully at this announcement, she smiled. 'They're much closer in age, after all, and Lydia will like to have some young company.'

Miss Preston, it appeared, had volunteered to take the dog for a long walk over the hills to Ladywell, the other side of the railway. There are some beautiful hills in that direction and I was grateful. Bobs and Miss Preston are both full of energy and not only would it do them good but the house would be much quieter.

'Did I tell you that Wilfred called for Addy?' Granny asked in passing. 'He offered to take her to listen to the band in the park to take her mind off everything.'

'Really? That was kind of him,' I nodded and Granny twinkled at me.

'I suspect an ulterior motive,' she remarked. 'For the life of me though, I can't imagine what it could be!'

Penny announced that dusting and tidying the new schoolroom would be her task henceforth and I heard her clatter happily down the cellar stairs. My fingers are very tightly crossed (they always seem to be!) but so far, what Miss Bembridge of the High School, the quieter Vera's aunt, has termed our 'social experiment' seems to be a success. Early days, though.

Mother was sleeping off a long and fruitful night of creativity and Judith was taking it easy in the drawing room. 'I don't want to be in the way,' she explained, 'but I don't want to be away from all the news!'

Time for me to add to the bustle and busyness so I wandered out into the garden to inspect the hens. Six nondescript hens were pottering about the garden, pecking placidly and watched by three of the younger kittens, with twitching tails and bright eyes. There was no chance of a battle, thank goodness, as the older cats have their offspring well trained. A determined hen can inflict a fair amount of damage on a small, inexperienced cat!

In the hen coop Kaiser Bill and I observed each other rather hopelessly. Or at least, I was worried she might have lost interest. Do broody hens simply give up? Bill peered beadily at me with her usual contempt.

'Is anything ever going to happen, Bill?' I felt an unaccustomed affection for the vicious old chicken and she rewarded me for sentimentality by pecking the finger I foolishly held out to her.

'Serves me right,' I said aloud and heard hasty footsteps on the path.

'Christy?' Henry grabbed me by the shoulders, hugged me tightly to him and I think he was going to kiss me except that our noses bumped together quite painfully and we sprang apart, both of us with bright red faces. It all happened in about two seconds! I was too taken aback to do or say anything but he went on, words falling over themselves in his haste. 'I've just got off the Birmingham train and heard the news. Are you sure you're all right? They were all talking about it down at the station and someone said you'd been carried home, covered in blood?'

'N-no,' I stammered. 'I wasn't hurt at all but it was dreadful. Oh, Henry,' He gingerly put his arm round my shoulders and I leaned against him for a moment.

'Come and sit on the bench,' he said. 'You look exhausted and no wonder.'

There was no more attempt at kissing, if that is what it was and I was relieved in a way. Henry is my best friend but we're both very reticent, and very young, and I wasn't ready to take the next step. Or any steps at all, come to that. Instead, he reached into the overnight bag he had dropped when he arrived and fished out a box of chocolates.

'However did you manage to buy those?' I asked, eyeing them greedily. Suddenly, chocolate was the very thing I craved!

'They were a gift from one of the businessmen at the meetings I attended,' he said complacently. 'Besides Birmingham and chocolate go together, think of the Bourneville factory. Come along, choose one. I know you'll want to share with Alix and Addy and I want to be sure you have first pick.'

Feeling so much better I sketched out the events of the previous afternoon, ending with what Alix had said about Miss Diplock's death.

'It does sound plausible,' he agreed. 'Bertha will be sorry, though from what I gather she's practically the only person who will.'

At that moment Addy and Wilfred bounced into the garden via the side gate. Wilfred looked pleased with himself, but then – he always does – and I noticed that Addy was carrying something awkwardly in her arms.

'That had better not be a baby,' I scolded, sitting up straight and glaring at her.

'Of course it isn't,' she snapped. 'What a very vulgar mind you must have, Christy. It's a present to make you feel better after yesterday's horridness.'

'If you're hoping to wheedle me into some foolish scheme,' I wasn't convinced. 'It's not going to work. I'm not in the mood.'

She narrowed her eyes at me, looked at Henry for support and failed to find any, though I could tell he was trying not to laugh. Wilfred came to her rescue.

'We thought we could be helpful,' he said with an ingratiating smile. 'Alix said Captain Trellis would be meeting Henry's cousin Mr Makepeace at Miss Diplock's house at about half-past ten, and as he's been wounded, we wondered if he'd like us to fetch and carry things.'

I gave a cynical sniff and he was all injured innocence while Addy leaped in feet first as usual.

'Cousin Edgar wouldn't even let us in the house, the mean thing. He kept us on the doorstep and said today was just a tour of inspection and he was sure Captain Trellis could cope. He did say we might be useful in the days to come.'

'Well done, Cousin Edgar,' I said and Henry nodded vigorous agreement. 'You still haven't explained what that's in that bundle. I warn you, Addy, we are not taking in any more cats. We simply can't.'

'You're so ungrateful, Christy,' she declared indignantly. 'I told you this is a present. And why would you think I'd bring a baby home? Or another cat?'

Wilfred nudged her and she recalled her burden.

'I hope you're sorry for being so suspicious because this is a present from Mr and Mrs Seymour,' she said severely. 'Here, I'll put it down and you can be properly grateful.'

It proved to be a wicker hamper containing food! The kind of delicacy we hadn't seen for years.

'Father was upset when he heard about the accident and that you had been caught up in it,' Wilfred explained. 'He admires you all, the whole family, and he told the gardener to pack up some treats for you. The flowers are from Mother.'

'Oh, what beautiful tulips, Wilfred. Your mother is so kind, I must write to her at once.'

'Look, Christy,' Addy tugged at my sleeve. 'Look what Mr Seymour has sent.'

'The first asparagus,' Wilfred pointed out proudly. 'And mushrooms and a cucumber, There are grapes too. They aren't home-grown but the figs are. The gardener forces them on and won't let anyone touch them, so he and Father had quite a tussle over those; but as Father pointed out, it's his greenhouse and his figs. There are chocolates from Mother and there's a bottle of wine too.'

His eyes sparkled as he held it up for me to admire. 'Father says it's a very good vintage and you're not to give

164

this to the lady lodgers. It's just for the family and you should drink it tonight to make you all feel stronger.'

Henry glanced surreptitiously at his watch and I remembered that he was on his way home from the station.

'You must go and report to Cousin Edgar,' I said. 'And change too, you're far too smartly dressed for Ramalley on a Saturday.' I gave him a little push and smiled at him. 'We'll be all right, honestly; but do drop in whenever you feel like it. We're trying to keep everything normal and everyday for the lodgers and...' I glanced at Addy who was showing Wilfred the hens and scolding him because his only interest was in their possible appearance on the dinner table.

'Understood,' Henry nodded, gave a brief salute presumably out of habit, and waved to Wilfred and Addy as he departed through the side gate.

Bella's prediction regarding visitors was borne out. News travels fast in a small town like Ramalley and disaster and catastrophe are meat and drink to the locals. Bella, in fact, refused to go home and instead opened the door to a stream of local ladies all seeking details and sweetening their avid curiosity by various kind offerings of flowers, cake, biscuits, a pork pie and a baked custard.

'The ladies are not at home to visitors today,' Bella told them firmly. 'Her ladyship will be most grateful for your kind enquiries.'

Mrs Camperdown had been so kind and helpful that rather than expect her to find a meal in town, our lodgers' usual Saturday custom, I boiled an egg each for her and Lydia Trellis, who was still looking tired and shaken but with no repercussions – so far!

Miss Preston and Bobs reappeared tired but happy having stopped at the riverside café for a hearty meal for one of them and a bone for the other – donated by the proprietor who adores Bobs, a dog with a cheerful doggy smile that wins him friends and treats. Even though we are often driven to despair by his unsavoury habits, loud barking and muddy feet but we can't resist him either.

Wilfred and Addy, having deposited the magnificent hamper in the kitchen, agreed to convey my letter of thanks to Wilfred's parents and, if they hurried, they would be able to join them for luncheon, which would be lavish. It would certainly offer better pickings than a jam or cheese sandwich at home.

'Why don't you go and write some more of the new book?' Granny suggested later. 'Everything is peaceful here and we don't even have to think about dinner tonight because there's that big pork pie.' She took it out of the meat safe and examined it sceptically. 'Hmm, it's supposed to be home-made, Bella said, but I take leave to doubt that. This came from our friendly butcher's shop, unless I'm mistaken; and much the better for it too.'

The thought of disappearing into my new story was too good to miss but before going upstairs I looked in on Lydia.

'Are you feeling refreshed?'

'Much better, thank you, Miss – er – I mean Christabel,' she whispered. Interestingly we seem to have slipped into the habit of using first names, or at least we younger ones have. I think Mrs Camperdown began it when she took care of Lydia and it has carried on from there. It's not usual for our lodgers to be on such friendly terms with each other or with us, but these are not usual lodgers and certainly far from usual circumstances.

'Cocoa,' I told them cheerfully. 'It's always comforting and I thought you might like to finish up the last of the oatmeal biscuits.' I hesitated. 'Lydia, I believe Addy and Penny are planning to keep you company later on? If you get tired of them, just say you need a rest. They're eager to help but they might be too much for you.'

'Oh, no!' she reached out a hand in entreaty. 'I'm looking forward to it, they're such fun.'

Mrs Camperdown raised an eyebrow and smiled at me. 'As soon as we've finished these delicious biscuits,' she said. 'I'm going to leave Lydia to have a nap and probably have one myself.'

I wrote for an hour, gleefully placing my heroine in

jeopardy – it's a war story after all. Poor girl, I'll probably have to tone it down later but it's such fun to do. I've given the girls a really nice uniform, completely unlike the ghastly shapeless brown garments with orange smocking that our own dreadful school forced on us, and although there will be misunderstandings and woes, at least the headmistress will be sympathetic in the end. Mind you, I rather like the idea of writing about St Mildew's, heavily disguised of course, perhaps in another book. The Worst School in Town?

When I emerged from my work I found the older ladies, including Judith Evershed, had gone to Groom Hall and Lydia, animated and absorbed, was sitting up in bed with Addy and Penny perched at the foot, all busily talking, reading and laughing. It seemed that Wilfred had presented them with more bulls' eyes. There was a warm, friendly smell to the room.

Granny was also animated when she greeted me as I walked into the kitchen.

'Here's a really welcome present, Christy,' she exclaimed, holding out a platter containing four plucked birds.

'What are they?' I peered at them. 'Not more pheasants from Niggle?'

'Niggle certainly slid furtively into the scullery about ten minutes ago,' she nodded. 'He tapped his nose and left them on the draining board before he vanished again. Don't you recognise them? They're wood pigeons and bless him, he's plucked and cleaned them.'

'From the Groom Hall park,' I said. 'They'll catch him at it, one day! It's a kind thought but don't you think we should get rid of the evidence? What do you suggest? Roast pigeon tonight and save the pork pie for tomorrow?'

'An excellent idea,' Granny smiled blandly. 'In normal circumstances I might recommend serving a whole bird to each of us, but as there are eight of us and four birds, I'm sure we can eke it out with some of those wonderful vegetables from Mr Seymour. And there's that baked custard for pudding.'

She twinkled as she drew out her sharpest knife and I

collected vegetables and started to prepare them. 'It is always good policy, Christy, as I've told you many times, to keep on good terms with your neighbours. Casting your bread on the waters can certainly have practical results, as we see!'

Chapter Thirteen

The rest of Saturday was surprisingly relaxing after the turbulence of the previous day. Even Miss Preston lounged around in the garden next door before dinner, apparently writing letters though I'm fairly sure she was actually asleep. Mrs Camperdown reported that the patients at visiting hour up at Groom Hall had been agog at the many wild tales that had reached them.

Judith told me that she had been discussing Major Minton's plans with him. It transpires that in civilian life he is an historian and has asked her if she would help him with his new research. She sounded rather prim about it so perhaps she is shy? She believes this would be an interesting project and has promised all possible assistance.

I agreed solemnly that it would be an agreeable exercise and enquired about young Lt Camperdown. Alix was sitting with us at that moment and she started to laugh.

'Peter's thoughts have had a change of direction,' she told me. 'We have a new young volunteer arrived today, so I asked her to sit and talk to him and see if she could raise his spirits.'

'And has she?'

Judith and Alix both chuckled.

'Indeed she has,' Alix replied. 'You remember Essie Wakelin from school? Elder sister to our own Vera Double-You? Her mother is so delighted with the prospect of Judith's class for Vera during the week that she seems to have taken a look at the hospital when she learned I spend time there. Essie has been drooping around the house, bored to tears but doing nothing; refusing to attend tennis parties or be a proper daughter to her mother. Yesterday was apparently the last straw as she even refused to go to the May Day revels, though she did redeem herself by looking after the two Veras. Faced with an ultimatum: to be a proper support to her parents or serve her country, Essie chose the latter and turned up this morning.' She laughed. 'I don't suppose I need remind you that she is extremely pretty even if she has no discernible brains!'

'Lydia Trellis enjoyed her afternoon with Addy and Penny,' I told them. 'She was much brighter when I looked in at five o'clock and they were all very giggly because Addy had been teaching them some of those silly paper and pencil games. Consequences and so on. Neither of the other girls had come across them before and they had a great deal of fun. Mrs Camperdown says she'll see how Lydia feels at bedtime and decide then whether to stay with her all night. I don't think it will be necessary though, Lydia is recovering well from the shock.'

'An early night all round,' Alix said seriously. 'Doctor's orders!'

'From Dr Munro?' I asked innocently, and she nodded, blushing.

Sunday, 5th May, morning

Our early night must have done the trick because we all felt and looked much more relaxed on Sunday morning. I had insisted that Bella and Penny should not appear again until Monday morning. They had put in sterling work yesterday which, like Sunday, was not one of their working days and we had been extremely grateful.

'You must take your time off, Bella,' I had remonstrated. 'You work very hard as it is and you deserve a rest, so please – indulge me and do as I suggest? I don't want you to collapse with overwork! And Penny should just read a story book, just for fun.'

Last night's dinner of roast wood pigeon had been a great success and of course we had given our lodgers a taste of Mr Seymour's wine. Granny was doubly pleased, having disposed of the evidence and given pleasure to our guests. I must try to catch Niggle and thank him; and on a less happy note, I still haven't reminded him that it has always been his task to keep down the numbers of cats at Sandringham Lodge. It wasn't a pleasant prospect but things had got out of hand during his disastrous time in the army and strong measures would be necessary.

'What's the matter, Christy?' Granny looked up from her knitting – something small and white and woolly, I noticed – as I wandered into the kitchen. 'You're disturbing the peace with your fidgeting.'

'I know, I'm sorry. I can't seem to settle to anything this morning.' We usually have a roast joint on a Sunday, even though these days the butcher is practically in tears when he has to sell us something grey and full of gristle, but after last night's elegant feast we were going to eat the offerings from our neighbours and no cooking would be required today.

'I think I'll go and sit with Lydia,' I decided. 'Mrs Camperdown has been so kind but she should have a change and a rest from care.'

I suited the action to the words and waylaid our gentle lodger in next door's drawing room. Miss Preston was there too, looking as restless as I felt.

'I'm going to spend the morning with Mrs Trellis,' I announced. 'She would probably like to read another of my mother's books, I know she enjoyed the one I lent her. Why don't you ladies go into town and attend the service at the Priory?'

Mrs Camperdown looked apprehensive but I reassured her. 'I usually sit right at the back,' I remarked casually. 'All the clergy are in the Choir stalls and can't really see the congregation at the back of the church. It's easy to leave early and if you call in at The White Horse on your way to church you can make sure of a table for lunch. The landlady is a famous cook so it is always a treat, even in wartime.'

Miss Preston's eyes lit up and she bounded to her feet. 'What a splendid notion,' she said. 'Do say yes, Mrs

Camperdown!'

Ten minutes later I tapped on Lydia's door.

'May I come in? I've come to spend the morning with you if you would like that?'

My instinct was proved right. I had known there was something wrong somewhere in the house and as soon as I spoke, Lydia burst into tears. I hastily closed the door, dropped the two books I was carrying, and put my arms round her.

'There, there,' I soothed, patting her back as she hiccupped and wept. 'Tell me what I can do to help. It's not the baby, is it?' Mercifully, she shook her head and then gulped.

'No, yes… it is, but it's not what you mean. It hasn't started, it's just…everything!'

Well, that was comprehensive. I held on to her and waited.

'I'm so frightened,' she shuddered and clutched at me. 'It was terrible. I thought I would die. I can't go through it again. I'd rather kill myself first.'

'What do you mean?' I was horrified at the anguish in her voice. 'Have you already had a baby, Lydia?'

'It was at the orphanage not far from Salisbury; the vicar used to – well, you know. When they realised I was in the family way he got them to beat me but I didn't lose the baby, not then anyway.'

All I could do was hold her and let her cry on my shoulder.

'I was frightened when Canon Camperdown came to the hospital,' she whispered. 'He used to visit the orphanage every month. No, he never touched any of us, but he used to look. You know. And I'm sure he knew what went on.'

I was appalled but just made soothing noises, feeling quite at a loss because, no, I didn't know what she meant about the Canon looking. (A girl at school, the doctor's daughter, once tried to tell Alix and me something about babies but it struck us as ridiculous. Surely you would laugh. Is that why marriage is described as 'an excellent mystery'?)

'When I went into labour,' Lydia sobbed. 'They beat me again and again and it went on for days and days and the baby wouldn't come. They were horrible, just horrible and

172

my baby was dead anyway.'

I mopped her up and offered to fetch tea or cocoa or anything, even the last glass of wine, but she clung to me.

'As soon as I could, I ran away and got a housemaid's job in Woking and changed my name from Lizzie to Lydia.'

'It's a lovely name and it suits you.' All I could do was go on hugging her. 'Oh, Lydia, I never imagined anything so terrible. You poor, poor child, but you're safe now. We're looking after you.'

She seemed comforted but the dreadful tale was uppermost in her mind and I thought she would be better for telling me.

'The housemaid's job was where I learned how to talk nicely and all about clothes and manners. It was an old lady and she'd been a governess to a posh family and she made a pet of me. I'm a quick learner. There was only me and the cook and we did it all between us, it wasn't hard work and the mistress was kind. The cook's nephew used to visit her and a couple of months after I started there, he visited a lot more often and then we... Anyway, he was called up last August and told me he'd marry me on his first leave if I let him...'

I could understand. She was just a little girl, lost and lonely and desperate for affection. I cuddled her close and my own cheeks were damp as she sobbed in my arms. Taking a deep breath, she insisted on telling the rest.

'You can guess what happened. The cook was heart-broken when she got the telegram, and so was I, doubly so. I was afraid in case I might be in the family way again though it had only been a week but the thought of another baby nearly drove me mad. He wasn't killed in France, mind you. He was larking about on a wall, so we heard, and broke his neck when he fell off! It was his first day in camp; he never even got out of England.'

'What did you do?' We were both lying on her bed by now, her head on my shoulder.

'Mr Trellis lived next door, with his sister. He was really brave, you know, even though you wouldn't think it, because

173

he joined up as a private to begin with. Luckily, he was never sent abroad and I don't know if it was because he was a chartered accountant but he was commissioned quite quickly and later transferred into the Pay Corps. I never saw him till he came home on leave at the end of August. That was a week after cook's nephew died. I saw him, Mr Trellis, watching me when I pegged out the washing and he'd see me come out the door to go to the shops and I knew he'd grab his hat and hurry out too, making believe he was going for a stroll, or needed a bottle of ink, or a packet of envelopes.

'I made a plan,' she said, wiping her eyes. 'I'm not proud of it but it was all I could think of. One evening when I knew his sister had gone to stay the night with her friend, I could see he was weeding in the front garden so I dressed up quickly and went out. Where was I going, he asked? I said it was my birthday and as I had no family left I thought I'd go for a stroll, the weather was so pleasant.

'He took the bait and suggested a celebration dinner at the inn and I slipped some brandy into his glass of wine. I'd taken the bottle from my old lady's sideboard. Of course he got drunk really quickly so I helped him home and put him to bed. He fumbled around a bit but nothing much happened and I just put up with it and luckily he never tried again. In the morning he woke up with a thumping headache and a naked young woman blushing beside him in his bed.

'Of course he did the decent thing.'

She seemed calmer so I thought I could leave her for five minutes.

'I'm only going to find us some elevenses,' I reassured her. 'There's plenty of cake. I'll be back before you know it but you need to keep your strength up.'

She had more colour in her cheeks after something to eat and I ventured a question.

'You said Mr Trellis didn't... But you're expecting. Does that mean the cook's nephew...?'

'It must!' She was wide-eyed with despair. 'But he didn't look anything like Mr Trellis, he was really big-built – and anyway – he had ginger hair!' Her tragic wail set off more tears. 'The baby will look like him, I know it will. Everyone will know how bad I've been and Mr Trellis will cast me off.' She was shaking again. 'I'll have to run away as soon as the baby is born.'

'No, you won't,' I said, trying to disguise the quaver in my own voice. 'I'll think of something.' (Yes, Christabel, I asked myself. And what on earth do you think you can do?)

We sat in silence until Lydia looked at me from under those slanting dark brows.

'There's something else,' she whispered. 'Something terrible that I did. I'm going to die in labour this time, I know I am, but I can't. Not with a mortal sin on my conscience.'

I took a moment or two to shift from panicking about changeling babies, a vengeful Captain Trellis and an impending and terrifying birth to a bewildering digression into sin.

'Whatever are you talking about, Lydia? And you're not going to die, I won't let you.'

'I found out he had wealthy relations in Ramalley, a Mr and Miss Diplock. He told me that he was the only cousin they had, so if anything happened to them it would come to him.' She looked wistful as she recalled her daydream. 'I pictured a great big house and a park and gardens and when he heard that Mr Diplock had died last year, I thought it would be a good idea to move here and get her to like me. That's why I persuaded Mr Trellis, Digby, to put Ramalley as a choice when he was at Netley. I really thought she would be pleased to have a new family and a baby; an interest to occupy her when she'd lost her brother and was left all alone.

'You saw her at the hospital. She pretended to be nice about our marriage and about the baby and Mr Trellis was pleased, but when she caught me alone she was nasty. She said horrible things about me and I was frightened she would repeat them to my husband.

'When I saw her at that May Day maypole dance I remembered the things she'd said and I felt spiteful so I thought I'd trip her up. Make her look a fool. That's all I meant but my hat was making my head hurt so I'd just taken the pin out to fix it more comfortably when she came and stood in front of me. Right in front! It was deliberate, she smirked at me, knowing I couldn't see a thing past her. Without thinking I hooked my foot round her ankle and she started to wobble but instead of falling forwards she fell sort of sideways and knocked me down too. I screamed. I was frightened for the baby but she didn't really hurt me, it was more that I was squashed and couldn't breathe. It was terrifying. The thing was though, I was still holding the hat pin and I kept stabbing at her to get her off me. It must have gone straight into her heart.'

Lydia stared at me with wide, horrified brown eyes.

'I murdered her!'

She burst into a storm of tears and I felt battered by this new development, (though I admit part of me thought this would make a wonderful plot if only Mother or I wrote penny dreadfuls for women.)

'I'm very sure you didn't,' I said, soothingly, putting the idea firmly aside. 'We all know she never wore a corset so there was nothing to protect her – um – chest, and that was a thin cotton dress she had on, quite unsuitable. Alix told me that the doctor, the old one – Dr Salt – did say that she had multiple contusions and abrasions but that there was nothing to be learned from that. She was a large woman and she had a very big bosom so the injuries were consistent with her fall.'

Lydia was inconsolable. 'But I wanted to kill her by then. It had stopped being a game, to make her look foolish and I kept stabbing at her, on and on. It wasn't just to get her off me.' She was wild-eyed and hysterical now, small hands clutching frantically at me.

'Suppose even just one of those stabs pierced her heart, Christabel? That could have been the blow that killed her. I really, really wanted her dead. That's murder.'

'Lydia, you didn't murder her, you can't possibly have done. She died of a heart attack. Remember that was what the doctor wrote on the death certificate. It's official.' I wasn't at all sure about it but we were both far too exhausted to go on like this. I was glad to see her lean back against her pillows and try to compose herself.

'How old are you anyway, Lydia?' The question had been bothering me and at least it served to distract her from her obsession with murder. 'And don't tell me you're eighteen, even if that's what your husband believes.'

'You promise never to tell?' There was a sudden conspiratorial gleam in her dark eyes as she glanced at me. 'Well then, I was fourteen last August! It's perfectly legal.'

'I know!' And so it is though the idea that Addy too could be legally married if she took it into her head to do so, sent chills down my spine but I just exchanged a wry smile with Lydia 'My lips are sealed, and now I really must get on. I'm going to bring you some soup, and when you've drunk it you're to have a rest,' I told her firmly. 'You mustn't worry, I'll think of something and everything will be all right.'

I carried out my plan and settled her with soup and toast and a few grapes but as I made to leave the room, I remembered something else that had puzzled me.

'Your hat pin must have been extra sharp, surely, Lydia?' (What an irrelevant question compared to all the previous drama.)

'Yes,' Lydia laid her soup spoon on the tray and looked at me. 'I always keep my hat pins really sharp.'

I was curious. 'But why?'

Lydia gave me a world-weary look. 'In my walk of life you need your wits about you, Christabel. A sharpened hatpin can deter most unwanted advances.'

I made a mental note to discuss this useful snippet of information with Alix, and Addy. You never know.

Chapter Fourteen

I was relieved that Lydia seemed calmer because I was now terrified. The trouble with being a writer, particularly of thrilling yarns is that your imagination never stops picturing disaster. And Lydia was faced with what seemed to me to be insuperable problems.

Which of them was the more dangerous? There was no question which Lydia believed to be the one that would bring disgrace down on her. A baby that looked nothing like Captain Trellis would cause raised eyebrows for ever, and how could it possibly resemble him? (How many girls of my age would know anything about that anyway? Particularly when I'm not very sure of it myself?)

Could Lydia be persuaded to brazen it out for the rest of her life? I shivered, remembering what she had told me; the vicious cruelty of the orphanage, the hideous labour and the death of her baby. For a child to have endured so much was completely outside my comfortable existence. It broke my heart and I knew I was bound to help her, in any way I could. Perhaps it wasn't exactly, 'There but for the grace of God', but it could have been any of us – in another time or place.

We all, particularly the women – of this house, this town, this country – live under a dark shadow but it is rarely mentioned during everyday life. Why would we? So many of the men face worse horrors. The war dominates our waking and sleeping hours and is a constant in our lives; in fact the war is our life so although our lives are shaped by it, we manage and we pretend this is how life is always lived. Lydia's story shocked me out of this comfortable pretence so much that the darkness seemed to close in on me for a moment until I forced myself to acknowledge it.

I paced about my bedroom until it occurred to me that even Mother might hear me and be aware of a disturbing influence, so I sat down and thought hard, whereupon an idea actually flashed into my head. Papa! Could I send Lydia and her baby to Australia? We might not have an address for Papa but Miss Agatha Trubody did have a London account with our bank. Would it be possible to send a message to Papa somehow and ask him to help? I would gladly use some of our latest windfall to set her up.

Even in this moment of distress I wavered. Asking Papa for help? But he would really like Lydia, I told myself. Brave, desperate and possibly willing to enter into his schemes, she might prove to be the adventurous daughter he had never had.

I burst into tears, which was not helpful so I slipped into the bathroom and had a quick wash, tidied my hair and put my clothes straight. A pale, almost unrecognisable face stared out of the looking-glass and I sat on the edge of the bath and thought about Lydia and her mortal sin.

I could understand her guilt at having murder in her heart…I pulled myself together angrily. No you can't, you have no idea. You didn't like Miss Diplock because she was a nuisance and that was all, but Lydia saw her as a real threat, on top of all the other misery hanging over her.

I gave up. I had told Lydia we'd talk about it later and that in the meantime she was to stay in bed and try to keep calm. I looked at the pale Christy in the glass and told her the same thing, but I don't think she was convinced.

Sunday, 5th May, afternoon

'It's surprisingly peaceful,' I remarked as Granny found me sitting on the wooden bench by the hen run. Not that the hens were inside because they were pottering about the garden, all except Kaiser Bill, of course, who goes her own way even without being broody. This afternoon she was sulking on her untidy nest.

'Haven't we had more than enough excitement in recent

days to last us for a long time? Are you expecting even more alarms?' she asked, raising an eyebrow as she sat down beside me. 'Move over, Christy, I've spent an hour doing the mending and I need five quiet minutes in the sunshine. I can't imagine how Addy manages to poke holes in her stockings almost every week. I've never noticed anything sharp about her feet that could explain it.'

Granny says that kind of thing so seriously that most people don't realise she's joking but as it was just the two of us she did allow her mouth to quirk slightly as she caught my eye. I love my grandmother very much and I try to imitate her in as many ways as possible. We loved Mother and Papa, (though sometimes it has been a distinct effort!) but they have never inspired that kind of admiration. Exasperated affection has always been the major emotion evoked by our parents.

'You're looking very smart,' I said. 'You should go out more often.' She was wearing her best grey coat and skirt and looked elegant. '

'I could hardly refuse when Mrs Seymour invited me to tea. She is a kind, if nervous woman and as we know, she has an extremely good cook.' She raised an eyebrow. 'If I'm offered any pastries to bring home I shan't succumb to false pride and will accept them graciously.' She hesitated, glancing round the sunny garden. 'You'll be all right, won't you, Christy?'

'Of course,' I nodded. 'I've made a really good start on The New Girls at St Mary's School, it's much more fun than writing the serials for the boys.' I thought about it for a moment. 'I hadn't realised what a disturbing effect it was having on me. Trying to turn that hideous misery into entertainment – bread and circuses – and yes, I know the young men and boys enjoy the tales, but I can't tell you what a weight it is off my shoulders.'

Granny touched my arm lightly and I was comforted. I carried on ticking off my list of family and lodgers and their whereabouts.

'Alix has gone up to help at Groom Hall...' I looked

sideways at her and Granny actually grinned.

'As long as she doesn't get hurt,' she said.

'He won't hurt her. I've already warned him!' Granny's smile broadened and I shrugged. 'He's perfectly serious about her, but I think he wants to give her time to know her own mind and he won't hurry her. As for Addy, I believe she has invited Penny to spend the afternoon helping to sort out all our school story books and arrange them downstairs in the classroom. It seems a harmless enough occupation and I'm so glad to see them getting along so well.'

I went on with my list. 'Mother is lying down, I think, though I didn't linger. She's had a busy morning so that's good; the hens are enjoying the sunshine; the dog and cats are behaving reasonably well. Mrs Camperdown and Miss Preston were to lunch at The White Horse after church and will go straight to the Hall; and Lydia is having a nap. I looked in not long ago and she was sound asleep. Oh yes, and Judith is taking a book up to the Hall for Major Minton. Apparently they discussed it yesterday and he expressed an interest in reading it.'

Again Granny and I exchanged looks but said nothing. We are very fond of Judith although only I know of her doomed previous attachment. If there is a chance of a pleasant friendship for her, we will certainly not interfere.

I stood up when Granny rose at three o'clock and accompanied her to the front door. 'That's a very smart feather,' I said as she adjusted her hat. 'Nobody would ever know it came from a contraband pheasant. Give my regards to Mrs Seymour and enjoy your party.' I gave her a quick kiss because I knew how much of an ordeal the party would be to such a shy woman, but I also knew that she would be warmly welcomed. Besides, she has sent us off to countless parties with the bracing words, 'It will be good for you' ringing in our ears. Time for the tables to turn.

'Look in on Mrs Trellis now and then.' She hesitated at the door, casting a curious look at me. 'Are you all right, Christy? There's nothing to worry about. If anything happens you can send to the hospital. That poor girl was still very shaken up yesterday, and no wonder. She seems better today but we should keep an eye on her. She doesn't seem to know when her baby is due but it can't be far away.'

I knew better, regarding the 'nothing to worry about' but I reassured Granny and waved her on her way then I wandered round the garden to see whether I could find any eggs. It's remarkable how hens who have a comfortable, secure house to live in prefer to play a complicated game of hide-and-seek with us by choosing the most obscure hidey-holes to lay their eggs.

'Oh, well done, Bad Fairy,' I exclaimed as I retrieved a very small egg from behind the wheelbarrow. The bantam strutted towards me, clearly bent on defending her egg, but I skipped out of the way and made a dash for the back door. Now I was doing it, calling her by name. Alix insisted the bantam was sinister but I couldn't see it myself. She was assertive, that was true, but the other hens were frightfully meek and seemed resigned to being marshalled and chivvied from pillar to post from now on. But honestly, Bad Fairy? I ask you!

Reluctantly I turned my thoughts back to Lydia's dilemma. During the last hour or so I had pictured Mr Trellis and the way he doted on his pretty little wife. He glowed with pride in her youth and her condition. Could he reject her? Would he cast her aside even if the baby did turn out to be a hulking red-head with no resemblance to its slightly-built putative father? I thought not. He would wonder, of course, but all Lydia would need to do would be to exclaim, 'The baby looks just like my father, or brother, or mother. Long legs and red hair run in the family!'

There would be gossip but with our staunch backing – and I know my family well enough to be sure that it would be staunch – Lydia could get away with it. And so I would tell her.

No, it was the other suggestion that haunted me now, as it haunted Lydia. Not that she had murdered Miss Diplock, nobody would believe that for a moment, but what about that idea of a single stab wound causing instant death? Was that even possible? I don't know why the idea upset me so much but I couldn't leave it alone. It was fixed there at the back of my mind all the time now. The only person I could think of asking was Dr Munro and I shrank from the prospect.

I had reminded Lydia about the official cause of death and was sure the inquest would record the same, so I forced myself to go back indoors and calm down.

'Christy?' Addy looked anxious, which is very unlike her, and she and Penny were hovering uncertainly in the hall as I came out of the kitchen. Addy scuttled towards me.

'There's something wrong with Lydia,' she faltered, half excited, mostly apprehensive. 'I just put my head round into next door to make sure the cats hadn't sneaked in when I heard her making some strange noises. I think she's crying too.'

Oh Lord! Here it was! I summoned up a calm, competent smile, not that it deceived her, I could tell. 'I'll go and see what's up,' I said, carefully not letting my voice wobble, even though I was more and more worried. Here we were, with no Granny, no other lady lodgers, no Alix, nobody older or more experienced than I was. I suppose it's significant that at no time did I ever consider calling for my mother's help, even though she has given birth to four children. Which meant that to assist me, if it was what I was afraid it was, I only had two young girls of thirteen and fifteen, not to mention the fourteen-year old mother-to-be.

I didn't bother to knock, Lydia and I had been through far too much in the morning for such niceties and, oh, dear heavens, it was happening. It was really happening. Her face screwed up with pain, Lydia crouched against the pillows on the imposing walnut bed that we had rescued from the miscellaneous lot of furniture we'd inherited from our late neighbour, the hoarder.

'It's all right, Lydia,' I told her as calmly as I could, slipping my arm round her shoulder. 'I've got you and I won't let you go.'

In the doorway Addy and Penny looked even more anxious than I felt so I took some deep breaths. (Addy, faced with a real medical emergency rather than being allowed to dissect a chicken scientifically, looked both excited and apprehensive but she braced her shoulders and gave me an encouraging nod.)

'Penny,' I said quietly. 'I want you to run up to the Hall and ask Dr Munro or Sister Wisden to come down to us at once. Tell them Mrs Trellis is having her baby. As fast as you can.'

Bending over Lydia I asked, 'When did this start? You were sound asleep half an hour ago when I looked in on you.'

'About ten minutes ago,' she gasped, halted in mid-sentence as a pain struck. 'It hurts, Christabel, it hardly stops at all. I'm so frightened.'

'I'll keep you safe,' I said again, praying I could make it true, and I waved Penny off on her errand. 'Addy, I know people in books always boil water, so will you do that, please? Kettles in both houses and the big saucepans too.' I had no idea why boiling water was needed but at least we would be sure of a constant supply of tea.

'Addy,' I whispered, out of Lydia's hearing. 'Do the water first then and see if there's anything about childbirth in The Family Health Book or any of your medical ones.'

She made a face but nodded and ran off to set the water boiling.

With both girls out of the way I helped Lydia to the cloakroom while I tidied her bed, only to hear a shriek of dismay from her.

'What is it? Oh...' I surveyed the puddle on the floor. 'Don't worry, that saves us having to change the sheets again.' This inanity struck me as extremely lame but seemed to cheer her up so I left her in the cloakroom while I dug out an ancient rubber sheet from the scullery. No need to mention that it was what we use for feline maternity matters if the cats decide to produce their litters in a good armchair, or worse, in one of our beds – provided we get a chance to intercept them in time. I swiftly tucked it under the top sheet as a further

184

precaution; (the mattress had cost a fortune and even at a moment like this, my practical mind rebelled at the prospect of further expense). I smoothed it just in time as she reappeared. I helped her into a fresh nightgown, arranged a stack of towels old and new on the dressing table, and manhandled her into the big bed.

What else might we need? A sponge to cool her face and – oh yes – a jug of water and a glass so she could sip as required.

There was no time for dainty sips of water. It was like nothing I had ever imagined and I still don't know how on earth any of us survived it.

Lydia suddenly started to make noises like an animal, deep in her throat, and to my horror she clambered to her knees at the head of the bed, hanging on to the bed post. I tried to hold her but she struck me away, still grunting like a pig until the pain receded and gave her a brief respite.

As soon as I held her writhing body I was slippery with sweat, just as she was, and I barely noticed Addy come into the room and let out a small shriek of her own at the sight of us. 'There's no sign of Dr Munro,' she mouthed at me, but at that moment we heard our own doorbell ring, the offbeat clang unmistakable. Addy and I exchanged thankful glances and she ran to answer the door.

'Oh, goodness!' I heard her exclaim. 'Well, you'll have to do, we need help here now this minute! Take off your hat and coat and I'll find you an apron. Come on, Christy needs you. Hurry!'

Who on earth could it be? It was obviously nobody from Groom Hall and I just prayed it wouldn't turn out to be Wilfred!

Chapter Fifteen

Addy opened the bedroom door and thrust a flustered Bertha Makepeace into the room. She stared aghast as Lydia shifted down the bed on to her side and panted.

'Have you ever delivered a baby, Miss Bertha?' I whispered and she shook her head, looking terrified. 'Nor have I,' I confessed. 'However, we'll keep that quiet for the moment, and anyway I've watched lots of kittens being born.'

'That's bound to be a tremendous help,' Bertha managed a shaky laugh. 'What do you want me to do?'

'Pretend you've done this dozens of times; she needs reassurance – and so do I!'

Addy reappeared with some old sheets from the linen cupboard. 'The textbooks are useless,' she said scornfully. 'We'll have to make it up as we go along!'

Suddenly, everything started happening again, and it was the most primitive, messy, noisy business. I'd had no idea. In paintings and books the new mother lies pale but exalted, languidly holding a sleeping infant clad in a priceless lace christening gown.

There was nothing languid about what was happening in this room. Some kind of instinct made me lie down on the bed, facing Lydia and holding her hands, and that seemed to comfort her. I cuddled her and sang and stroked her hair and felt as close to her as I do to my sisters.

'You're the bravest girl I've ever known,' I whispered. 'Such a strong, brave little girl. We won't let anyone hurt you, not ever. Granny and I will look after you and your baby if the worst happens. We all will, you won't have to do it alone, I promise.'

We soldiered on like that for a while, leaping to attention to help Lydia uphill and downhill, with less and less rest in between. It was all happening so fast. I kept thinking we're too young to do this, and with an inward whimper that demanded to know where were the grown-ups? And why didn't they come?

I managed to catch Bertha and whisper that somehow or other we had to find out whether the baby's head was in sight and that it was going to be her task. It took her a moment or two to understand what that would involve but although she gave a faint squeak, she nodded and gingerly set about it. It was a daunting prospect for a middle-aged spinster. Or, come to think of it, for an eighteen-year old one, but it had to be Bertha. I couldn't let go of Lydia and there was no question of Addy, prospective medical student or not. Fortunately she didn't think of it.

Suddenly, the strange compulsive rhythm of the contractions changed yet again and Lydia began to pant heavily then, with a huge groan, she pushed and – oh my God – we all saw the baby's head emerge. It was the most astonishing thing I had ever seen. Lydia lay back in my arms for a moment, panting and gasping, then there was another of those terrifying animal grunts and with a great push, the baby was born, yelling his head off.

Lydia, laughing and sobbing uncontrollably, reached out for the baby and clutched him to her, and Bertha hastily wrapped an old sheet round the pair of them. We had no idea what to do next. The mess was indescribable and all I could think of was how on earth we would manage all the washing. Even more disturbing than the sight of ourselves, the dishevelled amateur midwives, was the presence of the baby's pulsating cord – it was alive! – so we all averted our eyes.

I was so exhausted I could barely hobble to the head of the bed, but with the spectre of Lydia's fears of the morning, I had to know.

'Tell me,' I croaked. She knew what I meant and nervously pulled the towel away from the baby boy's face.

'But...but how is that possible?' she gasped.

'Well,' Addy broke the silence. 'There's no doubt who's the father!'

We all gazed at the button nose in the round red face, and the tuft of mouse-coloured hair on the little bald head. Then Addy whispered in my ear. 'He's even got the Queen Anne bandy legs!'

Lydia raised herself on an elbow and stared at her baby, while Addy was fascinated and I struggled with hysterical laughter.

'He only needs a pair of gold wire spectacles,' breathed Bertha and she was right. The baby was the image of Digby Trellis.

We had no time to do more than stare at the baby and exchange startled glances because the next minute there was a ring at the front door, a tap on the bedroom door, and what seemed like a dozen people surged in.

'Oh, thank goodness!' Grown-ups at last. I could have burst into tears at the sight of Sister Wisden, my sister Alix, and Dr Munro, except that tears were already pouring unchecked down my cheeks.

'I thought I told you to not to overstretch yourself, Christabel? Good girl, though. Let's see what you've been getting up to now,' Fergus smiled, surprising me by putting his arm round me briefly before he went on to attend to the exhausted young mother.

When Sister Wisden bent over Lydia, who turned back the sheet to show off the baby, I saw a smile spread across her face as she recognised the likeness.

'Oh, well done, Mrs Trellis,' she said warmly and Lydia glowed at the praise. 'What a dear little fellow. The image of his father, and how healthy. Listen to those powerful lungs!' She looked over her shoulder at me. 'I'll take over here, Christabel and don't worry, one of the nurses will come down tonight and the hospital will take care of mother and baby. You have done quite enough.'

Alix hugged us all then pushed Bertha, Addy and me

towards the kitchen where one of the hospital orderlies was filling a pail at the sink with hot water - I knew it would come in handy! However, we were soon stripped of our messy garments which were put to soak in cold water in the scullery, even Bertha. (We were all on first name terms now and I doubt we will ever go back to any kind of formality.)

Alix fetched dressing gowns for all three of us and made us go upstairs. She pushed Bertha into the lodgers' bathroom first.

'You'll feel better for a good wash,' she urged. 'And then you're going to lie down and have a rest.' She led Addy and me to our own bathroom. 'You two can share,' she said. 'I won't suggest a rest for you, because I want to know all about it, so I'm going to make tea. You'd better get dressed though, the house is full of strange people.'

It was such a relief to have her arms round me and I gave a sigh of relief, knowing I could rely on her to organise dinner, beds, washing, and whatever else was needed.

I listened for Bertha and caught her looking lost on next door's landing.

'Come and lie down on Judith's bed,' I suggested. 'I'll make sure someone sends a message to your brother and he can send a car and some fresh clothes for you, but you must have a rest first.'

'I – I'm quite bewildered,' she confessed. 'I only called in to let you know that Edgar and Henry were spending the day going through Portia's affairs, even though it's a Sunday. Edgar is anxious to expedite matters under the sad circumstances.' She dashed a hand across her eyes and I showed her Judith's small room.

'Go to sleep, Bertha,' I said gently, covering her with the eiderdown.

Downstairs, I found Penny jiggling up and down in the hall, her eyes round with wonder and I was about to suggest to Addy that they should keep to their original plan for this Sunday and catalogue our books for Judith, when Sister Wisden slipped out of Lydia's room.

'Do you know anyone who could lend you some baby clothes,' she whispered. 'That poor girl seems not to have made any preparation at all and of course the husband has no idea!'

'Oh my…' I was so tired I could hardly think, then… 'Penny? Do you think your neighbour would lend us some things for the baby? She doesn't have a small baby at the moment, does she?'

'I'll go straightaway,' she said joyfully. 'And I'll bring our Bella back with me to help, she won't want to miss out on all the excitement.'

Addy decided to go with Penny which was a relief and as I wondered what to do next, Sister Wisden touched my arm.

'I completely forgot to tell you,' she said looking guilty. 'We brought Captain Trellis down with us. I think your sister put him in your own house somewhere.'

Captain Trellis? My heart sank but there was no-one else to deal with it so I sidled out into the hall. There was no sign of the new-made father but I heard male voices in our own drawing room. Surely that was Wilfred? But surely not, at a time like this?

'Hello, Christy.' There is no end to that boy's self-confidence – or is it cheek? I stared wearily as he beamed at me, welcoming me into my own home. 'I've brought Captain Trellis over here to keep him out from underfoot next door and Alix says she's making tea for everyone.' He leaned towards me. 'Have you got anything stronger? He's rather shocked.'

'The very thing,' I said gratefully. 'Wilfred, I do apologise. I was cross when I saw you here but if you'll take care of him, I'll be eternally thankful. I'll get the brandy.' He twinkled at me. 'Oh, very well,' I added. 'You may have a drop too but only a drop or your mother will never let you come here again.'

Alix produced biscuits and cake – mostly seed cake from the kindly townsfolk. (Not that we mind, we all like the taste of caraway). Wilfred dosed Captain Trellis with a generous measure of brandy and Alix and I huddled in our dining room while I described the birth in all its detail, crying on her shoulder as she held me in stunned silence.

The grandfather clock in our hall wheezed asthmatically and chimed the half hour. Half-past what though? Half-past four! Four? Was that all? Granny had left our house at three o'clock, intending to walk into town and arrive at Mrs Seymour's tea party at four. They would still be chatting politely and not even have started on the bread-and-butter, let alone reached the cake stage by now. It felt as though a lifetime had passed since I'd cheerfully waved my grandmother goodbye.

I dragged myself back into our drawing room to see what was happening, only to find Wilfred still acting as host and jollying along the new father. At that moment, Dr Munro appeared and shook Mr Trellis by the hand.

'They're ready for you now, old chap,' he said heartily. 'Your wife has been splendid and your son is as healthy a little fellow as I've ever seen.'

I shed another tear – I couldn't seem to stop myself – and Wilfred thrust a glass into my hand.

'Here,' he urged. 'Drink this, Christabel. To wet the baby's head.'

Without thinking, I obeyed and spluttered.

'That's neat brandy,' I objected, feeling warmed all the same.

'I know,' he chuckled and poured himself a tot and held it up in a toast. 'Here's health, wealth and happiness to baby Trellis!'

Sunday, 5th May, evening

As Granny said later on, 'Thank goodness for this large pork pie!' That was the one donated by one of our kind and inquisitive Ramalley ladies the day before. With lettuce and radishes from our own garden, the cucumber from Wilfred's father, and some splendid tomatoes from another well-wisher's greenhouse, we were able to cater for our lodgers as well as the family. Someone had even sent in a bread-and-butter pudding so we were very well fed.

Sister Wisden despatched the orderly back to Groom Hall with all our soiled linens to be dealt with by their own laundry and he had driven back down, bringing the night nurse to take over the nursery. 'You don't need to feed her,' Sister said. 'She brings her own rations! Our patients rarely need attention during the night so she can easily be spared. She is very eager for this change of routine. A baby makes such a delightful contrast to caring for wounded men.' The nurse's rations included ample supplies for us too and Alix fell happily to work cutting sandwiches to keep our visitors going.

Sister Wisden also kindly undertook to send a telephone message to Bertha Makepeace's brother, Cousin Edgar, asking him to collect her discreetly and with a change of clothes. Fortunately, a solicitor must receive many unorthodox commissions and Bertha was safely home by now.

Granny had arrived home from Mrs Seymour's tea party laden with cheese straws and cream puffs for which the Seymour cook was renowned. I heard the back door open and our eyes met as she rapidly took in the situation. (It didn't take a Sherlock Holmes, you could hear the baby in both houses!) Touching my shoulder she made her way to her room to take off her hat and coat.

'An eventful afternoon, I see, Christy?' was all she said. I knew she could tell that although I had been through something momentous, I was now in a slightly calmer frame of mind. That's one of the restful things about her, she sums us up instantly and doesn't fuss. Once in a while Mother used to wake up to her maternal duties and make our lives hideous while she tried to behave as a model parent. Granny never does that.

She was followed shortly by an agitated Mrs Camperdown and an intrigued Miss Preston agog to be told the whole story. Inspired, I pushed them into our drawing room and handed them over to Wilfred who was still there. As always, he acted with perfect aplomb and arranged a light meal for them.

Fergus Munro emerged from Lydia's room, smiled at the impromptu tea party, and beckoned me out into the hall.

'How are you feeling, Christy?' I noted the friendly abbreviation and managed a smile. 'I just wanted to tell you that you three amateur midwives did done a fine job. I'm very proud of you all, but Mrs Trellis insists that you were her main support.'

I glowed with pride. 'We did it together,' I told him. 'And Fergus? Make sure you praise Addy. She was a tower of strength. I relied on her at every turn and she didn't let me down, not once.'

Wilfred's tea party broke up when Penny, Addy, and Bella appeared pushing their neighbour's perambulator which was laden with baby clothes, sheets, napkins and everything Baby Trellis could possibly need in the near future.

'She says to keep it all,' Bella told me as she whisked into the house. 'Her husband has gone off with that brass-haired hussy from the Home & Colonial Stores, and she says he'll never darken her door again, so there'll be no more babies!' She patted my shoulder, put on her apron and went off to scrub anything that came her way. This was her idea of a really good time!

I was touched by the kindly neighbour's generosity – and of course I would be recompensing her first thing tomorrow.

By then dinnertime approached so our two lady lodgers repaired to their own rooms and I pushed Wilfred out of the house and, to my surprise, kissing him gratefully on the cheek.

'You've been such a help,' I said and tottered back into the house.

I left Granny and Alix in charge of dinner and suddenly remembered the hens. I need not have worried. Six of our chickens pecked happily around the vegetable patch while

Bad Fairy – and I'm beginning to agree with Alix that she might have the Evil Eye – looked sinister as she stalked a butterfly down by the old stable.

That left Kaiser Bill and I steeled myself to poke my head into the coop. How long could we bear to leave her sitting forlornly on a barren clutch? But what was this? An eggshell? Two? I was met with contented clucking, something we had never heard from Bill in her entire existence. Peeping out from under her fluffed-up feathers I counted three tiny chicks.

'Oh, Kaiser Bill!' My heart leaped. Suddenly our household had emerged from the shadows and here was yet more evidence of renewal, of life and birth and light. I might be grasping at straws but it was a great comfort at that moment. 'Oh, what a clever old lady you are.'

Monday, 6th May, morning

After the momentous events of the previous week it was almost a relief to settle back into our usual routine. Alix made a face at herself in the looking glass as she tilted her hat to a becoming angle.

'I wonder how Mrs Redfern has enjoyed her week in Bournemouth?' she said. 'She's bound to be irritable this morning, she always is when she's been travelling. Oh well, I'll have plenty of news to distract her today and at least I'll be up at the hospital this afternoon.'

Her blue eyes sparkled and we smiled at each other. There had been no time for confidences but I suspected she had solved the dilemma as to whether she really, truly was in love. Her joy made me feel warm and happy too.

She was still my sister though, however much in love she might be, and she hesitated at the back door.

'There's something on your mind, isn't there?'

I shook my head and said nothing so she made a face at me.

'Don't be silly, Christabel. Do you think I don't know when you're in a state?' She frowned. 'If you won't tell me or Granny (and I know you haven't said anything to her because I asked), Fergus is the proper person to confide in.'

I stared at her and she flashed a smile at me.

'I'm right, aren't I? Talk to him. I'll warn him you need a consultation. That way you'll have to talk to him.'

It was astonishing how the advent of one very small male person changed the atmosphere in our two entirely female households! Talk of the baby dominated every conversation and none of us could think of anything else.

I realised that far from worrying that we had only three new guests next door, as I had – was it only a week ago? I was grateful that the remaining beds had not been taken. How could we possibly have coped?

The night nurse reported that mother and child had spent a relatively peaceful night but she then said that she might have to ration visits. I smiled guiltily. I hadn't slept well, which was probably not surprising, so I think I was the first person that morning to pop my head round the door and ask Lydia how she was, but I certainly would not be the last. And yes, I did slyly pick up the baby and cuddle him for a few moments. He's a dear little thing and very healthy, despite the services of his makeshift birth attendants.

'Does he have a name yet, Lydia?' I handed him back to his radiant mother who had fallen utterly in love with her baby and could hardly bear to let anyone else hold him. I bent to give her a kiss.

'He'll be Digby, of course,' she said proudly and then... 'Oh, Christabel! I can't thank you enough for what you've done for me. Mr Trellis is so pleased and proud and he says that when he is discharged from the army we're to move into Miss Diplock's house and he will set up his own accountancy practice.' She looked ecstatic at this modest ambition. 'Just think! I'll be properly middle-class, a real lady!'

I thought her plans would succeed. She is clever and adaptable and now has Little Digby to fight for. And she has friends in us.

Breakfast in both houses was finished when I opened our own front door to Miss Acton who had arrived eager to attend to Mother's wants. For a second week too, for which I was – and am – sincerely grateful.

'Miss Acton,' I greeted her warmly as she entered the hall. 'I wanted to catch you and tell you how very happy we are that you and Mother are working so well together. I do hope you are equally suited? And settling into life Ramalley?'

'Indeed, indeed,' she clasped her hands together and her voice throbbed. 'Your mother is a genius, Miss Christabel and it is my great privilege to be her assistant. As to the town, I find it most agreeable and have begun to worship regularly at the Priory. Such a coincidence too! My first service was at Evensong on Wednesday and it was taken by the new curate. I feel a great affinity with him, two newcomers as we both are, and I believe he felt a connection too.'

Oh dear! I smiled weakly and scuttled into the kitchen. Bertha Makepeace would have to deal with this if it became a problem, I decided. I had too much to think about already.

I was intrigued to realise that Miss Acton, like Mother, appeared to have no interest at all in our new and noisy inhabitant although it was impossible not to be aware of him. I gradually worked out that although Mother lives in a literary world of her own, so does Elise Acton in her own way. She is so absorbed in her role as guardian and slave to a famous author, as well as her own romantic fantasies, that she has no room for real life. She and Mother are very well suited!

I ought to make it clear that we do not actually lock Mother in her room to prevent her from finding out how the household runs! On the contrary, one or other of us makes her come downstairs after breakfast so that Bella can turn out her room, change the bedlinen, and generally tidy up.

While this is going on we insist that she must take a turn round the garden though she has lately refused to go beyond the gate which is something I must think about. I worry that she might be afraid to leave the safety of home, and that must be avoided.

This morning she surprised me.

'I heard a baby crying,' she said abruptly.

'The neighbours have visitors with a baby,' I explained and she nodded absently.

'Are you sure?' I realised that for once my mother had lingered in the present day and was peering short-sightedly at my stomach. I was about to reassure her that the baby in question was not mine, when she pulled her note pad out of her pocket and started to scribble.

I leaned over her shoulder to read what she had written. 'Child of shame, dead of winter, aristocrat betrayed by Napoleon?'

Trying not to laugh I took the note from her hand and tore it up. 'No, no, Mother, really. Your readers would be shocked. Go back to Lady Griselda. Didn't you leave her pining for the Bonnie Prince? Why not let her have a new gown to impress him?'

She looked vaguely at me and I could see that the child of shame was already forgotten and Prince Charlie now uppermost, so I conducted her safely upstairs, settled her in her writing armchair and put a couple of Henry's Birmingham chocolates temptingly in front of her.

I had completely forgotten about Judith's students but they arrived in plenty of time, full of curiosity and eager to be part of the excitement, but she soon shooed them downstairs. During the morning I looked in at our dining room and was impressed to see both Addy and Wilfred concentrating hard on some exercise they had been set. When I tiptoed down our own cellar stairs I understood why they had retreated upstairs because I could hear both Veras singing. Singing? When had that been added to the curriculum?

Judith had noticed me and she slipped out to explain.

'They're learning lullabies and nursery rhymes in French,' she giggled, sounding most unlike the slightly severe school mistress we had first encountered. 'They are under the impression that Mrs Trellis will let them mind the baby as long as they teach him French!'

'I'm sure she will,' I was taken aback but was confident that Lydia would take all offers of help in good part. 'This is part of your French conversation class, I gather?'

Judith nodded. 'Not only that, but they are collaborating on actually writing an original lullaby for the baby, also in French.' She glanced into the schoolroom where the two girls were now frantically scribbling and humming snatches of song.

'This class is so much more fun than I had imagined,' she laughed. 'Oh, by the way, have you seen what Penny has made for the baby?'

I shook my head and she added, 'I'm so glad she is part of this experiment, she's a real asset. Go and see him now.'

Baby Digby was now arrayed in the most beautiful nightgown, one of a pair that Penny had apparently stayed up late to make the night before.

Lydia's eyes glistened with grateful tears but Penny brushed it aside.

'He shouldn't have to wear old clothes,' she declared stoutly. 'He's lovely and he's our baby. He deserves to be dressed properly.'

I almost joined Lydia's tears at that 'our' baby but instead I flung my arms round Penny. She is such a kind child.

'I cut out some more nightgowns this morning,' she told me. 'I'm going to teach the two Veras how to sew them after lunch, if you don't mind, Miss Christy?'

Everyone seemed to be busy apart from me, though I did remember that we had other babies to care for. After my discovery of the previous evening I had whispered to Alix and Addy to come and admire Kaiser Bill and her chicks and we had all gazed in awe at her.

'Who would ever have thought it?' Alix said it for us all. 'It's your turn, Christy. Name them, you know you want to!'

'April, May and June,' I answered without hesitation. 'I know those aren't sensible names but I like them. You do realise that they're probably all cockerels, don't you? And then what shall we do? We'll never be able to eat them.'

Chapter Sixteen

Whatever else occurred today we would always have to think about meals, especially as we were charging such an exorbitant amount for board and lodging but help was at hand.

First of all, I was chewing the end of my pencil and tried to plan our meals for the next day or so, when Miss Preston offered to take Bobs, our dog out, for a long tramp across the hills every morning and I was so grateful I barely allowed her to finish her sentence before I accepted and thrust his lead into her hand.

He is large, young and even more energetic than Miss Preston herself so that meant the two most restless members of the household would be out of the way and happily occupied for hours. Every day!

Surprises came thick and fast after that. Miss Preston and the dog marched away towards the river just as a large chicken (plucked and prepared too, such a help) arrived, courtesy of our dear friendly farmer, with a message that he had heard the news and hoped the enclosed would be useful. His youngest son and Bertie were boon companions as boys and he cherishes their memory. He is particularly kind and generous to us for the boys' sakes, and our own, something we truly appreciate.

I made coffee for a change for Judith who left her students to their musical endeavours and I took elevenses for the nurse and Lydia into the newly designated nursery. On my return to our own kitchen Judith indicated a neatly covered basket on the table.

'Your gardener handed this to me,' she announced, looking mystified. 'He said it came from a well-wisher.'

'Niggle?' I pulled away the cloth and there were four handsome, shining trout. 'Heavens! What has he been up to now?'

Judith shook her head. 'I asked him and he insisted that a gentleman had asked him to deliver the basket and that was all.'

'That's odd,' I said thoughtfully. 'Niggle has his own little ways but he never tells outright lies. I wonder who… Wilfred, perhaps?'

'Wilfred is not at all what I expected,' Judith suddenly laughed. 'I hear he was a tower of strength to you yesterday, or so he modestly informed me himself this morning. Is he a fisherman?'

'No…' I stared at her. 'He isn't but his next oldest brother is.'

She was interested so I briefly explained Wilfred's half-brothers. 'We don't know them well but the Seymours are all very well-respected businessmen in Ramalley. The eldest runs the whole concern for his father these days and was furious when he found himself in a reserved occupation, while the second one served for two years before being gassed and is fortunately able to work for the family firm now. The youngest, Richard, is only seven years older than Wilfred and he was turned down by the army because of his poor eyesight.' Yes, I thought, and he is a renowned angler and knows the Groom Hall trout stream as well as we do. Time to put a stop to any speculation and just be quietly grateful.

Mrs Camperdown dragged herself reluctantly out of the house after lingering over coffee and said she would call in here on her way up to the hospital before visiting time. I could see that the baby's claims now almost outweighed even those of a delicate son and difficult spouse. Mrs Camperdown had a joyful gleam in her eye that suggested a sudden realisation that she might, after all, attain grandmother status in the future. Miss Preston, although clearly fascinated by this new small creature, seemed to regard him as some kind of new pet.

'Welsh rarebit for luncheon, Granny?' I asked. 'We have bread, cheese and mustard. Judith's students have remembered to bring their own food and we don't have to cater for Lydia. Shall we have the trout for dinner tonight? Just in case it turns out to be contraband rather than a generous and respectable gift?'

Granny agreed, laughing, and I stood up and stretched. 'In the meantime I'm going to pack up the first episodes of the girls' serial and send them off to my magazine editor. I wrote and told him about it and he's eager to read it. To celebrate, I might be very bold and find some lunch in town!'

It was a relief to march briskly over the bridge into town. Exciting as the last few days had been I was now finding the intensely domestic atmosphere at home quite stifling. I must be a fickle creature, needing change far more than I previously believed.

To my delight, I bumped into Henry as I came out of the post office. We shook hands politely and he surprised me by ushering me into Bracewell's Department store.

'Why are we here?'

'Bertha has commissioned me to buy some wool so she can knit for this baby at your house,' he said. 'And you are going to help me, because I have never, ever set foot in a haberdashery department.' He held the door open for me. 'As a reward, I'll treat you to coffee and cake in their Cosy Café and you can tell me all about yesterday. Bertha is still worn out and hasn't said very much, but I believe she has sent you a note.'

I bought wool for Granny too, she was already knitting tiny garments and would certainly wish to knit many more for Baby Digby, but I thought I would let the lady lodgers make their own arrangements. I could imagine Miss Preston teaching the baby to play football or cricket, but it seemed unlikely that she would be a knitter.

'Why aren't you dressed for the office, Henry?' I surveyed him and he was wearing his grey tweed suit, rather than his formal black.

'Because Cousin Edgar has asked me to take charge of going through Miss Diplock's possessions,' he said, his eyes gleaming. 'Edgar and Captain Trellis removed all the official papers, her will, and her valuables on Saturday, and you know we spent yesterday dealing with her affairs. Bertha says the house is crammed to the rafters with miscellaneous furniture that will have to be disposed of.'

'It is,' I remembered Addy's and my one visit, and how – in spite of ourselves – we had experienced that moment of sympathy with Portia Diplock. Only last week and now…

'Captain Trellis is happy to leave it to Makepeace, Makepeace & Makepeace to make all arrangements and dispose, however we think fit, of anything surplus to what he and Mrs Trellis will need. Miss Diplock's maid packed her bags yesterday and has gone to London to stay with her sister. Apparently, she couldn't possibly stay all alone in a house of mourning.'

'Good riddance,' I said callously. 'The house isn't well kept and it will be easier to empty the house without her.'

'I know you are thick as thieves with all the tradespeople in town, Christy,' Henry ignored my comment. 'You have to help me. Please?'

I haughtily overlooked that slur but I knew he was joking. 'Let's call in at the auction house now,' I said eagerly. 'They will be delighted when they see what that house contains.' I looked pensively at him, struck by a thought. Henry guessed what I was thinking.

'I gather Addy and Wilfred don't join Miss Evershed's class in the afternoons? Edgar and Captain Trellis have no objection if I want to recruit them to help me.'

Our eyes met and we burst out laughing. 'I'll send them into town after lunch,' I promised. 'And you must come back with them, for a cup of tea at least, and to meet our newest lodger!'

'Come with me now?' he wheedled. 'You can tell me what furniture they'll need when they move in. I don't want to find the auctioneer has taken it all and they don't even have a bed or a table to their names! I'll send a note to summon Addy and Wilfred, but not until we've taken a look..'

The auctioneer recognised me and his eyes lit up when we explained our business so Henry and I hurried down Paradise Row to make sure we had first pick for the Trellises.

'It's a much bigger house than we realised,' I said thoughtfully. 'I didn't know it was really sideways on to the road. It goes back quite a long way and there's a carriage house and stable too.'

Henry opened the door but I lingered outside, staring down at the small yard that opened up into a garden behind. 'I say, Henry,' I exclaimed. 'Mr Trellis could use the carriage house as his office when he starts up his accountancy practice, with Wilfred as his first employee.'

'Don't fuss about that now, Christy,' Henry said, sounding quite unlike the shy, diffident young man we had met only a couple of months ago. 'You really don't have to arrange everyone's lives for them, you know.' I hid a smile and followed him indoors. Henry was learning how to escape the shadow of his terrifying father.

'Addy will never forgive you if you simply throw out all these boxes and bags and cases of what is probably rubbish but might be treasure,' I warned him. 'If we take them straight to the stable it will make it much easier to clear the rest of the house and Addy and Wilfred can take on that task and not get under everyone's feet. Meanwhile we can use those labels you brought with you and identify some usable furniture.'

I stuck my head round the dining room door and gazed in awe. 'Heavens, look at this monstrous dining table and chairs. The auction house can definitely have those, I can't see Lydia presiding over something that she would need a ladder to climb up on. It's that nasty yellow maple too, she wouldn't want that.'

When the auctioneer – attending in person and accompanied by two of his workmen – arrived, he shook his head at me.

'I might have known, Miss Christabel,' he said in mock reproof. 'You have an excellent eye and blow me, if you haven't kept back all the best pieces.'

'They must have furniture,' I said mildly, though I was flattered at his remark, nonetheless. 'And we've saved some treasures for you. Have you seen the hat-stand in the hall? I'm sure you'll have eager bidders after it when they see the carved life-sized wolves on either side!'

The auctioneer sent for beer and sandwiches from the Monk's Head just down the road and shared it with us. At least, Henry had a glass of beer with them and I had lemonade after which we left them to it. We had set aside some of the nicer furniture for Lydia and her accountant – lighter and less overbearing than the large mahogany pieces favoured by Miss Diplock's family. There were beds, chairs, sofas and whatever I thought they would need as well as a smaller dining suite that would be far more suitable than the monstrous one.

'Rugs, Henry,' I remembered as I was about to leave for home, having washed my hands and face and tidied my hair. I didn't want to be waylaid by Addy and Wilfred who must have received Henry's message by now. 'Don't get rid of any of them, we can always send them down for the auction later on if they're not wanted.'

As I reached the Priory green I was waylaid after all, but as it was Fergus Munro, I was relieved. The decision was made for me and I would ask for his help.

'Alix told me you're worried about something,' he said abruptly, after he had greeted me. 'She said you won't tell her what it is but she thinks it might be something I could help with?'

I hesitated. 'I think you might,' I nodded. 'Do you mind if we sit down? I don't want to be overheard.'

I sat silent, still wondering whether I had been dreaming up mysteries where none existed, the result of writing my yarns for boys and young men. Alix was right. Nonsense though my thoughts might be Fergus was the person to set my mind at rest. Or not…

'It's about Miss Diplock,' I said slowly. He nodded but

said nothing – a good doctor who knows how to listen. 'Lydia was very agitated on Sunday morning. It was before the baby was born and I think she must have forgotten about it since, in all the excitement. I don't believe there's anything to be done but I can't get it out of my head.'

I gave him a sidelong look. 'I know it's foolish but I kept waking up last night, worrying about it until I felt sick.'

I stared at the ground and then told him what Lydia had said about stabbing at Portia Diplock with her hat pin.

'You can understand why she did that,' I faltered. 'That very large woman falling on to a tiny, pregnant girl must have been terrifying and her reaction would have been instinctive. Anyone would have done the same but Lydia thought she must have stabbed Miss Diplock fatally and believed that would make her a murderer.'

He nodded gravely and I continued. 'Of course she wasn't, she isn't, and I hope I convinced her that Miss Diplock's death was a heart attack, as it says on the death certificate, but…' I bit my lip and tried to read his expression. 'Oh, Fergus, I don't know anything about hearts or wounds or anything, but could she be right? Could one of her wild stabbings have caused death?'

He stared across the green at the Priory clock, frowning and gathering his thoughts. 'I had no opportunity to examine the body, as you know,' he said slowly. 'If I had, I should have a better idea of the true extent of Miss Diplock's injuries.'

He rubbed a hand over his face. 'The trouble is, I have no experience of that kind of injury. My instinct is to say that death would not be instantaneous but I simply don't know. I certainly never heard anything of the sort mentioned during my training and went straight into the army after I qualified. We all did and were thrust pretty quickly into it. You've heard about battlefield surgery and the conditions in the dressing stations. It's brutal and violent and immediate. There's no time to consider whether death was instantaneous or took five minutes. It happens and to be frank, it doesn't matter. A patient is either already dead, about to die or, if he is very lucky, he has a chance of surviving.

'I think you must stop this; it's doing you no good and dwelling on it is utterly pointless. There is no mystery, Christabel, it's all in your head and you must drop it. All the evidence points to heart failure, brought on by over-exertion and excitement in an elderly woman who should have known better.'

He pulled a handkerchief out of his pocket. 'Here, mop yourself up. It won't do my professional reputation to have patients weeping all over me in public!'

I hadn't realised that tears were streaming down my cheeks yet again so I obeyed and managed a weak smile.

'You said you've been lying awake at night fretting about this?' he asked sternly and shook his head when I admitted it. 'This isn't like you at all, from what Alix says, Christy. You're overwrought and if you're not careful I'll prescribe a very nasty tonic for you.'

He gave me a searching look, hesitated and then... 'Sometimes, Christy, the mind seizes on something that might seem irrelevant or trivial when the real problem is an altogether different thing.

'When my sister Phoebe died my father became very agitated about her old dog. It was thirteen years old, a fox terrier, not in good health, and he was terrified the dog would die. He spent all his time feeding it, coddling it, doctoring it, and when the poor thing did eventually die, Father was bereft. We all knew it wasn't about the dog at all, but it was very real to him for a long time.

'You are very young and your youth has been lived against a background of darkness and the loss of your brother. There is no escaping the war, it's all around us, with the casualty lists and grief everywhere. You also have the hospital as a constant reminder next door to your home. You'll have read of mourners seeing visions, searching for messages from beyond the grave, that kind of thing. You're a sensitive girl and you haven't gone down that road that but I suspect this obsession with the stabbing is an attempt to escape, to fix on something you can identify as real rather than being engulfed by the shadows.'

He patted my shoulder as I stared thoughtfully at him, struck by his argument. 'That's better, and now let's change the subject because I have some advice for you.'

His advice concerned Addy.

'Alix told me about the High School plan for next year,' he said. 'It sounds very suitable, but I had an idea for the year after.'

'Oh?' He was full of surprises.

'I told you my sister Emily is married to our local vet? Her husband's brother is a doctor. He was invalided out of the navy a couple of years ago and I thought Addy could go and stay with Emily, who would look after her. I'm sure she could spend time with the doctor brother-in-law. He's not fit enough to practise but he loves to instruct people so handing over Addy as a pupil would benefit both of them. Mind you,' he chuckled. 'Emily would probably turn Addy horse-mad and she might end up wanting to be a vet instead!'

I was touched and grateful but he had more to say.

'It's a good thing Addy is so set on going to Oxford,' he said thoughtfully. 'Time spent growing up there would prepare her far better than unleashing her into a training hospital at the age of seventeen or so!'

The Priory clock tolled half-past three and I jumped up.

'You've been so kind, Fergus, I'm glad you're part of our family now.'

I tilted my head and looked at him.

'You look like an inquisitive robin,' he laughed. 'Very well, then, I shall be asking you for Alix's hand in marriage one of these days. Will that do?'

'Will you stay in Ramalley?' I shivered at the thought that he might take Alix away from us.

'Yes,' he said, suddenly fierce. 'I'll never part you, don't worry. I've started making enquiries about a practice in town once the war is over and the hospital finally closes and I've been assured of a welcome. Don't tell anyone but I've made an offer which has been accepted and although everything will have to wait until the war is over, I'll have a future to offer Alix.'

I couldn't speak but rubbed my hand along his own and he smiled down at me. 'I want to deal with warts and mumps and bunions, not broken boys,' he said. 'Old ladies too, whose grumbles are nothing to do with illness but really a token of loneliness. I want to make people and not just patch them up. And most of all I want to bring order into their lives.' He shook his head and smiled at me. 'I have a passion for order after the disorder of recent times.'

'You realise that permission for Alix to marry doesn't lie with me,' I warned him, pleased, but wondering just how much order he would find in our family. 'Only Mother can do that, and I don't think you would enjoy having to ask her.'

He looked aghast and I giggled in sympathy as I set off home. 'You'd better just call it an understanding for now.'

Tuesday, 7th May, afternoon

Our days gradually settled into a routine and the presence of a baby in the house became normal, though always a delight.

Miss Acton appeared every morning, eager to serve at mother's right hand and to confide interesting details of her 'warm friendship' with the new curate. I, in turn, alerted Bertha Makepeace who said it was all nonsense and one of Elise's silly infatuations. Also that the curate was, in any case, only twenty-three and terrified of Miss Acton. She promised to make sure that whatever happened, Elise Acton would continue to be Mother's devoted slave.

My mind at ease about Lydia's confession and my helpful talk with Fergus (which had actually made sense of my anxieties) I wrote and wrote and wrote, delighting in the sheer frivolity of a story for schoolgirls after the harrowing tales I had been writing. How foolish I had been, not to understand what a distressing effect it would have on me – I know I feel as old as Methuselah sometimes, but as Alix pointed out, I'm still only eighteen, and not even nineteen until September.

Judith's classes prospered. Addy and Wilfred worked hard

in the mornings and after lunch they joined Henry at Miss Diplock's house where they found treasures every day. With all the boxes in the carriage house in the yard and the surplus furniture now removed to the auctioneer's warehouse, Bertha Makepeace, quite recovered from our adventure, was able to send in her housekeeper, accompanied by an eager gaggle of local charwomen, to scrub the house from rafters to cellar. The auctioneer was delighted with Addy and Wilfred's rummaging and rubbed his hands at what he termed 'interesting objets d'arts' that he added to his catalogue.

The two Veras and Penny had forged a firm alliance; with Addy too, though she was working with Wilfred more than the girls. Although the French lullaby had been abandoned, they were reading their way through all our schoolgirl books and telling me stories about their own school which was very useful local colour for me. I felt I could hardly use Addy's exploits in a book, considering the number of times she had been suspended for outright impertinence and disobedience. Nor was Alix's one outbreak of revenge edifying, though it had been satisfying; she had tied a bully into a chair using the girl's own plaits and had shut the her, chair and all, into a dark cupboard where she remained for more than an hour. I suspected that the magazine editor might find it a step too far.

Meanwhile, under Penny's supervision, the Veras' needlework was improving in leaps and bounds and Baby Diggy (as he had inevitably been nicknamed) was acquiring an outfit to suit a small prince because, of course, our neighbours had heard the news and gifts arrived at all hours.

I dragged myself away from my story and went downstairs in search of tea, cake and company, only to find Judith closing our front door behind a female figure.

'Who was that?' I asked idly, on my way into the kitchen.

'Miss Bembridge,' she said, with a very odd expression on her face.

'Miss... Oh, Vera-Bee's aunt? The High School headmistress? What did she want? She can't possibly have any complaints, can she?'

'Far from it,' Judith followed me into the kitchen and sat down at the table. Inevitably she soon had a kitten on her lap but she is so used to our household now I don't think she even noticed.

'She came to offer me a teaching post at the High School,' she said bluntly her eyes wide and startled.

'Goodness,' I said. It seemed an inadequate response but was all I could muster.

'Yes, she has been impressed at the way her niece already seems more mature and is grasping the rudiments of mathematics, a subject hitherto a blank to her.'

'Maths?' I knew about the French and the singing and the needlework, but mathematics? 'When have you had time to teach that? The class has only been running for five minutes! What is she thinking? It's still only Tuesday, for goodness' sake.'

'Cutting and sewing baby clothes involves calculations,' she shrugged. 'You've been so busy the last day or two, Christabel, that you haven't noticed the girls are also helping Lady Elspeth with simple cookery which again requires concentration.'

I stared at her. 'Really? Miss Bembridge has offered you a position on the strength of that?'

'Not really, no,' Judith looked at me with dancing eyes. 'I am Miss Bembridge's last resort!'

'Stop being so mysterious,' I pleaded and she relented.

'It has come to her notice over the last term or two that several of her senior girls, although well-grounded in most subjects, are weak in mathematics. To this end she had appointed a new mistress to help with remedial exercises and coaching.'

She chuckled. 'The new mistress had the temerity to marry her guardsman sweetheart by special licence on Saturday. This means she will not now be available to take up her post, so Miss Bembridge thought of me. It would be a part-time post and more in the style of tutorials, which I would really enjoy.'

'Judith, that would be perfect! You're going to accept,

aren't you?' I seem to be growing much more demonstrative lately because I clutched at her in a warm, fond embrace. 'You know you don't want to go back to your horrid old headmistress and you can stay with us and be family. When does she want you to begin?'

'In September. She knows I am not supposed to return to teaching until then, though my headaches are improving rapidly.' Her eyes sparkled and she, also naturally reserved, hugged me back. 'Of course I'm going to accept. My parents can't possibly object if I live with you; you know how much my mother loves a title to boast about. Remember how she fawned on Lady Elspeth during that fleeting visit after my accident.' (Judith is thirty but her family resent her independence – from a great-aunt as well as her salary – so they insist on putting stumbling blocks in her way. Parents can be very strange, sometimes.)

To celebrate I made hot buttered toast and we drank Miss Bembridge's health in tea. I kept quiet about a snippet of news that Henry had told me, though Judith probably knew already.

Major Minton had decided to move permanently to Ramalley. He had no family, Henry said, and apparently found the town and its occupants 'most agreeable'. His batman had now been discharged from the army and the plan was that they would take rooms in town where the major would begin a new life and take up the reins of his former profession as an historian. I kept quiet about this with great difficulty but he and Judith both deserved some happiness.

Wednesday, 8th May, early evening

I strolled round the garden after dinner, alone for a change. It had been another busy day, full of domesticity, baby worship, inventing a suspicious-looking individual to lurk near my fictitious school, and being summoned by Bertha Makepeace to discuss Portia Diplock's funeral. This was to take place privately on Saturday, and Bertha didn't really need my assistance, so we discussed our shared experience instead, becoming even firmer friends over it.

The lodgers were sitting with Lydia while the night nurse had her own supper and Addy had taken herself off to bed early with a pile of books and an assortment of cats. 'I'm reading that Charlotte Yonge book,' she told me. 'The Clever Woman of the Family, the one where the heroine wants to go and inspect invalids in asylums in Switzerland. I wonder if you can still do that?'

I knew the book she was talking about. It's one I love, particularly where the hero teases that they might include the asylum tour on their honeymoon, so I kissed her goodnight and waved at Alix who, inspired by Penny, was embroidering a muslin collar to enhance her best blouse.

Granny had retired to her own room having made a supreme effort just after tea. Captain Trellis and Lydia had been startled to have a visit from her and, not to my surprise at all because I had suggested it, Granny very shyly offered to be godmother to Baby Diggy.

'Oh, Lady Elspeth!' Lydia flushed and turned pale, clutching at her husband's arm. 'That would be wonderful!'

And so it will. Ramalley is a small town and as I've said before, although everyone knows our circumstances, the townspeople are proud of Granny's title and there is that sense of deference. To have such an illustrious local figure as his godparent means that Baby Diggy's social success will be assured. As will that of his parents so I could see that Lydia was basking in a dream of glory.

I was even more touched after Granny had gone back to her knitting and Lydia hesitantly asked me my brother's name.

'Bertie,' I said, puzzled. 'Albert, really. Why?'

'We would be honoured if you would also agree to be a godmother and to allow us to give it as the baby's second name,' said Mr Trellis, clearing his throat. '

I couldn't speak but Lydia stroked my hand and smiled down at her baby. 'Digby Albert Trellis,' she said proudly.

The hens had made no fuss when I rounded them up earlier and a peek at Kaiser Bill and her chicks reassured me. There were still three of them and Bill was still remarkably placid. I wondered how long that would last. It isn't her normal state of mind.

It was pleasant sitting outside in the dusk and I was surprised but happy to see Henry limp through the back gate and came to sit beside me on the bench.

'What is happening at Miss Diplock's house? Are you still moving furniture every day? ' I said lazily. 'Does Cousin Edgar still want you at the house all the time?'

'I think we should start calling it the Trellis's house. It's capital fun,' he said. 'Edgar says it's a great help having someone young to tackle the job, his rheumatism wouldn't stand for it and none of the other staff are under fifty! Of course the firm employs all the tradespeople so my job today was to supervise the man who whitewashed all the ceilings. You won't believe the difference it makes. What have you been doing today? Addy and Wilfred have been very useful and I know they're enjoying themselves.'

I told him about Judith's new opportunity and we agreed to keep quiet about Major Minton's plans, just in case she had not yet heard them, though that seemed unlikely bearing in mind their flourishing friendship.

'Do you remember, not long after we first met,' he said suddenly. 'When I asked you what you wanted to do when the war is over?'

'Did you? Oh, yes, so you did.' I sat up straight and recalled the conversation. 'I said I'd like to go to Italy, to Sorrento, and watch the sun go down over Pompeii across the bay.'

'Drinking wine and eating olives,' he said, then…' I said it sounded romantic.'

'Well, it does,' I agreed.

'I thought it would be a romantic place for a honeymoon,' he murmured.

'Oh!' I stared helplessly at him and he took both my hands in his.

'Listen to me, Christy,' he urged. 'I don't mean now. You haven't even had a life yet, just hard work and sorrow and the war, and I wouldn't want to tie you to anything. We're both far too young anyway, but perhaps when I'm qualified we might think about it?'

I couldn't speak and after looking anxiously at me, he went on.

'You know I love you, don't you? And I'm pretty sure you feel the same way about me, but I promise that if you didn't want it, I would never make myself a nuisance.'

I leaned my head against his shoulder and was startled to feel him shake with unexpected laughter.

'Don't you dare say, 'Oh, Henry, this is so sudden!' because you know it's not sudden in the least.'

'Of course I love you,' I whispered. 'It's just that I don't know what to say.'

There was a gleam in his dear, kind eyes. 'Why not tell me if you've had any further thoughts about your future? Apart from drinking wine at Sorrento, which, let me tell you, sounds rather racy for such a very young lady!'

'What the auctioneer said the other day.' I heard the words spill out of my mouth but had no awareness of the sentence forming inside my head. 'Do you remember? He said I had a good eye for all that antique furniture and the oddities. Have you ever noticed that run-down house the other side of the bridge as you walk into Ramalley? It belongs to a very old lady and her bachelor son and it's crammed full of old furniture and books. That's what I'd like to do,' I warmed to the subject, which truthfully had never crossed my mind until now. 'I heard the other day that the old lady will reach her hundredth birthday at Christmas and is determined to see that out with a big celebration. I'd like to suggest to her son that I could go through the house and sort out all the contents.' I caught him trying to hide a grin as I said that and I added, with dignity: 'He's very reclusive but I'd be tactful, of course, and suggest it would make their lives more comfortable. I wonder if he would let me turn it into a shop? That would be fun and as I am acquainted with him slightly, it wouldn't upset him.'

'It sounds highly suitable,' I could tell he was trying not to laugh. 'And the schoolgirl books?'

'Oh, yes, of course, I shall go on writing those. They're far too much fun to stop.'

'We have a provisional agreement then, do we? To review the matter on your twenty-first birthday?' The parody of his Cousin Edgar's precise legal tone was exactly right and as I smiled, he bent down and kissed me.

Properly this time.

Epilogue

Thursday, 9th May, 1918.

It was teatime on Thursday and our lives had been shaken inside-out and turned upside down and yet, as I looked round our familiar, shabby drawing room, I could see they were just the same. There had been a death, and a birth, and the pattern of our family life had shifted and blended, changeable as clouds after a storm. And yet, here we all were, still ourselves but enhanced – touched by drama, elation, always overshadowed by the war, of course, and with our abiding memories of the grief that still crippled us and that would always do so, in some measure. But there was love; there would always be love.

'I'll bring in the tea, shall I?' I raised an eyebrow as I glanced at Granny. Our lodgers were still up at the Hall so we were just family, which now included Henry and Fergus. (Mother had sent her highland heroine to France, to Bonnie Prince Charlie's court in exile, and was busily concocting a ballroom scene – presumably to cheer the courtiers up – so she would not be joining us.)

Granny looked at the clock and shrugged. 'Knowing Addy, the very act of making tea will summon her at once. She and Wilfred are late home today.'

There was a ripple of amusement at that. Addy and Wilfred were always late home from their forays at Portia Diplock's house and it had become a household game to try and guess what particular oddity Addy might have persuaded Captain Trellis to bestow on her. He was certainly putty in her hands but very appreciative too. Still recovering from his perforated appendix, not to mention having his foot run over by a tank (which was less dangerous than the operation but still a nasty injury) he was unable to do any of the fetching and carrying that they relished. Besides, he was besotted with his wife and baby and spent all the time Fergus would allow him at our house.

'I don't see how she can possibly – um – improve on yesterday's offering,' Henry grinned. 'Your face was a picture, Lady Elspeth!'

Granny shook her head at him and if she had possessed a fan I swear she would have flicked it at him. I loved the way Henry was proving confident enough to tease my dear, austere grandmother and that she was happy to let him.

We had grown accustomed to strange ornaments and piles of books coming home but yesterday had been – different.

'Just look what dear Captain Trellis has given me,' Addy had cried as she'd bounced into the kitchen. She held out a small brown cardboard box and handed it to me. 'Go on, Christy, open it. You'll never believe it. It's supposed to be frightfully lucky!'

I gingerly slid the lid open and squealed in disgust. 'What on earth is it?' It appeared to be a length of pale, grubby string or something, coiled up on a bed of dirty-looking cotton wool.

'Read the note,' Addy urged so I did.

'Uncle George Diplock's umbilical cord, 17th February 1838.' I dropped the horrid thing on to the table. 'Addy, that's disgusting! Throw it away at once.' (She refused, of course, though Granny had conveniently managed to lose it, which made Addy furious.)

We all shuddered now at the memory and I had risen to go and fetch the tea when my younger sister arrived home, followed by her henchman who, I noticed suspiciously, hovered at the drawing room door, unusually diffident.

'We've brought you a present,' Addy announced, ignoring the assembled company and beaming at me. 'Just a moment, let me get rid of this old thing,' and she dragged the once-good but now threadbare Persian rug away from its place in front of the grate.

I began to have an inkling and prayed I was wrong though everyone else looked on in surprise and, in Alix's case, wild speculation. I made a face as she stared at me but there was no escape.

'We cleaned it up,' Addy told me eagerly. 'I know it was a bit grubby and you'd have made a fuss, but it's perfect now.'

Oh, dear Lord. I knew. I knew now and there was nothing I could do about it. She was so pleased at the thought of giving me a treat and I looked helplessly at Alix who came to stand beside me.

Addy beamed as we linked arms and she briefly laid her head against my shoulder. 'It's all been dreadful, but everything is all right now, isn't it? And this was Miss Diplock's most loved treasure, she told me so, didn't she, Christy? I know she would be really, really happy for us to have it.'

'She would be, and she did say it, you're quite right, Addy,' I whispered, choking back a sob as Alix and I stood with our arms round our own dearest treasure — our little sister, loving, eccentric, awkward, clever and full of boundless possibilities.

Fergus was smiling but when I caught Henry's eye he looked concerned so I managed a tiny nod just for him and turned back to Addy. She beckoned to Wilfred.

'Lay it down here,' she ordered and she, Alix and I, linked for ever by our unbreakable love and sisterhood, gazed down at the monstrosity that lay there: grey, flat, (mercifully dead), with its mangy Alsatian fur skittishly sticking up where she had washed it and its spindly legs and tail sticking out at all angles. Most horrible of all was the lumpy stuffed head with its unconvincing teeth and staring, lopsided glass eyes.

Alix and I stared at the repulsive thing, then I caught her eye and we both burst out laughing.

It was the Brother Grimm.

And it was here to stay.

THE END

Fantastic Books
Great Authors

darkstroke is
an imprint of
Crooked Cat Books

- Gripping Thrillers
- Cosy Mysteries
- Romantic Chick-Lit
- Fascinating Historicals
- Exciting Fantasy
- Young Adult
- Non-Fiction

Discover us online
www.darkstroke.com

Find us on instagram:
www.instagram.com/darkstrokebooks

Printed in Great Britain
by Amazon

46458922R00132